The Grump Whisperer

Also by Katy James

Too Much Man
Too Hot to Touch

Visit the Author Profile page at Harlequin.com.

THE GRUMP WHISPERER

KATY JAMES

Recycling programs for this product may not exist in your area.

ISBN-13: 978-1-335-57486-2

The Grump Whisperer

Harlequin Enterprises ULC
22 Adelaide St. West, 41st Floor
Toronto, Ontario M5H 4E3, Canada
www.Harlequin.com

Printed in U.S.A.

To Percy, the best boy

One

Bronwen stood with a wheelbarrow handle in each hand, staring at the overflowing manure pile, and it occurred to her that the universe's idea of a metaphor was a little too on the nose.

Somewhere back inside the barn a horse whinnied, impatient for breakfast. Bronwen raised her bare hands to her lips and blew hot breath on them. She'd optimistically dressed for spring that morning, and yet again, April in Massachusetts was being a real bitch about things. The water buckets were frozen, the dirt road down to the turnout fields was slippery with frost, and her gloves were somewhere in the tack room instead of on her hands where she needed them.

With a sigh, she picked up the wheelbarrow and began shoving it to the top of the pile. Manure was already starting the inevitable creep toward the barn—if she wanted to have any hope of keeping it contained until it could be hauled away, she needed to dump as far back as possible.

"Nothing like starting the day by climbing an actual pile of shit!" a voice behind her called.

Despite her frozen hands and gloomy mood, Bronwen smiled. "Living the glamorous life!" she called back over her shoulder.

She finally made it far enough up the pile to safely dump the manure where it wouldn't simply spill back down and onto the path behind the barn. Slowly, she maneuvered her way back down and set the wheelbarrow on the ground with a sigh.

"This is getting out of control," she groused. "It's not like I can tell the horses to stop pooping until the manure is removed."

Her friend Olivia looked dubiously at the mountain of shit threatening to overtake its designated space, dark braid over one shoulder topped with a thick, fleece-lined knit hat. "Don't the manure guys usually come every couple of weeks?"

"They *should*," Bronwen replied. "But I wouldn't come, either, if I hadn't been paid."

Olivia frowned. "They haven't been paid? Ruth was always so on top of that stuff. She'd never let this happen."

Bronwen sighed again, irritation rising for the hundredth time that day. And it was only 7:00 a.m. "Yeah, well, Ruth sold the farm in a big rush and is currently across the country visiting her sister, and she never gave me access to the farm account to pay bills—you know how she is."

Olivia nodded. "Too used to doing everything herself."

"Yeah. At least she set up direct deposit so Abigail and I can still get paid as long as I keep depositing the boarders' checks." If Ruth hadn't done that much, Bronwen and the barn assistant would have truly been up a shit mountain.

"She said just to coordinate with the new owner, but the phone number she gave me is out of service," Bronwen continued. "And now I can't get any of the bills paid, we're low on feed and hay, and Martha complained yesterday about the footing in the outdoor ring."

"Martha complains about everything," Olivia said with a grimace.

"Yeah, but this time she's right. I can drag it with the tractor, but it really needs to be replaced. It's just dirt and clay packed solid. And I can't authorize that big a project—I'm the barn manager, not the owner. Never mind that I can't pay for it."

Olivia glanced toward the old farmhouse, sitting forlornly at the top of a small hill. "I'm guessing the new owner isn't here yet?"

Bronwen grimaced. "No. I keep trying that phone number, and I've been up to the house almost every day, but nothing. Totally empty. Ruth moved out two months ago!"

Bronwen began pushing the wheelbarrow back to the barn, and Olivia fell into step beside her. She took a few deep breaths, taking in the earthy scent of the fields of damp grass, their frosty blanket melting in the morning sun. The trees surrounding the farm were still bare, the cold spring holding them to their winter barrenness. Blue-gray sky stretched endlessly overhead, vast and silent without the birds who in a few weeks would turn morning from quiet melancholy to a cacophony of celebration every time the sun rose.

Bronwen couldn't wait. She loved snow, loved the coziness of the barn with its dozen furry and warm residents in the winter. But she didn't love breaking ice in the water buckets. Or dragging herself out of bed in her sparely heated apartment over the barn, only to face a long day of chores with hardly a minute to warm up in the tack room that doubled as a lounge for the people who boarded their horses at Morning Song Farm.

She was ready for spring, but spring was in no hurry this year.

"The new owners have to show up, right? Or at least contact you?" Olivia's dark eyebrows knit together in concern. "What happens if they just...don't?"

Bronwen thought about the horses she spent every day caring for, and their owners, who had become almost like family—well, some of them, anyway. She thought about her little apartment, snug and simple and safe. She thought about the fact that she got to see her best friend, Olivia, every day. Her own horse, Charlie, was happy and settled here. And she loved most of all that every day followed the same dependable routine of feeding, mucking stalls and tending to the endless issues the enormous but fragile animals loved to toss her way.

Managing a boarding barn might not be the most fulfilling job she could imagine, but it was *hers*. Morning Song Farm had been her refuge when she needed one. When she'd been lost and untethered from the life she'd thought she'd wanted, the life she'd thought she could have. When everything changed, Morning Song had been a soft, sure landing. The farm gave her a life she could feel good about, even if it wasn't what she'd wanted before. She'd *built* something here, out of all the turmoil and breaking apart of her world. She made connections, friends, earned their trust and gave them hers. She knew every quirk and need of every horse, and those of most of their owners. They depended on her just as surely as she depended on them, not that anyone but Olivia knew why she needed the stability and comfort of the farm's unvarying rhythms so much.

The people and horses here were her responsibility, whether she owned the farm or not.

"They have to," she replied grimly as they entered the barn. A chorus of whinnies and snorts greeted their arrival. She smiled despite herself, once again shoving down the panic that rose up every time she thought about the farm's invisible new owners. "We're popular this morning."

Olivia laughed. "Only because we have opposable thumbs and access to the feed room."

"Want to help?"

"Always," Olivia replied with relish. She'd grown up obsessed with horses, but didn't start riding until college, where she was assigned a freshman-year roommate in Bronwen, who'd promptly dragged her down to the school's barn for a lesson. Olivia stopped riding for a while after college, but had fairly recently started up again, and currently rode Bronwen's horse, Charlie.

Which was perfect, because Bronwen certainly wasn't getting on him again.

As they passed the tack room, the sound of voices caught her attention and she stuck her head inside the door.

"Bronwen!" Brian greeted her with his usual cheerful grin. He was seated on the ancient couch in the corner of the large room, a mug of coffee in his hand and curly dark hair flopped over his forehead. "Another lovely morning."

Olivia rolled her eyes and edged past Bronwen to head toward the coffee maker. "Yeah, if you want to live in Antarctica," she said. "Where is spring this year?"

"We're in for a hot summer—that's what this cold spell tells me." Martha sat on a folding chair with her own mug. She was an older woman, short and stout. An opinionated person but a bit of a timid rider. Her horse, Percy, was a mischievous gelding who loved to stop dead while someone was riding him, refusing to take another step until he was steered in a tight circle and sent back the way he came. Martha believed he could do no wrong.

"I don't think that's scientifically accurate," Olivia murmured.

"Where's Scott?" Bronwen asked Brian. The two men had been married last year inside the barn surrounded by all the other boarders, family and friends. The event had gone off mostly without a hitch, except for Brian's horse, the Mountain, or Mount, slobbering all over him right before the vows.

"A little under the weather," Brian said. A sheepish look crossed his face. "And also, you know Sugar doesn't like the indoor ring, but…"

Bronwen groaned inwardly. Sugar was an ex-racehorse whose legs needed a lot of extra care—and decent footing. She much preferred—and therefore behaved better—being ridden in the outdoor riding ring, but she'd come up lame afterward at least twice due to the hard ground. They were lucky to have an indoor ring with good footing, but that didn't do Scott any good if his horse misbehaved the whole time she was in there. Scott wasn't a competitive rider; he just wanted to have fun. And for him and Sugar, that meant having a usable outdoor ring.

If the boarders couldn't ride their horses, the farm was going to be in trouble.

"I'll try to call the new owners again," she said, even though she knew she'd just get the out-of-service message. "Maybe I can get in touch with Ruth so she can give me the name of the real estate agent for the buyers, and I can contact them that way."

"Or..." Martha began with a knowing glint in her eye. "You could just go up to the house and talk to the owner there."

Everyone in the room turned to stare at Martha, who sat quietly on her chair with a smug smile, sipping her coffee. No one loved gossip—especially gossip no one else knew yet—more than Martha.

"But the house is empty!" Olivia exclaimed. "Bronwen's been going up every day to check. Right?" She turned to Bronwen.

"Well..." she replied slowly. "Yesterday, the day sort of got away from me. The vet was here, and then Percy chewed up his halter—sorry, Martha, I found a spare—and Olivia wanted me to help her with Charlie..."

"Oh sure, blame it on me," Olivia muttered.

Bronwen winced. She'd been trying to give Olivia lessons on Charlie, who wasn't a beginner's horse by any stretch of the imagination. Olivia had been taking weekly lessons at a nearby barn before accepting Bronwen's not entirely altruistic offer of a free horse to ride. But the match wasn't exactly working. While she could feel in her body exactly what Olivia needed to do, she hadn't found a way to articulate it.

"I just— I've been up there almost every day." Bronwen stared at Martha. "Are you saying someone moved in?"

It must have been in the middle of the night, and quiet, since Bronwen lived on the property. She would have noticed a moving truck, or any sort of action up by the house during the day.

"I *saw* him," Martha replied with satisfaction. "When I drove in yesterday, he was on the front porch—went inside as soon as he caught sight of my car. Tall. Young. Did I mention tall?"

"Hmm… Was he good-looking?" Brian asked with interest.

"You're married!" Martha reached over and swatted his knee.

"Not for *me*—Bronwen!"

"What? No. Definitely not for me." Bronwen glared at Brian. "I'm not in the market for a…whatever."

"Is that what we call them these days?" Olivia smirked at her.

"You've worked here for four years and there's been no sign of…whatever," Martha remarked.

Bronwen shook her head. "I don't need the new owner to be good-looking. Or tall, or young. I just need them to be *here*, and ready to throw money at this place. The outdoor ring, manure removal, hay…" She broke off.

She generally tried not to unload her worries about the barn onto the boarders. It wasn't their problem, and she also didn't want anyone getting cold feet and moving their horse to another barn. They'd already lost two boarders recently, and a small farm full of recreational riders like this one always needed as much income as possible.

"Well, you can go talk to whoever he is and get all of those fixed up," Martha said, as if everything was settled.

Which...maybe it was. But if the new owner was onsite, why hadn't they stopped down to the barn? Didn't they want to know their own boarders? The horses? Ruth had said that the new owner hadn't mentioned any plans to turn the barn into a private operation. That as far as she knew, it would continue as a boarding facility. Which meant that the owner *should* want to familiarize themselves with the running of the farm.

It was absurd, really, that they hadn't at least introduced themselves to her, the barn manager. It was mismanagement, pure and simple. They'd knowingly taken on responsibility for the farm and the horses, and they had an obligation to make sure that everything was running properly. Infuriating.

"Uh, Bronwen, are you okay?" Olivia asked, nudging her with her elbow.

Bronwen realized she was scowling into space. She glanced around at the others in the room, who were all looking at her expectantly.

Okay. If the owner wasn't going to come down to the barn, she'd have to take matters into her own hands.

"Let's feed the horses," she said, "and muck out. Then... I'm going up to the house."

Bronwen wasn't above a little light breaking and entering. After feeding the horses, turning them out into the chilly fields snug in their blankets and mucking out the stalls with the help of Olivia, Martha and Brian—who were as eager as she was for her to discover more about the farm's new owner—she marched up to the old house.

The building was a mishmash of styles, formal and elegant in the front with neat, symmetrical windows and a large wood door in the middle. Bronwen guessed that this section dated from the early nineteenth century, with a later Victorian section tacked onto the back, complete with a curved two-story bay window and an unbalanced roofline that made the addition look a little tipsy. At the far end of the house was a relatively modern greenhouse that Ruth had always kept stuffed full of plants and flowers. It looked empty now.

Bronwen traced the same path along the side of the house as she had so many times before, when she'd headed to Ruth's for dinner or tea, or just to put her feet up on one of the comfy footstools after a long day. Ruth would bring her a glass of sherry and they'd discuss horses until the sun had long set, and Bronwen would make her way back to her apartment in the dark, happy and tired.

Her heart gave a little twist as she thought not for the first time how much she'd miss those nights. How much she already missed Ruth. The older woman had been a bit eccentric, but there was nothing she cared more about than horses, and the farm had always run smoothly under her ownership.

She walked past the darkened windows. Ruth's beloved roses along the side wall were still brown and frozen, leaves from the past fall banked against the side of the house like an extra layer of protection for whoever was inside. Everything was cold and the unknown hung in the air like thick fog. Bronwen shivered in her heavy coat as she stepped up the creaking front stairs to the door.

Knocking on the door, she remembered all the times she'd just pushed her way inside when she visited Ruth, whose radio was always too loud for her to hear the door. It felt wrong, somehow, too formal, to stand and wait for someone to answer.

And...no one was answering.

She knocked again and looked around. A fancy SUV sat in the driveway on the opposite side of the house from the barn. No wonder she hadn't noticed it. She craned her neck to try to peer into one of the first-floor windows, and was rewarded with the barest hint of light from a lamp in one of the rooms. Someone *was* inside.

One more knock.

Then she tried the doorknob, just to see. Unlocked.

She rubbed her bare hands together, making a mental note to look for her gloves when she got back to the barn. It really had no business being so cold in early April, for God's sake. Especially not when she was standing still, frustrated, in the chilly shade of the house.

Bronwen knocked one more time, and then that frustration got the best of her and she shoved the door open.

"Hello?" she called, trying to sound friendly and not at all like a burglar.

She hoped against hope that the new owner would be a friendly old lady like Ruth. Except Martha had said "he." And young. And...tall. Maybe he was just overwhelmed with the move. Maybe he was shy, and needed an invitation to visit the barn. Maybe he needed help, a friend...

She crept down the hallway and poked her head through the sitting room doorway.

"Who the hell are you?"

The man's deep voice startled her, rough and rusty and loud in the silence of the old house. Whatever she'd been expecting, it wasn't this.

The big great room where she'd spent so many hours in front of the fireplace chatting with Ruth was nearly empty, although the fire was lit. The space spanned the width of the house, windows on the two short sides and doors to various other rooms opening along the long sides. Only now, all of the doors were closed except for the one where she stood. No radio cut through the silence, no scent of Ruth's cooking wafted through from the kitchen. What was once cozy and comfortably worn and *alive* was now...sad and unfamiliar. Ruth's old couch sat directly in front of the flames, while an old armchair that Bronwen recognized as one that used to sit in a corner of the kitchen was placed perpendicular to the fireplace. One small table lamp perched forlornly on the floor, trying its best to light the large room.

And in the armchair, glass of something that looked alcoholic in hand, sat the most beautiful man she'd ever seen. It took her a moment to realize just *how* beautiful—a moment she spent blinking at him in shock while he scowled at her—because of the darkness inside the house, and also because he was a mess.

Untidy scruff tried and failed to cover over a strong jaw, while thick golden-blond hair waved wildly as if it hadn't seen a brush or a good cut in a long time. His high forehead and long, elegant nose gave him an aristocratic air, which, combined with his overall unkempt appearance, made her think a little wildly of a prince who'd run off to become a pirate. A raggedy sweater and jeans did nothing to hide the height and lean strength of the man before her. He had to top her own not-insignificant height by half a foot, though it was hard to tell with him slouched in Ruth's chair.

A man who did not look pleased that she'd just wandered into his house. Assuming it *was* his house. She narrowed her eyes at him.

"Who are *you*?" she countered, hoping that offense really was the best defense. "Are you the new owner?"

Because if not, she was really going to wish she'd brought her cell phone with her, so she could call the police. She glanced back at the now-closed front door, the suddenly unfamiliar dark hallway, around the eerily empty room in front of her, and realized a little too late that it was highly unlikely anyone down at the barn would be able to hear her scream.

When she looked again at the man, he'd raised one single, perfect eyebrow at her. She'd never been able to do that herself, and it seemed unfair that someone could look like him *and* have full, individual control of their eyebrows.

"What if I said I wasn't the new owner?" the man asked, mild curiosity infusing his deep voice. The tenor was what she imagined the amber liquid in his glass would sound like, if you could hear a taste. "What would you do then?"

"Uh…" Bronwen was not prepared for this line of questioning. She didn't have her phone, and the house was isolated. "Um…run, I guess?"

One corner of his perfect mouth turned up oh so slightly, as if he was amused against his will. Then the scowl made a quick reappearance, and he turned his face away from her, toward the fire.

"Then go on and run. Get out of here."

But there was more resignation in his tone than anger or hostility. Some instinct told her that he wasn't a murderous monster, although her instincts had certainly betrayed her before. Still… She had a *mission*, dammit. She needed answers. She could hardly head back out to the barn and tell everyone assembled that yes, there *was* someone in the house, but no, she didn't know who they were or whether they could help with the rapidly mounting issues at the farm. She weighed the slim chance that he wasn't, in fact, the new owner against her responsibility to the horses and their people, and decided to give him another minute before bolting for the door.

"Are you…are you saying you're not the new owner?" She glanced around the mostly empty room and front hallway, once so cozy and cluttered when Ruth lived there. She could feel the heat from the radiator behind her in addition to the warm fire, but it still felt cold in the house. Freezing, even. She shivered despite her coat.

The man took a sip of whatever he was drinking, and Bronwen noticed a bottle sitting on the floor next to his chair. It was barely ten in the morning. She thought about everyone waiting in the barn, cheerful and full of laughter and whinnies and chatter, her favorite place in the world. What a contrast to this lonely scene. She'd almost feel sorry for whoever this guy was, if she wasn't so annoyed.

"I am not," he said firmly. "So feel free to see yourself out. I'm busy."

Bronwen snorted. Busy drinking first thing in the morning, and nothing else. "Uh-huh. Listen, either you do own this farm and you're just being weird about it—in which case I have things to discuss with you—or you really aren't the new owner and I need to call the police. Which is it?"

She crossed her arms in front of her chest, still more than ready to beat a hasty retreat if he ended up being the least bit threatening. But if he didn't own the house he was making himself…uncomfortable in, then she had a responsibility to deal with that situation, too.

He turned his head to look at her again, a spark of anger in his eyes. They were blue, crystalline light blue and cold as the water in the frozen water buckets this morning.

"My sister is the owner of this farm, and I'm here at her invitation," he said, as if it was an enormous imposition to have to answer her. Which, given that she'd basically broken into the house, it might be. But…

"Great. Can you give me her contact information? The phone number I was given is out of service."

The scowl returned in full force. "She's out of the country, on some island somewhere, and she deactivated her old phone for…personal reasons. You won't be able to reach her, not for a few weeks."

Wow. So, this was one of those rich families she was dealing with, where people went AWOL to random islands because they didn't have jobs or responsibilities. Any hope that she could get around having to deal with this surly man in favor of a more reasonable person evaporated.

She took a few steps forward into the large room, now that she was reassured he wasn't someone who'd wandered in off the street.

"I need to talk to her—or someone who's responsible. Bills aren't getting paid, so I can't schedule the farrier or get the muck pile taken away. And we're going to run out of feed if the feed store account isn't paid up."

Now that she wasn't afraid for her life, her anger at the absentee owner—and her brother—bubbled back to the surface. She needed to make this man understand the seriousness of the situation. Surely even the grumpy person in front of her would understand that things needed doing at a boarding barn?

He stared at her as if she was speaking a foreign language.

"Who are you?" he finally asked, those blue eyes intense. He really was gorgeous, but there was something unsettling about the stiffness of his body, even sitting down, a resigned tiredness in those intense eyes. Something that spoke of isolation and pain, two things she was familiar with herself. She almost felt sorry for bothering him.

Almost.

"I'm Bronwen. The barn manager."

He sat back in his chair as if he'd just received the worst news imaginable. "Barn manager..." he murmured to himself. "I thought I saw lights down there."

"Um, and all the horses around." She gestured vaguely toward the fields. "And the people coming and going?" He still stared off into the distance, trying her patience. "You *do* know that Morning Song Farm is a boarding barn...right?"

His gaze snapped to hers, sharp as wire cutters. "A boarding—" A bark of laughter escaped him, rusty like old hinges. "Of course it is. Anne…" he muttered, a twist to his mouth that on someone else would have indicated amusement.

She didn't think he was amused. And honestly, neither was she. The problem was not complicated. His sister owned the farm. Unreachable, yes, but he was here in her stead. Horses needed feeding, things needed fixing. *Someone* had to take responsibility. Bronwen wanted to stamp her foot in frustration, like one of the horses when they had to wait too long for their dinner.

"Are you telling me that your sister bought this farm from Ruth, and you're staying here in the house but had no idea this was a working barn?"

This was so much worse than she'd thought. No way to contact the owner, and only this man to deal with. Did he even know anything about horses? Did he have any way to pay off the mounting bills? What on earth was she going to do?

"I probably should have guessed, given Anne's enthusiasm for letting me use the house."

"Huh?"

"Never mind." He focused on her again. "Well, Ms.…"

"Jones. Bronwen Jones. The barn manager."

"All right, Ms. Jones, barn manager. No, I had no idea that my sister's new farm was a boarding barn. And I have absolutely no intention of getting involved with any of the operations, whatever they may be. She'll be back in the country in a few weeks, and you can contact her directly then. Until that time, do what you need to do—but leave me out of it."

She noticed that he hadn't offered his name. Or his sister's.

He turned to face the fire again, clearly dismissing her.

Frustration flared again, hot and urgent. This man would *not* get rid of her that easily. She stepped around his chair, directly in front of him, so he had no choice but to look at her.

"I can't leave you out of it, not if you're the closest thing to the owner. Ruth—the former owner—thought the new owner would be moving in immediately, and she didn't give me withdrawal access to the farm account. I *need* the bills paid. There are horses out there depending on it, not to mention their owners. If we can't keep up with feed and maintenance, people are going to move their horses out of here."

And she'd lose the small family she'd gathered around herself, the familiarity of even the people who got on her nerves. The horses she cared for like they were her own. And if the barn went out of business, what would she do with her own horse, Charlie? Where would she go? The farm was her home. It was safe. She couldn't let the boarders and their horses down, and she couldn't lose the place she called home.

"That's really not my problem," the man said coolly, as if the whole thing bored him.

Which was infuriating. Absolutely *infuriating.* There were few things she hated more than people who refused to accept their responsibilities. In her experience, there were far too many people like the man in front of her, which was why she'd learned to depend solely on herself. Still, in this case she needed him to do the right thing.

"It *is* your problem if this is your sister's farm and you're living here in her place. Your family is responsible for the well-being of these horses and of the farm. You have an obligation to the people who trust the care of their animals to you."

"To my *sister*," he contradicted, as if none of this mattered. As if he had something better to do than act like a responsible human being, when quite clearly, lounging around alone was all he had going on.

Must be nice.

"Your sister's on some fancy island somewhere while you're sitting in an empty house with a bottle and nothing else!" she all but shouted, her voice echoing through the vacant house.

Bronwen wasn't usually a shouter, but she was desperate, and enraged at the dismissive attitude of the man before her. Even if he didn't own the farm himself, even if for some wild reason his sister hadn't thought to mention that the barn was full of boarders, how could he act like their care was beneath his notice? If nothing else, didn't he want to maintain the business his sister had paid good money for?

Their eyes locked, hers no doubt shooting sparks of frustration, his deceptively cool but with dark fire beneath the chill. She'd touched something, some nerve, and she was finally getting the barest reaction.

Good.

"If all of the boarders leave," she continued, pushing for something more—any emotion, any sign that he cared at all, "your sister will have spent all her money on an empty farm—the business will completely dry up."

That earned a smirk. "I doubt she cares too much about that."

"Right." She suppressed an eye roll. It didn't matter if someone had money, but she had no patience for those wealthy people who seemed to think money excused them from being human. "And the horses? What about them?"

His hand tightened almost imperceptibly around his glass. Then he downed the rest of his drink in one gulp, leaned forward and set the glass heavily down on the bare wood floor. Gaze fixed onto hers, he rose from the chair, and she took an involuntary step back.

Martha was right. This man was *tall*. She wasn't exactly short at five foot eight, but he easily cleared six feet. More. He wasn't overly broad, but he had a lean solidity that spoke of strength and power. He loomed over her, glaring.

She glared right back.

"To hell with the horses," he said fiercely, but with a shadow of his previous resigned exhaustion.

Who was this man? He was lurking around the empty old house like Mr. Rochester from *Jane Eyre*, looking like a fallen angel, eyes chilly as the early spring sky and anger that came out of nowhere.

He took a step forward, and she took another step back.

"To hell with the farm," he continued. "And to hell with you."

He folded his arms in front of him, and Bronwen reminded herself to breathe. She wasn't scared, exactly. But he made an intimidating picture, and she still wasn't 100 percent sure she should trust that he wasn't a danger to her.

"I told you to get out. If you're the barn manager, that means you're my sister's employee, and in her absence I am telling you to *get out*."

She wanted to; she really did. Her heart was pounding in

her chest, whether from the confrontation with this strange man or from the fact that he'd stepped even closer—close enough that she could see the whiskers of his stubble, the way his jaw ticked with tension. She had the absolutely ridiculous urge to reach up and smooth away that tension, even as he was ordering her to leave.

Absurd. Probably she just needed more coffee. And a vacation. And for someone to fix the problems all around her.

She should leave and call…someone? She couldn't call the sister, either to help with the barn's situation or to confirm that this guy was, in fact, supposed to be here. A vague memory surfaced of Ruth saying the new owner was someone tangentially involved with horses. If that last part was true, shouldn't her brother care a little more about what happened to the animals? Even someone who was just a casual rider should care deeply about the welfare of horses—certainly someone who purchased an entire boarding barn would. Was this man so distant from his sister that he didn't understand how important good care was to most horse people? Or was he just a terrible person who didn't care about either the animals or his own sister?

She wasn't sure *what* she should do, to be honest. But one thing was for sure, and that was that she really didn't appreciate this man looming over her, angry and bossy, uncaring about the farm's problems and refusing to see reason.

She didn't like it at all.

"If you can order me around on your sister's behalf, then you're admitting that you're standing in for her while she's away," she snapped.

Faulty logic pissed her off, but in this case it worked in

her favor. She raised a hand and pointed her finger at him, nearly jabbing him in the chest. He glanced down at it like she was filthy. Which, to be honest, she probably was. She'd started the day climbing up a pile of shit, and it had been downhill from there.

"You're *not* my boss, but you are responsible. Or at least, you should be."

Bronwen turned and marched back to the door to the room, then swung around. She'd retreat for now, but if this guy didn't act soon, she'd tell the feed store and the farrier and anyone else needing payment to come right to the front door of the house. Nothing would stop her from getting things back on track, one way or another, even if it meant an army of cranky vendors invaded the man's strange solitude.

He glared at her, mouth open as if he was stunned by her audacity. Or maybe he was just about to snark at her some more.

"There are nearly a dozen horses down there who are going to run out of food. The manure pile is out of control. The outdoor arena footing is a hazard. Someone's going to get hurt, or go hungry, and if anything at all happens to any one of those animals, or to their owners, it will be *your* fault." She pointed at him again for good measure. "Anything at all. It will be on your head."

She turned and stormed out the front door, slamming it behind her, and tried not to slip on the remaining frost as she stomped down the steps and headed for the warmth and safety of the barn.

Two

Ian Kingston lay in bed and listened to silence.

He'd thought, during that week in the hospital a couple of months ago, that he'd relish quiet after he escaped all of the endless beeping and murmuring and shuffling around that went on in every medical facility. Time had escaped him then, even as his life before had been scheduled down to the minute. In the hospital it was always daytime, always bright in the hallways and always busy, even in the middle of the night.

Here, night was pitch-dark, especially since only one lamp sat in the nearly empty bedroom, and there was no point in turning it on when all he was doing was lying still. Alone. Moping, his sister, Anne, would say.

The silence was, in fact, almost unbearable. He shoved the blankets off his body and tossed around, as if movement could dispel his thoughts and allow him to finally rest. But it only caused a familiar twinge in his hip and ache in his back, pain he hadn't felt in a week or so.

At least the headaches had left him alone.

With a sigh, he swung his legs around to the cold floor and sat up. He peered out the window, bare of any curtains. It could be any time of night. He might have slept for an hour or for ten. But his well-tuned internal clock told him otherwise. He was all too familiar with the early morning period before dawn, and he guessed it was around five o'clock.

"Shit."

He knew exactly what was keeping him from sleeping in as he'd planned to do now that he had nothing to keep him occupied, other than the aforementioned moping. It certainly wasn't the bourbon, which he'd put away after *she* left, feeling more than a little pathetic. Which only added to his resentment of the intrusion. It wasn't the aches and pains. It wasn't even an existential crisis about his future. Not on this particular night, anyway.

He'd fully intended to continue secluding himself in the house, heading out only for necessities, until he decided what to do next. He knew that Anne believed he'd had enough time alone, but he hadn't expected that she'd go to such extremes to push him out of his self-inflicted exile.

A *boarding* barn. What could she have been thinking?

He had to hand it to her, though. Instead of sleeping late and puttering around the house in peace, here he was, awake before dawn, thinking about what that woman—Bronwen— had said about the horses.

He didn't really care about the people. They could move their animals to a different facility, for all he cared. That wasn't his problem. But the danger to the horses... If some aspect of neglect or lack of action on his part caused harm to any of the horses, he didn't know how he'd face himself. Because Bronwen was right, goddammit. He was the farm owner's brother, and the only one of the two of them in residence. Without him, the horses would suffer.

Apparently there was at least one thing he still cared about.

With a groan, he stood and pulled on the jeans he'd worn yesterday.

He'd have to go now, if he was going to go at all. He didn't want anything to do with any of the boarders, and even less so with Bronwen. The woman had caught him at a particularly low point, stuck in his head and in a house that he'd expected to be secluded and private but also warm and cozy.

"A quaint little farm in Massachusetts!" Anne had gushed. "Just a little outside of Boston. It should be gorgeous in a few weeks for spring, and you can house-sit for me until I move in."

House-sitting while she took off for vacation to celebrate her divorce from a real estate mogul who had doted on her—until he hadn't. But she'd been able to get a good settlement, as she deserved, considering how much she'd supported her husband and his business during their few years of marriage. Anne deserved a vacation. She deserved every happiness she could find, and she'd certainly deserved the money after the way they'd grown up. And it wasn't like Ian had anything else planned or anywhere to go.

So he'd agreed, expecting a small farmhouse overstuffed with comfortable furniture. Maybe in the woods, where no one could find him. Instead, he found himself in a big old monstrosity with the bare minimum of furniture and no comforts other than the downstairs fire and the bourbon he'd bought in town.

And, worst of all, he'd learned that the farm was a boarding barn, with people coming and going all day and a pushy barn manager to boot.

It was exactly what he didn't want, and yet knowing Anne the way he did, he should have seen it coming.

He looked around for his slippers, and not finding them, he headed downstairs barefoot, the wood floor unpleasantly chilled. No matter how high he cranked the ancient heating system, it was always cold in this house. Always empty. Always quiet. It should have suited his mood perfectly.

He stuck his feet into his old work boots and shrugged into his coat. Outside, everything was still and dark. His feet crunched on the gravel path down to the barn, and he stepped sideways onto the grass, even though no one could possibly be around to hear him at this hour. The horses, maybe, if they were expecting their breakfast—and horses were *always* expecting food.

And then he was there, the absolute last place he wanted to be: outside the door to the barn. His breath tightened in his chest and his skin overheated uncomfortably despite the chill. He wanted nothing more than to run back to the house, barricade the door and dig the bourbon bottle back out of the cabinet. Silently he cursed his sister for her interference. She should have known better. Should have known he wasn't ready. Wouldn't ever be ready.

But he was nothing if not tough, if not able to compartmentalize his emotions and stuff the difficult ones into a box he might or might not open later.

He pushed open the barn's large sliding door, noticing that it wanted to stick about halfway, forcing him to muscle it the rest of the way. Another problem. The padlock also stuck out haphazardly, loose on its screws. Another potential hazard for a horse walking by—no one wanted their horse cut or scraped by a solid piece of metal.

Cursing everything he could think of, he stepped into the dark barn aisle. Nickers greeted him up and down the stalls, the soft rustling of hooves in wood shavings breaking the silence as a dozen animals moved to see who was entering their home. He could just barely make out the outline of the nearest ones, the shape of their large heads so familiar.

The earthy smell of hay, horse, manure and leather hit him like a punch to the stomach, and he closed his eyes as if that would do anything at all.

He told himself he was being silly, overly nostalgic and dramatic, and groped around for the lights. He flipped the switch and found twelve sets of kind dark eyes watching him curiously from either side of the wide barn aisle. He had the absurd urge to wave and introduce himself. Instinct told him to check each stall, give each horse a little attention as he made his way down the aisle, to see if anything was out of place after a night alone.

Instead, he trudged toward the middle of the barn where another sliding door opened outward toward the fields behind, and he got a good look at the manure pile a few dozen feet away.

Yes, it was definitely overflowing. Inconvenient at the

moment, but it would be unpleasant when the temperatures warmed up.

He wandered farther down the wide concrete aisle to the feed room at the far end of the barn, a small space lined on one side with large metal boxes of feed and on the other walls with cabinets and countertops. He opened one of the tightly lidded metal containers. Definitely low on feed. He didn't bother to look for the hay storage. What Bronwen had told him was true. There was work to be done here, work that had to be paid for. If the farm wasn't kept in good operating condition, if the feed store bill wasn't paid, the horses would suffer.

He groaned in frustration. He wanted to march back up to the house, get in his car and drive away from this place. Why had he ever accepted Anne's invitation? He should have known she was up to something.

A whinny pulled his attention from his thoughts. And then another. The horses were impatient to be fed now that they knew someone was up and in the barn. He smiled despite himself. Horses were in some ways so much more dependable than people. And in other ways, dangerously unpredictable.

He turned to leave.

A noise somewhere nearby stopped him in his tracks. It wasn't the sound of a horse shuffling in its stall. It sounded like…footsteps on stairs. But that couldn't be right. He assumed the only thing above was the hayloft, and no one should be up there this time of the morning.

Before he could sort out what the noise was, the door to the feed room creaked open and something came barreling toward his head. The dark shape came out of nowhere and he ducked instinctively as it whooshed over his head. He straightened and saw that the object that had nearly decapitated him was a shovel.

Heart pounding, he grabbed the handle and pushed it out of the way, then dived for the person holding the other end, shoving their body up against the wall and wrenching the shovel from their grasp. He let it drop to the floor.

"Oof," the other person gasped, and he grabbed their wrists and held them to the wall.

The person was much smaller than him, much smaller than he'd expect an intruder wielding a shovel to be. Small and, he noticed as he glanced down to the floor, barefoot. And wearing pajamas. Yellow pajamas with little blue horses printed all over them. And a tight-fitting tank top with a faded logo for some college printed on it. A tank top that left nothing to the imagination, as his eyes drifted up toward the face of his attacker.

Bronwen.

She stood frozen like a deer on a nighttime road, caught in the headlights of an oncoming car. Ian forced himself to loosen his death grip on her wrists, but he didn't release her, and she didn't struggle.

He swallowed heavily, taking in her long brown hair, messy as if she'd just rolled out of bed. Her full, parted lips. The delicate curve of her shoulder, bare to the cold air. Her chest, rising and falling as her breath came rapidly, nipples sharp points under her shirt.

Some alchemical reaction charged the air between them, turning the crisp chill into something warm and heavy. He licked his lips, not even sure how to name the thing between him and this woman he'd met exactly once. A woman who'd just tried to bean him with a shovel.

In the house yesterday, he'd known she was beautiful, of course. Striking, with a long, slim nose and pointed stubborn chin. Green eyes that had pinned him where he sat on the sad, lonely armchair. But he had been too distracted by his anger and shame to notice any sort of chemistry. Now chemistry was all around them, fizzing and sparking and doing things to his body that he was definitely not prepared for at five o'clock in the morning in a barn he didn't want to be in, with a woman he didn't even know.

Bronwen sucked in a breath and her gaze dropped from his eyes to his mouth. His body tightened in response, warmth pooling in his groin and an urgency squeezing a groan out of him.

"What are you doing?" she whispered, and he realized he'd leaned into her until their torsos nearly touched. Which would have been even more embarrassing than being caught drinking yesterday morning, given what his body was currently doing.

He jerked back and glared at her. He needed to break this spell and get ahold of himself. Anger would build that wall back up, just as it had been doing for him since his accident.

"Me? I live here. For now. What are *you* doing here? It can't be time to feed the horses yet."

She stared at him. "What do you know about horses?"

He swung away from her, crossing to the other side of the small room and bracing his arms on top of the counter there. Forced himself to take a few long, slow breaths, until arousal was fully replaced by annoyance. Then he turned back to face Bronwen.

She was still pressed against the wall behind her, looking a little shell-shocked. The shovel lay on the floor, inches from her bare feet. If it had fallen on one of them, she could have been injured, a thought that caused a twinge of guilt.

He pushed the twinge away. She was the one who had tried to attack him, when she shouldn't even be here at all.

"*Why* are you here, Bronwen Jones, barn manager?" He used his most authoritative voice, the one that people generally obeyed without questions.

She just looked at him like he'd lost his mind. "Yeah... *barn manager.* Manager. Of *this* barn." She pointed to the ceiling. "I live in the apartment over the barn. You know, while I manage it."

Bronwen pushed off the wall and placed her fists on her hips. Ian ran a hand over his face. *Stupid.* It was hardly unheard-of for a barn manager to live on-site, even in the barn itself. He'd just been too distracted by the fact that there even *was* a barn manager, or a barn to be managed. He wouldn't have missed the plot so thoroughly, before. This sudden and complete uprooting of his entire world made him forget the most basic things. He was more than off-kilter. He was completely upside down, and the disorientation was more dizzying than the concussion he'd allegedly recovered from.

"And do you usually greet visitors with a shovel to the head?" he asked, falling back on snark.

Jesus. Like his head hadn't been through enough. A shovel would probably have sent him right to his just reward. Or punishment.

She narrowed her eyes, and he had the distinct impression that Bronwen Jones was not easily intimidated. And that she didn't appreciate his snark.

"I do when someone's broken into the barn I'm responsible for in the middle of the night."

He glanced out the small window above the counter, where no thread of light poked through the gloom of darkness.

"It's morning," he said. Not his greatest comeback.

"I'd hardly know that when I just got out of bed and ran down here to stop an intruder," she said dryly.

She made a good point. But he was still on edge, from his worries about the well-being of the horses, from the unwelcome discovery that his retreat was anything but, from whatever the hell had passed between him and Bronwen when he had her pushed up against the wall—something that appeared not to have bothered her in the least, while his body was still suggesting all kinds of useful things they could do with that something.

He grimaced. He needed to get out of there.

"Look. I didn't know you lived over the barn. I thought you were breaking in."

"Funny, I had the same thought about you." She eyed the shovel like she was still considering using it on him.

"I just wanted to…see."

She waited, silent.

He sighed. "See if what you were saying was true. If there was any danger to the horses if things weren't straightened out."

Bronwen's cheeks flushed, probably with anger at him,

but it was still incredibly attractive. Why did she have to be so pretty? The last thing he needed—aside from this entire mess—was an unwelcome attraction to a woman he definitely needed to avoid at all costs.

"You think I came up to the house and lied about what's going on in the barn?" she spit out. "Why would I do that?"

"How should I know?" he snapped back. A horse snorted somewhere outside of the feed room, no doubt wondering why they were talking instead of scooping feed. "I didn't even know there were horses here, let alone a whole boarding operation. You could have been anyone, saying anything."

She rolled her eyes, and his patience began to fray. All he'd wanted was to be left alone. To forget about everything: his previous life, his injuries, the horses, the people who'd vanished on him...

He shook his head to clear those thoughts.

"Look," Bronwen began, irritation sharpening her words. "Your sister owns this farm. She's not here. You are. You are responsible—"

"I heard this speech the first time you gave it," he said, cutting her off.

He shoved his hands into the pockets of his jeans and stalked to the door, careful to give her a wide berth. He didn't want any of that strange reaction to make a reappearance. He had enough problems.

"And it's still as true as it was yesterday," she retorted.

Ian inhaled through his nose, then out. And a solution came to him. It wasn't perfect, but maybe it would get this woman off his back so he could go back to his solitude. And it would also relieve the guilt he'd feel if anything happened.

"Fine. I get it. Here's what I'll do. I'll look into the issues you mentioned—feed bill, farrier bill, hay delivery, manure removal. Anything else?"

He made a mental note about the dangerous padlock on the barn door, as well, and realized he'd have to do a full assessment of the farm, somehow. Without Ms. Bossy trailing after him. Any sharp edges of pieces of metal or wood sticking out from the barn could harm a horse. Pasture fencing needed to be checked regularly for holes or hazards. What condition was the grass in? Was the barn roof holding up? Leaks could damage the hay above, and it sounded like they didn't have any to spare to mold or dampness. He hadn't been looking for issues with the property, but having spent time in the barren old house, he hoped the rest of the farm was in better shape than that building.

"The outdoor arena needs new footing," Bronwen added.

Right. She'd mentioned that before. "That's a big project."

Bronwen shrugged. "A farm is a big project. If your sister didn't want to deal with it, she shouldn't have bought it."

They agreed on that, at least. But his sister must have had ulterior motives from the beginning. He was going to have it out with her as soon as he could reach her.

"Fine. I'll see what I can do. About all of it."

Ian had the money in savings, and he knew that Anne was good for repayment. He'd basically never spent more than he needed to live, out of force of habit. He could run a farm for a few weeks until Anne could pay him back.

"Really?" Bronwen looked skeptical, and he could hardly blame her. She had no idea who he was, which suited him just fine.

"You have my word. Leave contact information for the vendors in the mailbox at the house. I'll take care of everything I can."

Doubt creased Bronwen's forehead. She clearly didn't believe him for a moment. But that wasn't his problem.

"And in return..."

Doubt turned into wariness as he watched her. She folded her arms in front of her and lifted her chin.

"In return?"

Jesus, what did she think he was going to say? He was hardly going to ask for sexual favors in exchange for new outdoor arena footing, as expensive as that was going to be. He wasn't a monster, although of course she had no way of knowing that. He'd been monstrous enough yesterday when she'd caught him off guard, looming and snapping and growling at her like a wounded animal.

"In return, I want you to leave me alone. Completely. If there's a problem, put a note in the mailbox. Don't come to the house, don't look for me, don't bother me. Understood?"

Something flashed in her eyes, and he wondered what she thought he was doing up at the house. Something horrible, probably. Nothing as pathetic as lurking around the empty rooms trying to figure out who the hell he was. It was for the best if she thought he was terrible. She'd be more likely to stay out of his way.

And that was what he wanted, even if she was too appealing, holding her ground against him in her horse pajamas, even if he was impressed by her dedication to the animals and the people who owned them. Even if he'd felt more alive in the past few minutes than he had in two months.

She bit her lower lip, and he made himself turn away. This was what he needed. He'd do as he had promised, but he wouldn't have any further interactions with Bronwen Jones.

"Understood," she finally said, so quietly he wasn't sure if it was doubt that he'd follow through or something else tingeing her voice.

"Good," he replied shortly and strode out of the feed room back toward the house.

Three

"So, what was he like?" Olivia asked over top of Charlie's neck.

His brown coat was still fuzzy with its winter growth, and he'd been rolling out in the field that morning, so Bronwen was helping to de-mud him. The horse relaxed in the wash stall, cross ties attached to either side of his halter, back foot propped on its front edge and eyes closed. Every so often he'd nose Olivia affectionately, and Bronwen tried not to feel anything like jealousy. Or loss.

Her nose scrunched. She didn't really want to think of either of her two meetings with… Well, she didn't actually know his name. For all their back-and-forth, she'd never asked. She was too busy being annoyed by his refusal to take responsibility for the farm, then by the shock of finding him in the feed room when she'd thought he was an intruder, and then…

Well. As much as she definitely wasn't looking for any sort

of relationship or fling or anything at all, really, her body had apparently not gotten the memo. When a ridiculously attractive man had you up against a wall, various reactions were bound to happen.

"Are you...*blushing*?" Olivia's eyes widened and her mouth dropped open. "Oh, this is good. Tell me everything!" She patted the top of Charlie's back in excitement, but he didn't even bat an eye.

"Ooh, tell you what? What's going on?" Scott, Brian's husband, stopped in his tracks as he led his pretty copper bay horse, Sugar, down the barn aisle. Sugar was all tacked up in her saddle and bridle, ready for her ride.

"Wait—are you riding indoors or outdoors?" She didn't want to risk Sugar's legs on the outdoor footing.

"Indoors." Scott made a face, then rubbed a hand over his dark beard. "She's so spooky in there, but I can't take her outside."

Bronwen sighed. She knew Sugar would be a handful indoors—spooking and pretending every shadow was a monster, every mysterious sound from outside a threat. But Scott couldn't just leave her in the field all day. He had to ride somehow.

"I'm sorry," she said.

"I guess the new owner wasn't much help." Olivia gave her a sympathetic grimace.

"Did you actually meet the owner?" Scott leaned back against Sugar's belly, his head barely reaching her back.

"I did," Bronwen replied. "And he said he'd take care of the issues." She chewed her bottom lip, a bad nervous habit. "It's actually his sister who's the owner, but she's out of the

country and he's staying here for a while. He didn't—"
She stopped, although she didn't know why. It felt wrong
somehow to tell them everything she knew—little as it
was—about the man, but that was silly. She didn't owe
him anything, and he hadn't said his presence there was a
secret. Only that he wanted to be left alone.

Which was completely fine with her. She didn't need any
more time in the presence of a tall, blond, brooding man
who clearly had no use for her—or the farm she loved—
whatsoever. For one very short moment in the feed room
yesterday, when he'd leaned into her and the air shifted
around them like an electrical charge, she'd even thought
that he'd been about to kiss her. And the worst part was,
she'd wanted him to.

She didn't even know him—he was a complete stranger,
and an unpleasant one at that. Bronwen had no idea what
came over her, and was just grateful that he'd stepped away
and resumed being awful. She'd already extricated herself
from a man who'd been perfectly fine until he was revealed
to be awful. Kissing a man who'd started off as awful seemed
like a distinct step backward.

"Didn't what?" Olivia asked, going back to scrubbing
Charlie with a stiff currycomb.

"Yeah, didn't what?" Scott added.

Bronwen decided she may as well tell them everything.
"He didn't even know this was a boarding barn—his sister
didn't tell him. Really weird. And he didn't want to take
responsibility for it, for any of it. But then he agreed to deal
with all of the problems until his sister gets back, *if* we leave
him completely alone."

Scott shrugged as if any of it made any sense at all. "So, we leave him alone. If we get feed and hay and—dear Lord in heaven, please let it be so—new footing for the outdoor, who cares? No skin off our collective noses."

Olivia squinted at her from the other side of Charlie's body. "Okay... That's weird but fine." She pointed the currycomb in Bronwen's direction. "But what's with the blushing?"

Bronwen had hoped she'd distracted her friend from that little reaction.

"Yeah, what's with the blushing?" Scott repeated.

"Why are we blushing?" Rachel stuck her head around the door of the tack room.

Bronwen resisted the urge to bang her head against the side of the nearest stall.

Rachel was eleven years old, completely horse obsessed and as good a rider as Bronwen had seen at her age. She had the fearlessness of most child riders, as well as natural-born talent and a total understanding of her pony, an adorable little black-and-white paint named Applejack.

Unfortunately, Rachel was growing as fast as kids tended to do, while Applejack stayed the same height. No one dared bring it up around the barn, but Rachel's ability to ride her beloved pony would come to an end sooner rather than later.

Bronwen thought fast. "He was just... He was so rude. It makes me mad just thinking about it."

It was a weak excuse for her blush, but Scott and Rachel seemed to buy it. Olivia raised an eyebrow but kept brushing Charlie.

"Well...again," Scott said. "Who cares? If we're not going

to see him around, he can be as rude as he likes up there at the house. Alone."

Olivia's forehead wrinkled. "Didn't Ruth's grandkids take most of the furniture when she moved? How did he get all his stuff in there without you noticing, Bronwen?"

"He doesn't...he doesn't really have any stuff up there." The image of him, sitting in the near darkness by the fire in a cold and empty house, flickered across her consciousness. She wouldn't feel bad for him. She *wouldn't*. He clearly wanted whatever it was he had going on in the house, as lonely as it appeared. It wasn't her business.

"Weird," Scott said.

"Yeah, that's creepy. Is he a serial killer?" Rachel asked with some enthusiasm.

"Who knows?" Bronwen said, then thought better of herself. Sometimes she forgot that Rachel was just a kid. Rachel's parents wouldn't thank her for suggesting that the person in charge of the barn where their kid spent every free minute might be a murderer. "I mean, no. Of course not. He probably had his stuff shipped and it hasn't arrived yet. He said he's only here until his sister gets back, anyway."

"Well, as long as he does what needs doing, he can be as weird as he wants," Scott said, and he led Sugar toward the indoor.

"I'm going to get Applejack from the field," Rachel said. "I bet he's gross," she added with a glance at the caked mud on Charlie's side. "This weather sucks."

Olivia snorted. "It does. Where is spring?" And when Scott and Rachel were well out of earshot, she added, "And listen—don't think I buy that crap you gave us about this new guy being irritating."

"He *is* irritating," Bronwen protested.

"Okay. But he's also a grouchy recluse in a big old house, and I'm going to wildly guess from the color your face turned when you talked about him that he's attractive, too. Right?"

Bronwen made a face.

Olivia cackled. "He is, isn't he? He's a gorgeous beast, and you're the beauty!"

"Yes, look at me, the epitome of what everyone desires in a woman," Bronwen said dryly, sweeping her gaze over her shirt with the hole in the hem from where one of the horses had ripped it with their teeth, her stained jeans, her unspeakably filthy boots. She never wore makeup, and her plain brown hair was eternally pulled back in a practical ponytail.

"Oh please. You're hot."

Bronwen curtsied at her friend. "Why, thank you. But our perspective as official Horse Girls T-M might be a little different from the general public."

Bronwen was used to the looks she'd get when she ran into the grocery store in her muck-covered boots and her rattiest old T-shirt. She barely noticed the dirt or the smell herself, and since her life revolved around horses 24/7, it was hardly worth it to doll herself up just to go into town. It wasn't like she was looking to meet anyone, and if she ever decided she was ready for that again, they'd have to accept her as she was. Horses were far more important than trying to meet some artificial beauty standard she didn't care about to begin with.

"The general public is missing out, both on horses and hot horse girls."

"Too true."

"He *is* hot, though. Isn't he?"

Bronwen waited a beat. "Yes. Yes, he is."

"Excellent." Olivia grinned at her.

Over the weekend, Bronwen was caught up in the usual rush of boarders coming and going while they had whole days off work, as well as the extra grooming, blanketing and coping with the ice—and even a dusting of snow—that always came over the winter. Except it wasn't winter anymore, and she wondered yet again when they'd finally get the spring thaw.

She couldn't remember the last time she'd had to break solid ice in the horses' water buckets this late in the year, and while the frost-covered grass across the six large fields out back sparkled cheerfully in the morning sun, the dirt road dividing them was an eternally muddy mess. And that same sun seemed to have no interest in actually warming or drying any part of the farm. But the horses were snug in their winter blankets, and they didn't mind rolling in the cold mud, even if their owners were less pleased with the results. They all gathered in the heated tack room for hot coffee and the doughnuts that Brian brought with him almost every day between grooming, riding and the other never-ending chores that accompanied horse life. And the wait for spring continued.

Bronwen spent a not-insignificant amount of time cursing the Man of the House, as she'd started thinking of him, for lying to her and convincing her to leave him alone while he took care of the various issues around the farm. He hadn't made another appearance, which was unsurprising. But she *was* unexpectedly surprised and a little disappointed that he hadn't kept his word about fixing the farm's problems.

She didn't know why she was surprised, honestly. She'd certainly had close run-ins before with men who promised big and delivered nothing.

But if this man thought she'd continue to stay out of his way while he failed to hold up his end of the bargain, he was sadly mistaken. Still, she hesitated to stomp up to his doorstep and tear him a new one, telling herself that she wanted to give him a chance. That she was too busy to go up and have it out with him again. And after all, the reality was that she couldn't force him to do anything.

The *other* reality was she didn't relish the thought of being in close proximity to him again. The way the breath had whooshed out of her lungs when he'd leaned close to her, the heat that had begun somewhere just below her heart and melted downward to her pelvis—she enjoyed attraction as much as many people, but not when it was attraction to *that* man. She needed to hold him accountable, not swoon whenever he got too near to her.

So, she grumped around the farm for several days, and then… Then things started happening.

First, she went out into the crisp morning air one day and had to fumble around for the lock on the main sliding door because it was no longer sticking out. She'd meant to fix that issue herself and just hadn't gotten to it. Then she came downstairs to the tiny office next to the feed room one morning to find the farrier scheduled into the chalkboard barn calendar that hung on the wall, in handwriting she didn't recognize.

And the feed store called while she was standing there staring at the chalkboard and said they were all paid up, and would she like to pick up their regular order, or have it delivered? The hay delivery arrived a day later, just as their supply was getting dangerously low. And finally, incredibly, the manure removal truck came to take away their mountain of manure, just as Bronwen couldn't possibly dump any more on top without risking an avalanche.

It was all awfully productive and efficient for someone who'd appeared to neither care about nor know anything about horses. She wondered if she'd been mistaken about him, or if he'd intentionally misled her.

"Huh," Martha said. "Whatever you told the new owner really worked."

"The owner's brother," Bronwen said absently. "He's just here temporarily."

"Well, he can stay permanently if this is how things are going to be." And she stalked off to get Percy.

Bronwen wanted to agree. A hands-off owner who paid the bills and made sure everything was taken care of while also leaving her to do her job wasn't the worst thing in the world. She missed Ruth, of course, but Ruth had been her friend as well as her boss. Those sorts of relationships didn't happen every day, and she wasn't expecting a replacement. She just wanted the farm to be safe and well-run.

But she did wonder... The Man of the House hadn't seemed particularly happy on the two occasions when she'd seen him. And that wasn't her business, or her problem. She had her hands full at the barn with nearly a dozen horses and owners clamoring for care and attention. And maybe it was because Ruth was a good friend, and Bronwen had become accustomed to caring about the well-being of the owner. Maybe it was habit more than anything.

But she worried.

Not overwhelmingly, and not all the time. But every so often she'd remember the creases in his forehead when she'd been so close to him in the feed room. The grim set of his mouth as he hunched by the fireplace surrounded by emptiness. The way he'd lashed out and told her he wanted to be left alone.

Bronwen liked being alone. But not all the time. Not in an empty house. And not when she was so obviously unhappy.

She found herself glancing up at the house, trying to see if there were any signs of life. He'd been busy the past few days, fixing the things she'd told him about, and more. Surely he had to leave the house sometimes, if only to deal with those problems? But she never saw any sign of it. She wondered if he was sick. If he needed anything. If, despite her promises, it might be in everyone's best interest if she went up to the house just one more time, to check on him.

The thing that finally pushed her over the edge was the outdoor ring.

When Ruth had lived at the farm, she'd always made sure that Bronwen had two full days off each week. Usually Mondays and Tuesdays, since most of the boarders were back at work and things were relatively slow. For those two days, their part-time barn assistant, a college student named Abigail, handled feeding and mucking out.

Since Ruth left, Bronwen started splitting her days off to Tuesdays and Thursdays just so she wasn't away from the barn for too long at once. But this week, she'd taken Tuesday and Wednesday to go into Boston and visit her parents in Brighton, staying in their duplex overnight. She hadn't seen them in weeks, and while they were both healthy and happily retired, she liked to check in on them. Plus, eating two days' worth of her dad's cooking was always worth the short trip.

She'd returned home to her apartment late Wednesday night and collapsed into bed after a quick check around the barn. Thursday morning, after she'd finished her chores, she caught Scott chatting happily with Martha just outside of the barn, grasping Sugar's reins in one hand.

"Good morning, miracle worker!" Scott greeted her with enormous cheer.

"I— What?" Bronwen looked around like maybe Scott was talking to someone else.

"I told you before," Martha said. "Whatever you said to the new owner *really* worked."

Bronwen stared at the older woman. "What am I missing?"

"The outdoor ring!" Scott said. "Two days ago a big truck came and all these guys dug out a layer of the packed old dirt and replaced it with that fancy fiber-mix stuff. It's all dragged and leveled out—I feel like I'm at the Olympics or something!"

Bronwen blinked several times. The old footing had just been dirt and clay, so trodden down that even dragging it with the tractor didn't do much to soften it, especially in the freezing weather. But when she'd said they needed new footing, she was picturing a layer of good sand. Not only was the fancy fiber stuff more expensive, but it took some level of knowledge to know what to shop for. A level of knowledge she definitely wouldn't have ascribed to the Man of the House. Only someone with significant barn management knowledge could have pulled this off so quickly.

"And they fixed the drainage!" Martha added. "They were in there all day both days, doing whatever it was."

"Yeah, they put in a couple drainage pipes, did some leveling—the main guy said they were under strict orders to get it done in two days. They were here as long as any of us were, way past dark both times."

Bronwen frowned. None of this made any sense. The Man of the House obviously had been looking at—and writing on—the chalkboard calendar. He would have seen her days off. Why schedule the work for when she'd be away? And why spend more money than he had to on a farm he didn't even want to be in charge of? Because he must have paid for it out of his own pocket, with how tight the farm's books were, and he'd taken the expensive option.

Gratitude battled with confusion inside her. The expense and effort of everything he'd done recently was enormous. And yet he'd done it without ever speaking to her or any of the boarders. Without ever, it appeared, leaving the house.

Other than his nocturnal visits to the office to write on the chalkboard.

Nocturnal visits paid while she was asleep upstairs in her bed, which wasn't something she should find vaguely sexy. And yet...

She shook her head.

"Well," she said briskly, "that's great news, isn't it? The ring needed an upgrade for a while, and this is better than we could have hoped."

Martha eyed her. "You should go up there," she said, gesturing to the farmhouse with her chin. "See what's going on."

Bronwen shook her head again, even though she'd been thinking the same thing to herself.

Sugar sidled up to her and snuffled her pockets. "Sorry, Sug, I don't have any treats." She scratched absently between the mare's ears. "He made it really clear that he wants to be left alone. That he was going to take care of all this stuff *if* we left him alone."

Martha squinted in the direction of the house. "Alone all the time, though? He hasn't come down to the barn once."

Bronwen didn't mention the nocturnal chalkboard-writing or padlock-fixing visits.

"Yeah, we're not going to bite him or whatever," Scott added. "I mean, fine, if he wants us to stay out of his business, but...he never even comes out of the house. That seems a little weird."

It was more than a little weird. She didn't even know the man's *name*, for God's sake.

Was she doing the right thing by respecting his wishes

and leaving him alone? He obviously wasn't the complete ass she'd believed at first, an ass she was more than happy to avoid and ignore, as long as the barn was taken care of. But he'd gone to such effort on her behalf—and the horses', of course. He couldn't be as terrible a person as he'd seemed that first day. What if he was lonely, or worse, in trouble? She had no idea what kind of trouble someone could get into by themselves in that big old house, but she hated to think of anyone alone and struggling. No one deserved that. He seemed like the sort who could take care of himself. But still...

"He's already helped us so much," Martha said. "Even Ruth could barely keep up with the farm maintenance."

"Ruth did things her own way," Bronwen admitted.

Horse care always came first with Ruth, but she had sometimes needed nudging when it came to paying the bills or taking on large projects like, for example, the outdoor ring. She'd been a single woman in her seventies responsible for a whole farm, and for most of the decades Ruth owned Morning Song she'd done it all herself. Bronwen couldn't fault her. But having everything on the to-do list taken care of so quickly and without any effort on her part... It was pretty great.

And she was feeling pretty grateful, despite the unsettling effect the grumpy man up in the farmhouse had on her.

"And there are other things that need doing," Scott said. "Things Ruth talked about but never got around to—like new saddle racks in the tack room, and getting a new gate for the indoor. No, Sugar, no grazing with your bridle on."

He pulled his horse's head up from where she was trying to grab a snack.

Bronwen chewed her lip. "But those aren't things we *need*," she said. "The list I gave the new owner's brother were things that couldn't wait."

"You could still ask, though," Martha replied.

"You could," Scott said. "Just ask."

Bronwen looked suspiciously between the two of them. "Do you want me to ask for more because we need those things done, or because you're nosy and want more info on him?"

Martha grinned. "Both? It can be both, right?"

"I mean, you got to see him," Scott said. "None of us have. We don't even know his name. It's so mysterious!"

Bronwen rolled her eyes. "He's just a grumpy guy who's staying here until his sister can take over. It's not mysterious."

It was, though, she thought to herself. Mysterious and intriguing. She loved her life at Morning Song; she really did. The routine and unchanging pattern of her work had been a comfort when she'd first arrived. It was still a comfort. She wasn't wishing for it to change. She wasn't bored. She *wasn't*. But…she was intrigued. Curious. Things she hadn't been in a long time. It itched under her skin, this desire to uncover the mystery of the Man of the House.

And there *were* other things that should be done around the farm. Maybe it wouldn't hurt to ask. And to check up on him. And to see if the strange chemistry between them really happened, or if it had just been her imagination.

While she was at it.

"Maybe tonight," she said. "Maybe I can bring him dinner or something."

Martha scoffed. "We all know you can't cook. Remember that soup you made for the barn potluck?"

"Oh, yeah, that was…really something," Scott said.

"Takeout exists," Bronwen said defensively.

The sound of a truck at the end of the drive by the road interrupted them, and they all turned to look.

"Now what?" Martha exclaimed.

Bronwen quickly sorted through her mental list of things she'd mentioned about the farm, but there was nothing that hadn't already been taken care of. This was something else entirely.

As the truck approached, they could see that it was a horse trailer—a fancy one, with the name and logo of a well-known breeding farm on the side.

"Did you tell him we needed another horse, too?" Martha asked wonderingly.

"No." Bronwen watched the trailer as it came up the long drive under the old maple trees, and then passed right by the barn. Sugar whinnied softly, ears pricked forward.

"Where is it going?" Scott asked. "Barn's right here."

The trailer continued up the drive and maneuvered around to the front of the farmhouse.

"I guess it's not a horse," Martha said. "It must just be something for him up there." She shrugged. "I'd better go get Percy, anyway. I think he managed to get the whole field's worth of mud on his coat."

"I'm going to go try out the new ring," Scott said. "Ready, Sugar?"

The two boarders went their separate ways, but Bronwen stood for a while in the weak sunlight, staring up at the house. If whatever he was having delivered wasn't a horse, then why use a horse trailer? He hadn't indicated in either of their conversations that he even knew anything about horses, although given everything he'd accomplished around the farm, she was rethinking that assumption.

Mysterious and intriguing.

But still not her business. And after a while the brisk wind chilled her through, and she went back inside the barn.

Four

Ian turned another page in his book, then flipped it back, realizing that yet again he'd failed to absorb the words in front of him. After repeating the same process two more times, he tossed the book to the bare floor with a satisfying thud.

There had been a time when he'd been able to read anywhere—in bed, in the car on the way to a show, in the back of a horse trailer between classes. His focus had been legendary, on or off a horse. He'd had everything together: mentally, physically, in every way that mattered.

There had also been a brief time when he hadn't been able to read at all. In the hospital there had been too many distractions, but also the injuries. Not only to his hip and back, but to his head. His head, the source of that focus, his ability to laser in on the questions asked by any challenging show-jumping course and answer them systematically from the back of his mount of the day. Elegantly, even.

Now he couldn't read one damn chapter of one of his favorite novels without getting distracted. He knew there were many reasons for his lack of focus, but the one that worried him the most was the fact that it might be physical. And that while the doctors had all said he would heal, healing didn't always mean that you went back to exactly the way you were before.

He peeked out the window of his bedroom again, and was pleased to see the results of his rather high-handed demands of the local arena footing supplier in the distance. If he was going to do a job, he'd do it right. They'd suggested sticking with dirt or using sand, but Ian knew all too well the toll taken on a horse's legs over the years, and it wasn't in him to allow anything but the best.

Even if his savings account wouldn't thank him. Anne had better be good for a repayment, or he'd have to find another job sooner than he'd hoped.

With a weary sigh, he wandered down to the kitchen and stared into the refrigerator. Leftover delivery from last night and half a bagel were about all he had, other than the ridiculous cake that sat on the counter by the window. He didn't even want cake—he wasn't much of a sweets person, but as a kid he'd always distracted Anne from whatever had been going on in their home life by baking complicated dessert recipes. Now he was a confirmed stress baker.

The German chocolate cake with buttercream frosting and a dark chocolate drip had turned out perfectly, for what it was worth. Which wasn't much. He wasn't going to eat it, and he didn't have a crew of grooms, owners and fellow riders to share it with. Not anymore.

Some days the empty silence of the farmhouse was a co-coon, a safe landing place. A refuge from the chaos of his life, from a future that was wholly unknown and unimaginable. He was grateful then, to his sister. To her ex-husband, or at least his money. To the cold Boston spring that provided the perfect excuse to remain inside, tucked away where no one could ask him how he was doing, or what he would do next. He'd come all the way from Florida for just this refuge.

But other days, like today, the silence pressed in on him like the air had been sucked right out of the room. The dark corners crept in on the light that struggled to find its way through the dirty old windows, and he'd find himself with his palms against the glass as if he could draw the light in-side through force of will. Keep the shadows at bay with his own hands.

He wanted to be rid of the responsibility of Anne's farm, even if he could admit that sorting out all of Bronwen's is-sues had at least given his brain something to do instead of spinning in useless circles. Even if the thought of Bronwen bravely facing him in her horse pajamas, shovel in hand, brought a grudging smile to his face every time he remem-bered that moment. A flash of light and fresh air when the walls were closing in. But when his sister arrived, what would he do? He had no plans, nowhere to go. He'd be welcome to stay, but he didn't want to live in such close proximity to anyone. Especially Anne, who knew and saw far too much.

He knew in a deep, fundamental way that he needed this time to regroup, to lick his wounds in private. Whether he would ever be ready to emerge from the bottomless mental hole he found himself in, that was still a mystery. He sure as hell wasn't ever going back to his old life, or anything like it. He didn't want anything to do with horses, or riding, or the people in that world. Ever again.

Which made his sister's machinations just that much more infuriating. She thought he just needed a little push and everything would go back to the way it was. But he knew she understood just how much he'd lost, and how much he never, ever wanted the least bit to do with anything that reminded him of it.

A knock on the front door startled him, and he clutched at the kitchen counter. He swallowed, waiting. It couldn't be Bronwen again—he'd done everything she'd demanded, and she didn't seem like the sort to go back on her promise to stay out of his way.

He admired the barn manager, even as he resented her interference. And the way she made him feel. He wasn't ready to feel anything, and the one thing he'd done that morning in the feed room was *feel*. The attraction to her had come out of nowhere, knocking him off his precarious axis and overwhelming his already strung-out system.

The knock became a pounding, as if the person outside had no plans to leave until he answered.

Reluctantly, he walked to the door.

"Mr. Kingston? Ian Kingston?" the young man on the front porch asked breathlessly, as if he wanted to get the words out before Ian slammed the door in his face.

Which he was tempted to do, actually. He didn't know this man, and had no reason to find out why he was there.

But then he saw the horse trailer. Shiny, complete with

the logo of a breeding farm he recognized. The owners of that farm had regularly brought young horses down to Florida for the show season before they were put up for sale. Ian had ridden several of them. Top quality, across the board.

Cold slithered down his spine at the reminder of his past life. He took a step backward out of instinct, but the young man leaned against the door frame before Ian could shut the door.

He held out an envelope.

"This is for you," he said quickly, pressing the paper into Ian's hand.

Ian held up the envelope and stared blankly at it. Only his name was scrawled on the outside, in handwriting he didn't recognize. Slowly, because he didn't see that he had any other choice, and because this young man was simply doing his job, he opened it.

Ian—
Sorry for the telephone-game-style letter. I dictated it to the person at Clover Farm who arranged this. When you get this, I'll still be out of the country and inaccessible, which is probably for the best since I'm sure you'll be ready to cut my head off. You know Clover only buys the *best* horses. Well, they're in a bit of a jam, having bought this young stallion for breeding purposes, planning to compete him as usual to establish him before putting him up for stud. But as you can tell, none of that is happening. I suggested you might be able to help, and it turns out that not only do they want help, they want to be rid of him completely. They

just don't have time to work with him. So I bought him at a bargain-basement price, and now I'm sending him your way. I know you'll know what to do.

Please don't kill me! You know how I feel about the waste of a good breeding horse. He deserves a chance.

Love,
Anne
PS. His name is Hades.

"What the fuck," Ian muttered.

Anne had really gone through it in her life, her marriage and her divorce. And for the first time Ian wondered if maybe it all might have been too much for her. The note made no sense at all. Sure, Anne *had*, in fact, always been much more interested in breeding than competition. The baby horses held her interest most. And secondarily, horses who'd been mistreated and developed behavioral issues also held a place in her soft heart.

But she couldn't possibly mean—

"Should I try to get him out?" the man asked nervously.

And Ian realized that this young man wasn't just worried that Ian would shut the door in his face. Probably had been hoping for just that, if Ian's suspicions were correct, so he could turn the trailer around and go back to Clover Farm with no further involvement with the horse inside. It wasn't a good sign if someone who worked at the farm the horse had come from was afraid to handle him.

Ian pinched the bridge of his nose. "I'm assuming that

when my sister said his name was Hades, she was referring to whatever is in that trailer, and not you?"

The man cleared his throat. "Uh…yeah. My name's John." He grimaced. "Hades is an appropriate name, if you ask me."

Ian nodded. "Right. And while I'm guessing you'd rather do anything other than deal with…Hades, my sister provided a bonus for you if you convince me to take him?"

"I'm really sorry, Mr. Kingston. I'm a huge fan of yours— saw you win at Aachen that year."

It had been more than just one year, but that didn't matter now. He couldn't turn away a young groom who'd been offered money that could make all the difference to him. He knew how little they were paid. And Ian was sure that whatever Anne was offering was more than what he had on hand, especially after everything he'd done at the farm.

And now there was a horse.

"It's fine," he said tightly. He'd figure something out. He couldn't stick a stallion who was difficult enough to make a professional groom as wary of him as this one clearly was in a boarding barn and expect to remain hands-off.

And Anne had known that. He was absolutely going to murder his sister whenever she reemerged.

He walked over to the back of the trailer, outwardly calm but with his heart, lungs and stomach all lodged in his throat. Ian hadn't handled a horse since his accident, and he'd planned never to do so again.

"Here, let me get the door for you," John said. He lowered the ramp to the ground, unlatched the door and swung it open. Ian took a quick step back as a hoof went flying, banging sharply on the side of the trailer.

"Not exactly an auspicious beginning," Ian muttered.

He considered his options. Either the horse was flat-out mean, or he'd been ruined by someone's mistreatment. And he'd known very, very few horses who were naturally hostile. Nervous, sure. Aggressive, occasionally. Difficult, fairly often. But far more common was that some human wanted to dominate a sensitive animal, and the result was a whole hornet's nest of behavioral issues that a future owner had to figure out. Or, more frequently, the horse was written off as a problem, and subjected to increasingly harsh treatment.

Ian had written off horses generally—they were incredible animals, but his accident had shut the door on any desire to make them the focus of his life again. But like his sister, he couldn't stand to see an animal punished for the stupidity and cruelty of the people responsible for him. He had to get this horse off the trailer. He wasn't in a position to offer much to the world, but he could offer this one horse the same sanctuary that he'd found on this farm.

He could do that much.

"I've got a dressage whip in the front," John offered. "I could hold it against his hindquarters while you run in and get his lead."

Ian considered it. "No. No whips." Depending on what had been done to this horse, just the touch of a whip could be a spark to a powder keg.

He stared at what he could see of the horse, who was standing headfirst inside the trailer. He was enormous—easily seventeen hands, if not more. Black as ink, no white markings to be seen. The marks on the back leg that had shot out at him when he opened the trailer confirmed he was probably right about the whip.

Anger at whoever had mistreated this horse flooded through his body like he'd swallowed too-hot coffee. He wouldn't mind using that whip on whoever had put those marks there, who had harmed a horse in their care. There was a special place in hell reserved for people who abused animals. His spine stiffened in determination.

"Let's see how this goes," he said. He unlatched the bar behind the horse's butt and held out his hand for a lead rope.

He slipped into the trailer on the opposite side of the middle divider from where Hades stood. How many hours had he spent in a horse trailer? Loading and unloading his rides, making sure that everything was just so: horse, hay, equipment. Hanging out in an empty trailer at a show, a horse tied to the outside or in the show barn, finding a quiet moment to himself. It was as natural as breathing to slide next to the giant horse's head.

Less natural was the way Hades immediately reared up a few inches, kicking out with the front leg closest to Ian and then snaking his head around to snap with his large teeth. Ian backed quickly up against the far side of the trailer and then held completely still, murmuring reassuring nonsense that did nothing to calm the wild, dark eyes, whites on display, foam dripping from the horse's mouth.

The animal was terrified. And Ian was stuck.

"Uh…you all right in there?" John asked.

"Yes, everything's going perfectly," Ian snapped, and then guilt pricked at his conscience. It wasn't the other man's fault. It wasn't anyone's fault except whoever had done this to Hades.

And maybe his sister.

"Okay, big guy," he said quietly to the horse, who eyed him with a desperate fury Ian could certainly identify with. "What if I came just a little bit closer and put this lead on you?"

He slowly reached his hand toward Hades's head, managing to unsnap the lead that was tied to the front of the trailer. Another back hoof went flying, probably denting the trailer. And his enormous head—now untethered—turned toward Ian, who was now in range of the horse's impressive teeth.

"Shit."

Ian made his escape, quickly reversing himself out the back of the trailer and stumbling on the gravel of the driveway. His hip creaked in protest.

"Oh my God," John said in a horrified voice, snapping the butt bar behind Hades again. "That horse is the devil. I'll take him back to the farm—we'll never get him out of there. And no bonus is worth this," he added under his breath.

"Wait." Ian held up a hand.

He glanced down the slight hill toward the barn.

"Horses have good memories," he said. "At Clover, is there anyone who can handle him?"

John nodded. "Yeah. Maggie, the assistant manager, can. She's about this height—" He held his hand at about an average height. "Young. You think Hades remembers who abused him?"

Ian narrowed his eyes at the other man. "Of course. Do you know who owned him before?"

John thought for a moment. "He got to Clover about a month ago. I was there when he arrived. The man who brought him backed the trailer up to the field and unloaded him that way. Said it was best to let him back out himself."

"Not a red flag or anything," Ian murmured. "What did he look like?"

"Tall, athletic." He looked Ian up and down. "About your height."

"Great." Ian sighed. "And Clover was more interested in his breeding and conformation than whether they could handle him."

John shrugged. "We've never ended up with one like this before. Probably thought a horse this well-bred would be well trained, too."

Foolish. Any horse could be abused, no matter how well they were bred or how much they cost.

"And this...Maggie? What color hair does she have?"

"Oh, plain brown. Long."

Ian smiled for the first time in what felt like forever. "Perfect."

"Um...hi?" A familiar woman's voice came from behind him. "What's going on up here? I heard a bang."

"That would be Hades in there," John said, pointing at the back of the trailer. "Can't get him out."

Bronwen stared at the trailer, then turned her gaze on Ian. Green eyes met his and he tried to ignore the zap of awareness that shot through his system like static electricity. He didn't have time for that right now. Or ever.

"There's a horse in there?" Her eyes widened. "Named... *Hades*?"

"Pretty appropriate name, too," John said.

"That's...unfortunate. So—you do know something about horses?" she asked Ian.

John burst out laughing. "You're kidding, right?"

"All right, that's enough chitchat." Ian cut them off before John could say too much. "Here's what's going to happen. John, you're going to back the trailer down to that field away from the barn. Bronwen, is that field used for regular turnout right now?"

She shook her head. "No, we leave it empty for new arrivals, and riding for people who want some hills in a fenced area. There's a big shed in the far corner, too."

"Great." He loved when a plan came together. When he could solve a problem set before him. "Back the trailer up to the open gate. Bronwen, you're going to lead him out and turn him loose."

"He'll back himself if you poke him with the whip," John suggested.

"You mean explode out of the trailer in fear," Ian bit out. "We're not doing that to him. And horses need to be handled. I want to see if he'll let Bronwen touch him. If not, we'll...figure something out."

"Your funeral," John said softly, with a glance in Bronwen's direction.

"What?" She turned to look at the groom.

"Uh...nothing," John said quickly.

Ian looked at Bronwen. Her ponytail was mussed by the brisk wind, cheeks pink and full lips red. Her slim frame was bundled up in a puffy coat, coveralls and work boots. She wasn't short—average height, as John had indicated about the

Clover farm groom—but she hardly looked strong enough to handle a half-wild stallion.

But Ian had been around horses long enough to know that strength only got you so far, and often didn't get you anywhere at all. And he'd never underestimate someone in charge of a barn full of horses and their owners. Especially someone who had held the farm together in the absence of an owner, and who had advocated loudly and passionately on their behalf even when he'd tried to throw her out.

No, Bronwen could handle this. His only concern was for her safety. She was clearly a competent horsewoman, but he knew better than anyone just how unpredictable the animals could be.

One wrong move, one sudden movement, and you could end up in a hospital bed.

The thought of that fate befalling Bronwen sent a quick wave of nausea through his gut. Protective instinct told him to take John's advice and let Hades burst out from the trailer at the touch of the whip. But he couldn't do that to the horse. And he wouldn't speak for or make any decision on Bronwen's behalf. She was a grown woman, and she'd chosen horses as her profession. She could decide for herself.

He stepped closer to her, ignoring the way his body tightened in response to her nearness even with her layers of winter clothing between them.

"Can you do this?" he asked quietly. "Do you want to do this?"

She tilted her head, gaze darting to where Hades's rump was barely visible in the shadows of the trailer. A strand of hair blew across her face, and Ian's hands fisted so he wouldn't reach out and brush it back.

"He was abused, wasn't he?" Her eyes met his again. "Someone abused him, and that's why you can't handle him. A man, probably. So you want me to see if he'll let a woman touch him."

Ian nodded, keeping his gaze on hers. "John said there's a groom back at the farm he came from who can handle him, and her description sounds like you."

Bronwen bit her lip, and Ian's eyes followed the movement involuntarily. "And you're going to keep him? Give him a good home?" She blew out a breath. "That's kind of you."

Ian laughed harshly. "It's not kindness. I just don't have much choice."

He didn't want Bronwen to get the wrong idea. He wasn't softhearted like his sister. His heart was buried under so many layers of pain and bitterness it may as well be encased in stone. But while his sister had stuck him in this entire godforsaken situation, he wasn't going to punish a horse for that. He had that much humanity left in him.

"Still…" She regarded him with perceptive eyes, and he wanted nothing more than to stalk back into the house, slam the door and lock himself inside its silence once again.

"So, what are we doing?" John asked, rubbing his hands together against the cold.

Bronwen pressed her lips together. "Bring the trailer down. Let's see what we can do."

Five

Bronwen had put on a brave front, but her knees were a little weak inside her thick coveralls as she stood by the trailer, now parked so that the back opened directly into the field away from the barn.

Her hair had come loose from its ponytail in the wind, and she dug futilely around in her pockets for another hair tie.

"You need a rubber band?" the groom who had brought the horse asked her, in the voice of someone asking for last-dinner requests before execution.

"Yeah. Thanks." She took the band he pulled out of the front of the trailer and tied her hair back.

"I'm John, by the way." He shook her hand solemnly.

"I'm Bronwen," she replied automatically.

"Good luck in there."

"Um…thanks again."

She almost thought he might salute her, but instead he

took several steps backward and waited in the gap between the trailer and the fence. For easy escape route purposes, she assumed.

The Man of the House walked around the trailer toward her and handed her a lead rope.

"He wouldn't let me put this on his halter," he said in his serious, velvet-thick voice. She let her eyes wander across the field in front of her, not wanting to be distracted by looking directly at his admittedly extremely distracting face. "Snapped at me and kicked out instead."

"Oh. Great," she said faintly.

His mouth pressed into a thin line. "I'm guessing that Hades was abused by a man, given what John said. And since horses tend to remember things like that, and act accordingly, that's why the smaller woman at Clover Farm has been able to handle him."

"Usually," John called from his spot by the fence. "He's still a handful, even with Maggie."

"Great," Bronwen said again.

The tall man in front of her handed her something else— sugar cubes, she realized.

"John had these in the trailer," he said. "A little bribery can't hurt."

"Okay." Apparently she had been reduced to one-word responses.

He stepped closer, and she tilted her head back to look at him. "You don't have to do this if you don't want to," he said quietly. "My sister sent this horse to me because— Well, she has her reasons." His lips twisted into a wry smile. Or grimace. "He's my problem. But he can't stay on the trailer, and I don't want to send him back."

She understood why. Clover Farm wasn't going to hold on to a horse who couldn't be handled safely—no matter his pedigree. They were a huge, busy operation, not to mention that temperament was essential in marketing breeding stallions. Hades would be sold to someone who'd be willing to take him on, and there was no guarantee that someone would be kind.

"John said he could get him out with the whip, but…"

"But we don't want his first experience here to be a negative one."

He nodded.

"It's fine," Bronwen said, in what she hoped was a reassuring voice. "I do have responsibility for any horse on this farm, and I don't want him to end up somewhere he'll be mistreated, either."

He looked at her for a long moment, those pale blue eyes mesmerizing. Then he nodded again.

"Okay. Good. Just go slow and gentle. Talk to him. Let him get a good look at you so he knows it isn't me again. Then see if you can back him out slowly. If he pulls or tries to get away, let him go, and if…if he lashes out, get out of there."

"All right."

She could admit that even as she was a little nervous, she was also curious. Like the man in front of her, she couldn't help but want to know the potential of any given horse. If this one was a Clover Farm breeding stallion, he was probably nicer than any of the horses she'd ever worked with—

much as she loved them all. If she could handle him safely, then there was hope he could be rehabilitated. And more importantly, go on to live a safe, happy life.

The Man of the House watched as she turned and took a step toward the back of the trailer. Then she whirled around.

"Wait!" she exclaimed a little wildly, especially given that she was the only one going anywhere. "What's your name?"

She didn't know why it was suddenly important to know his name after going so long without it. Despite the groom's gloomy demeanor about the whole thing, she knew how to handle a difficult horse, and how to evade a dangerous one. There were risks around any large animal, and she faced them every day. She'd be fine.

He stared at her for a moment, and she wondered why he'd avoided introducing himself before now. Well, aside from not wanting to have anything to do with her or the farm.

"Ian," he said shortly.

"Okay. Hi, Ian." A smile tugged at the corner of her mouth. The name suited him, she thought. Elegant, a little abrupt.

As she watched, Ian took a deep breath, as if his name from her mouth was a surprise. She bit her lip.

And then she jumped a little where she stood as a bang from inside the trailer broke through the silence between them.

"I think he wants to come out," John said.

"Right." Bronwen took her own deep breath and tightened her hold on the lead rope. "Let's do this."

She turned away from the distraction named Ian, and

began murmuring soft nonsense as she made her way up the ramp into the empty side of the trailer. She waited for a moment, a short distance from the stallion's stomach with only the divider between them, talking to him all the while.

Hades was enormous and, as far as she could tell inside the trailer, a shiny, solid black with no white markings whatsoever. His tail reached down nearly to the floor, thick and luxurious, and he was heavily muscled like a dressage horse. She wondered if he was a Friesian cross, one of those big, black fairy-tale horses. She'd always wanted to ride a Friesian. Of course, she probably never would now. Or any other horse.

As she spoke to him, both of his ears pinned back in a show of extreme displeasure, and Bronwen swallowed tightly, her eyes on his enormous hooves. But as she continued talking, one ear relaxed to the side as if he was listening to her. A good sign.

She moved slowly into the horse's line of vision, not wanting to startle him, but needing him to see her. To understand that she looked nothing like the man who had likely abused him in the past. He turned his head toward her. Soft, moist nostrils fluttered as he breathed out, sniffing her scent. A tremor skittered across the surface of his shoulder.

"Poor guy," she murmured. "I know there's no reason for you to trust me, but you can. I promise I won't hurt you."

Hades snorted softly, as if in response to her words. Cautiously, she held her palm flat about a foot from his velvety nose. Slowly, so very slowly, he turned his head to snuffle her palm, legs braced and muscles stiff across his back.

He snorted again and stamped a front hoof, and Bronwen

barely stopped herself from jumping in surprise. Instead, she inched closer, lead rope in hand, and held it up next to her palm for its own snuffling. Hades's eyes widened and he stamped twice. Bronwen thought she might hear Ian call out to see if she was in trouble, but she figured that he was silent so as not to further startle the horse.

She was alone in this, but only because Ian was mindful of her safety and his effect on the horse.

She brushed the snap on the lead rope against the metal ring on the bottom of Hades's halter, once, twice—and then fastened it on. The horse remained almost eerily still, clearly not trusting her but not committed to trying to either flee or attack.

Bronwen realized she'd stopped breathing, and forced herself to take one deep breath, and then another.

She remembered the sugar cubes and slowly pulled one out of her pocket, holding it flat on the palm of her free hand. Hades immediately inhaled it like a vacuum, drawing a laugh from Bronwen. Maybe they'd be okay.

"Okay. Let's see if we can do this. Together, Hades. Also, please don't rip me apart with those big teeth of yours," she added.

She inched backward along the trailer divider until the lead rope in her hand went taut. She didn't pull the horse back, but let the light pressure of the rope hang there. A suggestion rather than a demand. As she watched, he arched his neck and took one step back, then another.

Suddenly, he kicked out with his hind legs and scooted forward instead of backward, pressing against the chest bar in front of him. Bronwen held her breath and tried to remain calm. There wasn't anywhere for Hades to go but backward, she reminded herself. And then, miraculously, after one endless moment, Hades took one halting step back, and then another, and then backed right out of the trailer as if it was no big deal. As if they did this every day.

Bronwen followed his lead rather than the other way around, letting him dictate the pace. He backed down the ramp, and she quickly unsnapped the lead rope in case he startled. She stood in front of him and watched as he stared back, neither relaxed nor as tense as he'd been in the trailer. He reached out with his nose again and brushed his whiskers against her coat, probably smelling the sugar in her pocket.

And then he shook himself all over like a dog after a bath, and Bronwen laughed in surprise. He spun on his back legs and took off across the field, bucking and whinnying at the horses in the field next door.

"That's as easy as I've ever seen him," John commented from beside the trailer, already moving to close up the back ramp and doors.

Bronwen had almost forgotten anyone else was there. "It was a little dicey, but I think he finally decided he wanted out more than he wanted to kick me into oblivion."

John glanced off into the distance, where Hades was now rolling, all four legs waggling in the air. "You might never catch him again. He'll just be out in this field forever."

"A lawn ornament." Bronwen smiled. "But at least he's safe."

"He'll be more than decoration," Ian said, striding around the back of the trailer from where he'd hidden himself from Hades's vision. "If I have anything to say about it."

Bronwen had the distinct impression that when Ian had something to say about a situation, he usually got his way.

"You never said you knew anything about horses," she said without thinking.

Mysterious and intriguing. And more so by the day, unfortunately. He'd made it clear that he wanted nothing to do with her or the farm. But here he was, standing in the field like a blond god, arms folded in front of him, jaw set with determination. Who was he? Why was he here?

John sent her an odd look. "Ian Kingston?" He laughed. "Yeah, he knows something about horses." He fastened the latch on the back of the trailer. "Anyway, I'm off back to Clover." He glanced over at Hades, now peacefully grazing in the corner farthest away from where they stood. "Good luck, I guess. And thanks for taking him—I wasn't looking forward to bringing him back."

"He'll be fine here," Ian said firmly.

And then John was in the truck, starting the engine and pulling the trailer back up the hill toward the driveway.

Bronwen shoved her frozen hands in her coat pockets and shifted awkwardly from one foot to the other. Half looking at Hades and half trying *not* to look at Ian, who was watching the trailer's progress as if it was the most interesting thing he'd ever seen.

Finally, she broke the uncomfortable silence. "You don't have to tell me anything," she said. "We're all pretty nosy around here, but you don't owe us anything."

It was clear that not only did he want nothing to do with her, the boarders or the farm, but he'd also had no intention of revealing who he was or anything about his history with horses. She was, of course, burning with curiosity. But she also didn't want him to feel pressured into talking about himself. His personal business was his alone.

She understood that, more than he could know. She didn't talk about her past, either, and she was eternally grateful that the boarders' prying was of the most gentle and least obtrusive type.

"Anything except payment of all of the farm's bills," he said wryly, turning his gaze onto her.

Bronwen's cheeks flushed with heat. "Well, somebody has to pay for all of this. It's my job to make sure everything keeps running, no matter what."

"Because otherwise the horses would suffer. And the boarders," he said consideringly.

She nodded. "It's my responsibility."

"Hmm." He turned and watched as the stallion raised his head to look around at his new surroundings. "He seems to tolerate you."

A short laugh escaped her. "That's me. Tolerable."

Blue eyes met hers, and she swore the ghost of a smile played around his lips. Lips she shouldn't be staring at. "I suppose so."

She squinted at Hades, more to stop looking at the man in front of her than anything else. Restlessness consumed her in his presence, like he was a puzzle she was itching to start solving, but had no business even trying to figure out.

"I was a professional rider," he said abruptly. "Show jumping."

"Ah." She didn't know what else to say.

"So, yes. I know something about horses."

"And you're going to help this one." It seemed safer to turn the conversation back to Hades than try to prod Ian for more information about himself.

His shoulders relaxed slightly, which probably meant she'd made the right decision. "If I can. He doesn't seem to think I'm tolerable like you, though."

"Whatever happened to him before, it was probably a man. And a tall one."

"He's a Friesian–Dutch Warmblood cross, according to the papers John shoved at me," Ian said. "Top lines on both sides. Probably too heavy for a show jumper or eventer, but could make a good dressage horse. And definitely a great foundation for any breeding program."

"We're hardly a breeding farm here," Bronwen said absently. Then frowned. "But you'll probably take him with you. When your sister gets here."

Something crossed Ian's expression, but it was like trying to read an unopened book. *Mysterious yet again.*

"He'll be fine in the field for now," he said shortly. "He's still got his winter coat, and we can bed down the shed with shavings. He'll have to be kept apart from the boarders, obviously."

Unless they wanted a crop of foals out of the mares next year. Breeding stallions were well outside of her area of expertise, but she knew what happened when mares and stallions were left to their own devices.

"Yep." She turned her mind back to what *was* her expertise. "Let me know what you want him fed, and I'll add it to the feed schedule. I'm happy to bring it down here for him until—if—we can get him into the barn. There's a big box stall at the far end, separated from the others by the tack and feed rooms. We used to use it to store shavings until we moved that to the other side of the barn."

"I can pay board for him," Ian said.

Bronwen smiled. "It's your—your sister's—farm. You should work that out with her."

"He's going to be more work for you. Another horse, a stallion who has to be kept separately."

Bronwen shrugged. "What's one more out of all the ones we have now? Besides, I don't think you'd be able to get him out of our hair even if you wanted to. I'm not going to try loading him into another trailer, that's for sure."

Ian gazed down at her in that way that made her feel like he could see inside her head, directly to her thoughts. She really hoped he couldn't. Not when his muscles were bunched against the chill in his long-sleeved T-shirt, or when his cheeks were flushed with cold. Her thoughts weren't something she wanted him to access, right at this moment.

He was close—maybe three feet away—and she imagined that she could feel the heat off his body, even though that was impossible. Her breath caught in her chest for no reason whatsoever, and once again she was stuck in the web of her attraction to him. He pulled her like a magnet, and it was a struggle to resist. To keep her feet solidly on the frozen ground and her expression neutral. She wasn't exactly sure what she was resisting, only that if he relaxed that armor around him for a moment, if he held out his hand, she'd willingly offer whatever he was seeking.

She'd never felt that sort of call toward another person,

not like this. And not to someone who would so obviously reject what she offered.

But he turned and strode toward the open gate, turning only to say, "I'll write in the feed for morning and evening. If you don't mind leaving it here at the gate, I'll feed him." He glanced over toward the happily grazing horse. "Maybe if he associates me with his dinner, he'll be less likely to try to stick a hoof in my side."

And then he was gone, back toward the house. A silhouette shrinking as his long stride took him away, while she stood shivering in the field.

Six

Ian sat on an overturned bucket one evening, just inside the field shed. The plastic was uncomfortably cold through his jeans, but he sat quietly anyway. Hades chomped his dinner happily, snorting and chewing. And occasionally stamping his feet just to make sure Ian knew that his presence was unwanted.

But not unwanted enough to forgo food.

He'd learned over the past week that the way to Hades's heart was definitely through his stomach, although they hadn't progressed enough for the big horse to allow any sort of physical contact. Ian had tried, first standing close enough to the feed bucket in the shed that he would have been able to reach out and touch the stallion. Hoping Hades was hungry enough to allow it.

He wasn't.

But a distance of about ten feet seemed to do the trick, and it allowed Ian the chance to look over the horse twice each day, to make sure he didn't have any scratches or any other issues from his outdoor exile.

He'd tried approaching Hades while he ate a couple of times, and was rewarded with pinned-back ears, snapping teeth and flying hooves.

But time, he knew, was the best way to deal with a traumatized horse. And if nothing else, he had time.

The weather was still unseasonably cold, and while Ian had thrown on a jacket before leaving the house, it wasn't enough to protect him against the plummeting temperatures now that the sun had set. He shivered, trying to stick it out in favor of more time with Hades, but he could feel his fingers turning numb.

"All right, big guy," he said quietly. Hades flicked an ear in his direction but didn't stop chewing. "You win this time. But I'll be back tomorrow."

He rose and stretched, taking his time before leaving the shed. Partly to give Hades those additional few moments of having a human in his space, but also because the wind was bitter today, and as soon as he left the shed, he was going to regret not finding his warmer coat and some gloves before he left the house. He grabbed the bucket he'd used to carry Hades's feed to the shed, which Bronwen had prepared and left by the fence earlier that day.

He hurried across the field, head down against the wind, and nearly ran into Bronwen, who was headed down the hill toward him.

She stopped when she looked up and saw him, twisting her hands—sensibly gloved—while she waited for him to reach her.

"Hi," she said awkwardly, not quite meeting his eyes. She shoved her hands into her coat pockets. "You didn't leave the bucket by the gate."

He glanced down at the empty bucket in his hand. He usually dumped the feed into the shed's bucket, then tromped across the field to leave it for Bronwen to take and clean with the other horses' buckets while he went back to sit in the shed. In this way he'd managed to avoid all human contact for several days. But he hadn't been able to make himself take multiple trips across the cold field that afternoon.

"Right. Sorry, I should have. It's just cold today."

"No, it's fine—"

"But you've had to make two trips in this wind."

He was an ass. It wasn't any farther across the field from the shed than it was from the barn to the gate, and while he'd avoided one trip, it meant Bronwen had to make two. He'd told himself that other than preparing the stallion's feed, he wouldn't impose on Bronwen's work any more than he absolutely had to. But the cold had frozen that thought right out of his mind.

She shrugged and smiled a little. Shifted from one foot to the other like a restless colt. "I've either been outside or in the unheated barn all day—I'll survive."

He supposed that was true, but still...

"How's he doing?" Bronwen nodded toward the shed, where Hades still stood. Probably avoiding the windchill himself.

Ian glanced back over his shoulder. "Doesn't want anything to do with me other than food delivery," he said.

"Stubborn," Bronwen said, then paused, chewing on her bottom lip in that distracting way. "I could help, maybe."

Ian should have seen the offer coming. Bronwen obviously cared deeply for all of the horses on the farm, and now that included Hades. Of course she'd want to help. And God knew he needed it—especially from the one person who'd been able to get near the horse so far. He'd seen a few of the boarders gather by the fence gate to look at the new horse, and Hades had always kicked up his heels and taken off to the other side of the field.

"I'll think about it." He wouldn't. Probably.

He absentmindedly brought his frozen hands to his lips and blew warm air onto them.

"You must be freezing—why don't you come up to the tack room? It's heated, and there's a fresh pot of coffee on."

He stared at her. Another offer he should have seen coming. And equally enticing—and dangerous. A series of images of past tack rooms, past barn lounges, flickered through his mind like a movie. Laughing, talking, sharing community with everyone he'd left behind. He'd sworn to himself he'd never go backward. Horses, the people around them—he'd left it all for a reason.

When he didn't answer, Bronwen sighed and gave him an apologetic smile. "Sorry. I know you want to be left alone. It's just—it's warm in there."

"It's warm in the house," Ian replied.

At that, Bronwen laughed. "Is it, though?"

Point taken. The old heating system did its best, but on a frigid day like this one, it barely kept the place habitable.

He looked down at his hands, red and chapped. "No. No, it's really not." And he laughed, just a little, rusty and rough.

"No one's in the barn," Bronwen said, cajoling him like he was a spooky horse. "Slow day, and the ones who showed up to ride left already. And if I drink all the coffee myself I'll be up all night."

He was *not* thinking about Bronwen at night, in her pajamas, which he'd already seen. In the apartment above the barn, which he hadn't. Was she lonely up there? He hadn't seen any evidence of a romantic partner, but that didn't mean she didn't have one. And it was ridiculous, that he'd feel even the slightest sting of jealousy over that thought. Over a woman he barely knew.

Still…he could admit that maybe, just maybe, he was the one who was lonely. He'd pursued solitude because he thought it would help. Because he thought no one should have to endure his moods, his bitterness. But Bronwen had seen him bitter, and angry, and she was still inviting him for coffee.

Maybe it was pity, which he hated. But he didn't think Bronwen was a person given to pity. She was kind, but he suspected she wasn't overly sentimental. Which was another point in her favor—and honestly, she was gaining too many points for his own good.

"Okay," he said, surprising himself. He told himself that he was just cold, and the thought of a well-heated tack room and fresh coffee was too good to pass up.

Especially if no one else was around.

A stunned expression crossed Bronwen's face for a split second before she covered it with a smile. Her astonishment was so obvious he nearly laughed again—twice in one day, some kind of new record.

He started up the hill without another word, Bronwen behind him. In the barn, everything was quiet. Just the occasional rustle of a horse turning in their stall, or grabbing another mouthful of hay.

"No radio?" he asked, just for something to break the silence. In most of the show barns he'd ridden for, there was always music on.

Bronwen shook her head and reached out to pat a horse—a big draft cross with hay sticking out of his mouth—as they walked by the stalls. "I don't like to make any more noise than necessary. This is the horses' home, you know? They don't need all our human racket." She chuckled and pushed open the door to the tack room. "The boarders already make enough noise."

He liked that she put the horses' well-being and comfort above the entertainment of the people in the barn. Most—though sadly not all—of the people he'd worked for and with cared deeply about animals, but it didn't always carry over into the details, into the careful considering of the ways horses were different from people, with different needs and wants. More points for Bronwen.

In the tack room, neat rows of saddles on racks lined one wall, and hooks with bridles hung above several large tack trunks that probably belonged to the boarders. Cabinets that likely held all of the miscellaneous equipment associated with horses—leg wraps, blankets, extra saddle pads, spare pieces of bridles, extra girths—sat under two small windows. And in one corner was a kitchenette, with a hot plate, sink, coffee maker and minifridge, surrounded by an old couch and two other chairs.

It wasn't as fancy as what he was used to, but it was neat and practical and comfortable. He liked it.

And it was warm.

"Help yourself to coffee," Bronwen said. "There's milk and everything. I'm just going to toss another flake of hay in with Charlie. Otherwise he'll eat his bedding."

He did as directed, stirring milk into his coffee in a mug that read My Best Friend Has Four Legs and taking a seat on the sofa.

When he heard a thunk and muffled cursing from out in the barn, he rose and set the mug on the counter. Out in the barn aisle, Bronwen was nowhere to be seen. A little black-and-white pony stuck its head over the stall door nearest where he stood.

"Where is she?" he asked the pony, who snorted unhelpfully. A tall brown horse who looked like he might make a jumper or eventer regarded him solemnly with kind dark eyes. "How about you?" Ian asked the horse. "Did she just disappear?"

Another thunk came from a stall down the aisle, and he followed the sound. He'd been in the barn a few times, always in the middle of the night to avoid the boarders. Which was absurd. Dramatic. Maybe a little unhinged. And maybe he was all of those things.

Now he took a moment to notice details he'd missed. The way each horse's halter and lead rope hung tidily next to their stall. The gleaming brass nameplates on the stall doors. The wood worn smooth from years of human hands and equine teeth and bodies. The neat broom marks left after an evening sweep of the aisle. The silhouette of a barn cat's ears just visible in the shadows before the animal darted off to do its job keeping mice from getting into the feed. This was no slick, polished show barn, but everything here was both well used and cared for. He inhaled deeply, old wood and hay and leather in the air, the scent achingly familiar.

He made his way to the door of the stall in question and watched as Bronwen tugged at a hay bale at the very top of a pile of bales. This must be where they stored some of the hay for easy access. Although the access wasn't looking so easy at the moment, at least for someone of Bronwen's height.

"Let me help," he said, and Bronwen whirled around. "Sorry, I didn't mean to startle you. But it sounded like you were trying to murder that hay bale."

A smile turned up the corner of her mouth. "Wow, a joke?"

Ian didn't know how to take that. He used to make lots of jokes. Now…he supposed not so much.

"A bad one, but yes. Here—" He moved to her side. The hay bale wasn't out of his reach, and he hooked a hand through the twine holding it together.

"I don't need—"

"Just let me get it."

His hand slipped out of the twine as she tugged at his arm, and he turned toward her. Her face was tipped up toward his. And in the dim light of the stall, filtered through where the hay bales partially blocked the window, she looked as warm and inviting as the comfortable tack room had compared to the frozen field he'd been sitting in.

He leaned down, much as he had in the feed room that night, the same charge of attraction sparking in the air between them. Electric and bright and everything that had been missing in his life for so many months. He *was* lonely, and wholly deprived of companionship and physical touch.

He blamed his actions on loneliness and deprivation, when he knew full well that it wasn't only that. Not entirely. It was her. She brightened his thoughts when he moped around the old house alone. A glimpse of her from his seat in Hades's shed as she picked up the empty feed bucket at the other side of the field was the highlight of his day. Her fierce determination on behalf of the horses and their owners reminded him that there was humanity outside of the fortress he'd built around himself.

But he told himself that it was simply physical deprivation that made him place a hand on her waist, waiting a beat to see if she pushed him away. As she should have. But instead she stood perfectly still, as if she didn't want to scare *him* away.

Instead, she placed her own hand on his shoulder, right at the juncture of his neck, cool on his heated skin. Somehow, the bone-deep chill of the field had vanished, and warmth sparked from his insides out, warmth that her gentle touch ignited into a flame. Warmth that burst into fiery heat when he closed the distance between them and pressed his lips to hers.

None of it made sense. He wanted solitude, time and space to lick his wounds. And then he wanted to leave the horse world behind forever. Bronwen wanted nothing more than to honor her commitment to her little section of that world.

But at that moment, surrounded by the sweet smell of hay and the irresistible taste of the woman in front of him, that all slipped to the side, things to worry about later.

Right now, Bronwen was brushing her mouth against his, fingers curling into his shoulder, tongue tracing the seam of his lips. He couldn't do anything other than kiss her back. Not when he was more lightheaded now than when he first woke up in the hospital, not when he could move his mouth to her soft cheek, the firm line of her jaw, the tender skin of her throat. Not when she pressed closer to him, gasping with pleasure. Not when she was so willing it made him weak with desire.

She made a noise that went directly to his dick, which was suddenly extremely interested in its surroundings in a way it hadn't been since his accident. When Bronwen pressed her body against his, he was sure she could feel his reaction to her even through her thick coveralls.

He told himself, *Slow. Careful.* There were a million reasons why this was a terrible idea to begin with, but since he didn't have the sense to stop, he could at least make sure they didn't do anything they'd really regret.

But Bronwen slid a hand under his jacket, under the hem of his shirt, and her palm moved up his side from his waist and around to his back. Nails digging into his skin when he moaned at her touch, a delicious sharpness heightening the sweet feel of her. And that was it for him—no chance for slow or careful.

He was hungry—starving, dazed with lust as she took

his mouth, demanding more from him. He couldn't resist. He spun her around and gently pushed her back against the tall stack of hay bales, kissing her a little more roughly than he'd intended. His control was legendary—on horseback, off, in relationships and everywhere else.

But he didn't feel in control now—this was the worst idea imaginable, kissing this woman he'd leave behind, a woman who deserved more than he'd have been able to offer before his accident, let alone now.

He did it anyway, her tongue soothing the sharp edges of his lust, her grasp on his shoulders telling him in no uncertain terms that he was wanted, *wanted*, just as he was right now. And how he wanted in return, groaning as he moved his thigh in between her legs, stroking her lips with his tongue, breath coming in ragged gasps.

He both cursed and sent up a prayer of thanks for her thick coat and coveralls, wanting nothing more than to tear them off her body to see what treasure lay underneath. And knowing that the kiss had to end, and the more layers between them the better.

Eventually, she tipped her head back, breaking contact. Her eyes were hazy and lips parted. An earthquake of lust tore through him, shocking him to his core.

She gazed up at him, mouth red and swollen, eyelids heavy. Her hair was a messy halo around her lovely face, so expressive and delicate even as she was strong and resourceful. Whatever he'd expected when he'd fled to Morning Song Farm, it wasn't this. It wasn't an angel in thick coveralls, bits of wood shavings stuck to her coat, a smear of dirt dashed across the side of the hand she now pressed to his cheek. If he'd known she was what waited for him when he arrived, he'd have run far and fast in the other direction.

Maybe he still should.

"You're unfairly beautiful," she said, her thumb tracing his cheekbone.

It surprised a laugh out of him. "I was just thinking the same about you." If he couldn't be honest now, when they were both flushed and panting, when could he?

She blushed adorably and bit her lip. "I'm pretty average." Her eyes flicked to her hand, and she moved to pull it away. He pressed his palm to it to hold it in place. "Filthy most of the time."

He couldn't help a smile. "Filthy can be good."

She laughed quietly. "I guess."

He sobered quickly, desire warring with the beginnings of regret.

"We can't do this," he murmured, releasing her hand. She lowered her arm to her side, and immediately he missed her touch.

She raised an eyebrow. "Can't or shouldn't?"

"Both," he said on an amused huff of breath.

"I'm not looking for...anything."

"Anything?"

She glanced to the side. "Relationship. Commitment. Whatever. I'm not looking for that."

He should feel relieved. Not only was he not looking for any of those things, but he was actively avoiding them. Yet some discomfort, some dissatisfaction, sat unpleasantly in his stomach at her words. He ignored it.

"Okay," he said, because he didn't know how to reply.

"But maybe you're right," she said on a sigh.

She shifted to the side and he stepped back, giving her space. She smoothed her hands over her hair, which did nothing to tame it. She gave him a sidelong glance, a little wary. He supposed he deserved it.

"Right about what?"

He'd already lost the thread of the conversation, distracted by the way her expression had closed so very slightly. He wouldn't have noticed it if she wasn't so close. If he hadn't studied her so avidly the few times they'd been near each other. He suppressed the urge to grab her hand and pull her back against him, to try to cajole her back into the openness and warmth he found irresistible.

She shrugged and stuffed her hands into her coat pockets. "This. Or not this. Not doing this."

"Ah. This."

She inhaled deeply, then blew the breath out audibly. "Yeah. It could get complicated."

As if it wasn't already complicated. As if she hadn't stormed into his solitude and blown everything apart just by being there. But...

"You're right. You have enough on your plate." She didn't need this—whatever this was. She didn't need the darkness inside him spilling all over her sunshine.

She made a noncommittal noise. "Anyway. I should probably give Charlie his hay before he eats all his bedding."

He glanced from her to the hay bale still on top of the pile, unmoved. "Right. Let me just..."

This time she allowed him to pull down the bale, and with scissors she pulled from somewhere she snipped apart the twine. The bale fell into neat flakes of hay. Bronwen grabbed one and headed for the door, then paused.

His heart beat somewhere up in his throat as he wondered if she'd come back to him. Change her mind, even though that was a terrible idea for both of them.

But she only said, "Don't forget your coffee."

Which he had. And he didn't care about the coffee. He only cared that something felt off, that he was left with the impression that he'd hurt her somehow. Or disappointed her. He wasn't sure which was worse.

But she smiled and said, "I think I'll skip the coffee and head upstairs. Have an early night."

And he was left thinking about her just upstairs in her apartment, in those pajamas, doing whatever it was she did each night, and wishing ridiculously that he could do it with her.

Seven

In the barn aisle, Bronwen placed a reassuring hand on the side strap of Percy's leather halter as Martha finished clipping his heavy winter coat. Olivia stood a few feet away, watching the action with a mug of coffee warming her hands.

The weather had grudgingly acknowledged spring that morning, if barely. Instead of frost in the fields, there was now mud. And after riding Percy for about an hour in the relative warmth, Martha had announced she wasn't going to keep walking him for another hour as his sweat dried under his coat until he finished shedding, so she broke out the clippers after she gave him a bath and let him dry in his stall.

Bronwen was glad she could stand in the aisle for a period of time without her fingers going numb for the first time that year, so she offered to help. Percy was a character, much like his owner. He had a tendency to stop dead in the middle of the ring and refuse to budge, and he had a wildly out of proportion aversion to all machinery. Including cars, the tractor, the riding lawn mower Ruth used to use around the house.

And clippers.

"Okay, I think that's about it." Martha straightened from under Percy's belly, an iffy position given the way the horse's ears were pinned back. But they pricked forward easily when Martha turned off the clippers and came around his side to give Percy's neck a pat. "Good boy."

"*Good* might be a bit of an overstatement," Olivia commented. "I thought he was going to take you out with his right hind leg for a minute there."

"Never. Who's the best-behaved boy?" Martha planted a kiss on Percy's nose.

"Not Percy," Olivia muttered under her breath.

Bronwen laughed and released the halter. Martha ignored both of them.

"Are you going to clip Charlie?" the older woman asked Bronwen.

She shook her head. "His coat's not as heavy as Percy's. And Olivia doesn't mind walking him until he's dry."

"Nope," Olivia agreed. "The more time at the barn the better, even if it's with a sweaty horse."

"When are we going to see you on your own horse?" Martha asked Bronwen, not for the first time.

She exchanged glances with Olivia, who as usual stepped in to deflect the question. "Bronwen's too busy to ride," she said. "And I monopolize Charlie. And I don't plan to stop," she said with a grin.

"You can ride Percy anytime, you know," Martha insisted. "Either of you."

Olivia choked on her coffee, earning a glare from Martha.

"Thanks," Bronwen said. "I appreciate it."

Martha opened her mouth, probably to continue being pushy in the best-intentioned way possible.

Bronwen didn't mind Martha's mild insistence that she should ride. The older woman didn't know any better, and it probably seemed more than a little strange that despite spending the vast majority of her life in the barn, she was never on top of a horse. Only Olivia knew the truth, and she could trust her friend to help brush off any questions on the subject.

Before Martha could speak, however, a figure appeared in the large doorway to the barn. Bronwen turned to greet whichever boarder had arrived for an afternoon ride, but was struck silent when she realized it wasn't a boarder at all.

Ian stood there, tall and broad, his face in shadow as the sunlight streamed in through the large opening behind him.

"Oh!" Martha exclaimed.

Olivia stared at him silently, eyes wide.

"Is this...is this *him*?" she finally murmured to Bronwen, who nodded and shook herself out of where surprise had frozen her to the spot.

She wiped her horse-hair-covered hands on her jeans.

"Ian. Hi."

He took three steps into the barn, then stopped.

"I'm sorry to interrupt," he said politely.

Martha broke out into a broad grin. "Interrupt? You've got to be kidding. We've all been dying to get a look at you!"

Olivia rolled her eyes. "Subtlety, thy name is Martha."

"Hush," Martha threw back at her. "Come in! Come in!"

She waved Ian forward like she was welcoming him into her living room. "Watch out for Percy," she warned him as he walked past the horse, who had fallen asleep in the aisle. "He gets a little kicky when he's clipped."

"What happened to 'the best-behaved boy'?" Olivia asked.

"Shush. Do you want any coffee…Ian, was it? We might have tea, if you prefer that. Have you met all the horses? Bronwen said you'd been in the barn, but I don't know if she properly introduced you to the residents. How long will you be around, anyway?"

"Oh my God, Martha." Olivia pressed the heels of her hands to her eyes. "Let the poor man get a word in."

Bronwen knew she should step in. Ask Ian what he wanted. Whisk him away from Martha's barrage of questions. But he came to a stop about two feet from where she stood, and all she could think about was kissing him in the hay storage.

She'd meant it when she said she wasn't looking for a relationship. She'd been burned too badly by her last couple of boyfriends, the most recent of which had been nothing but a string of broken promises leaving her second-guessing herself and her ability to trust anyone with her heart again. She was no more ready to commit to another person than she was to hop up on Percy's back and ride off into the sunset.

But that didn't mean she didn't like to be kissed, and kissed well. And Ian kissed *well*. Gentle and sure and just forceful enough to know there was a volcano of passion somewhere under that icy exterior. And he'd smiled. Joked, even. Both of which were nearly as appealing as being kissed by him. Nearly.

But he'd made it abundantly clear that kissing—and anything else—wasn't on his agenda. Not exactly a surprise, but still…a disappointment. She shouldn't care, shouldn't question why, when he'd barely wanted to be in her presence since he'd arrived, let alone push her into the hay bales and have his way with her. But it still stung a little.

She'd tried not to think about it in the days since, but here he was, tall and looking so adorably uncomfortable that she wanted to kiss him again. Instead, she pulled herself together.

"Ian, this is Martha and her horse, Percy. And this is Olivia—she rides Charlie."

He nodded politely at both of them, and they smiled back. Then Bronwen noticed that his hand was bleeding.

"Oh! What happened? Not one of those nails on the fence, was it?"

"Fencing needs to be replaced, too," Martha added helpfully.

Ian wisely pretended he didn't hear her and turned to Bronwen. "Do you have any bandages in here? There aren't any up at the house."

Bronwen refrained from saying that, as far as she could tell, there wasn't anything up at the house—whether it be decent furniture, heat or the sign of a living person other than Ian. But that wasn't her business.

"What happened?"

"Hades," he said through gritted teeth. "I tried to force

the issue and got too close, and he snapped at me. I don't think he even meant to make contact, but..."

She instinctively reached out for his hand, which had a small but nasty gash just below the thumb. Probably didn't require stitches, but definitely needed cleaning and a bandage.

As soon as she touched him, she wished she hadn't, as her brain—and other parts—immediately recalled that kiss. Again. She dropped his hand and took a half step back.

She almost missed the way Ian let out a shaky breath, as if he was affected by her touch, too. But he clearly wasn't affected enough to want to kiss her again. As great as the kiss had been, she couldn't forget how he'd tensed up and closed off immediately afterward. Things had gone from hot to teasing to awkward remarkably fast. As much as she wasn't looking for a relationship, the quick turnaround had stung a little, and she could take a hint.

She tucked any kiss-related thoughts safely away and waved him toward the tack room.

"We have plenty of bandages. Antiseptic, too. Come on."

The weight of all the questions Olivia and Martha would bombard her with later pressed down on her as Ian followed her into the tack room. She tried very hard not to think any more about the last time they'd been in this room, and what had come after. Instead, she opened the drawer that held the first aid supplies.

"Why don't you wash it off in the sink, and then we can disinfect it and get a bandage on there."

Ian obliged, standing over the sink and washing his hand thoroughly.

"Here." She beckoned him over to the counter where she'd laid out the antiseptic ointment and a large bandage.

He took the tube of ointment and she watched as he applied it to the painful-looking cut, then stuck on the bandage. Finally, he turned and leaned back against the counter, staring at the row of saddles on the other side of the room.

"I don't know what to do," he said glumly. "It's been almost two weeks since he got here, and I've been feeding him myself twice a day, spending at least half an hour with him every time, if not more. I've tried bribery. Patience. Walking around the field randomly like I'm just another horse."

She'd seen him, out in the cold. Inching his way closer to Hades until the big horse decided enough was enough and took off to a far corner. She'd been amused, frustrated for Ian and worried for Hades. What would Ian do with a horse who couldn't even be handled? Eventually he'd need to see the vet, the farrier. What if there was a big storm and they couldn't get him in the barn? And what would he do with a beautiful, wonderfully bred horse if he couldn't be ridden or used to sire foals?

"What are you going to do?" she prompted when he fell silent.

He slid a look in her direction, then went back to staring unhappily at saddles. "I need...help."

She wanted to smile, but stopped herself just in time. Ian sounded utterly appalled at the idea that he might need assistance from anyone. And given who he was, she wasn't surprised.

"I looked you up, you know," she said casually.

His gaze snapped to hers, and she swallowed. But she didn't think she'd done anything wrong.

"John, from Clover Farm, said your full name. And I was curious about the person we're depending on to basically hold this place together."

"I'm pretty sure that's actually you," he said with a wry smile, and she sighed with relief. He didn't seem offended that she'd done her research on him.

"Okay, but financially. Your name was a bit familiar, and now I know why. Ian Kingston, 'King of Show Jumping.' It was all very impressive."

A self-made man, as it were. Born poor and made his way catching rides from his teen years, going where the horses were, until he'd made enough of a reputation that he'd been offered the best horses, from the most prominent owners and trainers. There had been talk of him as a shoo-in for the next Olympics.

He looked down at his hand, picking at the bandage. "A stupid nickname. I'm a regular person from the middle of nowhere Virginia, who happens to be good at riding horses. Or I *was* good at it."

"And what happened...?" She'd read about his accident, a horrific fluke of a fall when his horse caught a foot on a fence and sent him flying. The horse had walked away without a scratch. Ian had gone straight to the hospital. "Obviously I don't know the details, or why you're here now. And I'm not going to ask. It's not my business. But I didn't want to pretend I didn't know who you were."

"You didn't know, though. Not until you looked me up."

She shrugged. "I've been out of that scene for a long time," she said without thinking.

One perfect eyebrow raised itself in her direction. "You *were* in that scene, though?"

She shook her head, not wanting to get into her past, or what she was doing at Morning Song Farm. "Not like you." She lifted her chin. Enough talking about the past. "So. You need help with the big guy?"

He sighed heavily. "I guess I do. And you're the only one who's been able to handle him since he got here."

"Well, technically no one else has even tried." All of the boarders had a healthy respect for—in addition to avid curiosity about—the beautiful stallion. "Not that I want them to," she added quickly. "I don't want anyone to get hurt." She glanced down at his hand. "Anyone else."

Ian's eyebrows knit together as he frowned. "I don't want you to get hurt, either."

She told herself it didn't mean anything that he was concerned about her safety. But then he moved closer, and his gaze was so warm she let herself wonder, just for a moment. What would it be like if this gorgeous, intense man cared for her? Protected her well-being, and grumped his way around anyone or anything that threatened to harm her? Not because he felt obligated, but because he *cared*—cared enough to take on a little of the responsibility that she hadn't even realized until now sat heavily on her shoulders. Perhaps more heavily than she cared to admit.

Those were dangerous, destabilizing thoughts to have in the middle of the tack room, about a man who'd made it clear that caring was not on his agenda.

"It's my job, dealing with all kinds of horses," she said, her voice a little shaky to her own ears. "Even the mean ones," she said with a little smile. "Not that Hades is mean," she added quickly. "He just needs to know he's safe."

"And you're willing to help me show him that?" Ian asked quietly.

He was maybe a foot away, and she had to tilt her head back to meet his eyes. Her heart was beating too fast, considering she was standing completely still. It figured that the first person who'd had this effect on her in years—maybe ever—was a man who wanted nothing but distance. Whenever his sister showed up, he'd likely be gone.

And the chill that spread through her chest at that thought was absurd. She'd only known him a short time, and other than one kiss, she had no reason to feel any sort of attachment to him.

"Of course," she answered him. "I'm glad to help. Maybe tomorrow I can help you with his evening feed? See if he'll let me get close?"

Ian made a face like he didn't have much hope of her success. "That would be great. If you're willing. And as long as you're careful." Worry crossed his face again, and Bronwen tried to ignore the little thunk of her heart.

Maybe he wasn't so iced over after all. She knew all too well how a bad accident could throw you for a loop. Everything changed in an instant, and sometimes it took a long time to rearrange the pieces of your life that had been scattered.

Some pieces never found their way back into place.

But similar to Hades, pushing Ian would probably only

result in him lashing out. So, she made things easy for him instead.

"There's a side door to the outside over there." She jerked her chin over by the tack trunks. "You can make your escape without running the gossip gauntlet, if you want." Martha and Olivia would be mad at missing the opportunity to grill Ian about anything and everything, but they'd get over it.

"All right." With a grateful look, Ian stepped away from her, and Bronwen turned to put away the bandages and antiseptic so she didn't have to watch him leave.

Eight

Ian watched as Bronwen stood in the corner of the shed, one hand on Hades's shoulder. Every so often the skin under her hand twitched, but otherwise he seemed unbothered.

"I am going to murder that horse," he muttered irritably.

Bronwen chuckled quietly, and Hades turned to snort at her. She smiled. "He doesn't like having his dinner interrupted, does he?"

"The only thing that horse likes better than food is giving me a hard time."

"Aww. I think he just needs time. Come here."

Ian raised his eyebrows at her, but stood up from his usual place on the overturned bucket. Bronwen had come out to the shed with him for Hades's evening feed, and instead of dumping the feed in the bucket and retreating to the corner, as he'd been doing, she waited a couple of feet away.

Ian knew from past experience that if he'd tried the same thing, the horse would have given him the stink eye until he moved away from his food. But Hades had come right into the shed, clearly not seeing Bronwen as much of a threat, and settled in happily to eat. Ian had kept his distance, and to his astonishment, Hades had let Bronwen inch closer as he chewed his grain, until she was touching him gently at the base of his neck.

Ian moved slowly now, coming up behind Bronwen until he was an inch away. This close, he could smell whatever floral shampoo she used, probably something as no-nonsense as she was. But combined with the scent that was hers alone, it smelled like spring and sunshine and warm grass.

He closed his eyes briefly, letting himself soak in her nearness, careful not to touch her. Still, they were so close he could have easily pulled her into his arms and finished what they started the other day. Desire slammed into him at the thought, and he swallowed heavily.

"Put your hand over mine," Bronwen said, apparently oblivious to the riot in his body.

He did as she said, his hand covering her smaller one completely. He felt like a tightly strung bow, trying to focus on the single point of contact and not on the nearly over-whelming need to press himself into all of her.

One of Hades's ears flicked back toward them, but he kept eating.

Slowly, Bronwen slid her hand out from under his, and he resisted the urge to hold it in place. *The horse.* That was why they were here. Why she'd asked him to touch her hand. That was all.

She turned her head slightly to the side, and his eyes raked over her profile. Long, slim nose, that determined chin, lips full and turned up at the corners as Hades stood still, unconcerned about the man now touching him. She had a tiny dimple, only noticeable now that he was so close. It would be so easy to lean down and press a kiss there. He wondered what she would do if he did.

"Okay," she said quietly. "Now stay there."

She ducked under his arm and slowly moved behind him, placing a hand on his back as if to hold him in place. The imprint of it branded him through his thick sweater.

Hades stopped eating, and Ian held his breath. The horse turned his big head and stared him right in the eye, as if taking his measure. Ian held perfectly still, and when the horse nudged his chest with his nose—like he was telling Ian in no uncertain terms that he knew exactly what he was doing—and then went back to eating dinner, Ian couldn't help but let out a soft laugh.

He stroked his hand down Hades's muscled shoulder, then back up to the top of his neck. Amazing. Apparently the stallion had needed Bronwen to vouch for his character, and now found Ian an adequate companion.

Bronwen's hand still lay on his back, and she leaned in toward him, her front pressed lightly against his back. He knew it was an unconscious movement, stemming from her excitement over Hades's grudging acceptance of him. But he still wanted to turn around and haul her into his arms, find out if the kiss in the hay storage room had been a fluke, or if he'd go up in flames again.

"You'll be riding him in no time," Bronwen said from behind him, a smile in her voice.

That was enough to dash ice over the heat that consumed

him. What was he doing, lusting after a woman he'd be leaving behind as surely as he'd fled everything he'd known down in Florida? She deserved better than his mess. But maybe she also deserved to know the truth.

"I won't," he said a little more roughly than he'd intended. He took a calming breath. "The accident— I've got a metal pin in my hip and my back is basically held together by force of will at this point." A sad joke, but he was trying. "And my head didn't get off scot-free, either. I was out for hours afterward. Woke up in the hospital and the first thing I learned was that I'll probably never ride again."

There. That was as much as she needed to know. The rest… How the people he'd counted on as friends had turned out to have no use for an Ian Kingston who couldn't perform like a circus monkey. Maybe that wasn't fair. So many of them had been sponsors, owners, trainers. They had their own lives and issues, and he was just one rider among many. The upper levels of competitive riding were unforgiving, and they had to look out for their own interests. Still, it had felt like betrayal when not one of them had visited him in the hospital. And it still burned.

And as for his future… Bronwen didn't need to know about that, either. His vow to leave everything related to horses behind had hit a snag thanks to his sister, but he still intended to fulfill it.

She'd gone silent behind him. And then: "I'm so sorry, Ian. That's truly horrible."

The sympathy in her voice was real, but he didn't want it. He was so tired of sympathy, pity, words that did nothing to actually fix his situation.

"Maybe we'll get you up on his back, though," Ian said, ready to change the subject. He let his hand drop from Hades's neck and turned to face her.

Bronwen glanced at him, then away. An unreadable expression crossed her face, and he wanted to ask about it. But he didn't want to press for secrets he wasn't willing to return.

"Yeah. Maybe," she said tonelessly.

He wanted to soothe whatever it was that lay under those words, but what did he have to offer, really?

A tug at the bottom of his jacket had him turning toward Hades again. The horse had finished his food and apparently decided that Ian's clothes made a decent dessert.

"Hey," he said in a low voice. He didn't want to startle the animal now that he had his interest. "That's not food. Here."

He rummaged around in the pocket of his pants and came up with a horse treat—a little ball of apple, oats and honey. Hades's large dark eyes lit up—truly, the horse's first love was food—and he shoved his way between Ian and Bronwen, slurping up the treat from Ian's hand with his soft velvet lips. He chewed contentedly, and Bronwen walked around his head and gave him a careful pat as she moved toward the shed opening. The horse nudged her with his nose, leaving a little slobber on her jacket.

Bronwen laughed, and the sound warmed his insides more than it should have. Unlike him, she seemed able to leave disappointment or hurt behind without much trouble.

Treat finished, Hades snorted and stamped his feet a little as if to remind them that he was on his best behavior—but that he didn't *have* to be.

Ian let out a long breath as they watched the horse amble

peacefully out into the field. A far cry from his usual tantrum when Ian tried to approach him, mostly comprised of snapping teeth and hooves flying as he tore out of the shed like it was on fire.

He felt a rush of gratitude toward Bronwen, who hadn't been obligated to spend the better part of an hour out in the field shed, helping him with the horse he hadn't even asked for. He knew she had more than enough to do, although she'd said their part-time barn assistant would handle the evening feed.

"Do you want dinner?" he asked and had to smile at the astonished look Bronwen turned on him. It hadn't been the most elegant invitation.

"I mean…yes, but you don't have to provide it." She returned his smile.

This was probably a terrible idea. He had no business asking this woman up to the house, not when he could barely keep his hands off her in the middle of a shed with a horse between them. Having her in the same building as an actual bed would probably cause him to spontaneously combust.

But he owed her, and he might be a different person now than he had been just a few months ago, but he still fulfilled his obligations. And that was all it was, he told himself. An obligation.

"I was going to make something simple—soup and bread, maybe a chicken."

Bronwen's eyebrows shot up. "Just that? Like…a whole actual chicken in the oven?"

He frowned at her. "How else would you cook a chicken?"

She laughed. "I wouldn't. My apartment has a microwave and a hot plate. So chicken is entirely a take-out food around here."

Ian liked to cook more than most people he'd met—he'd learned out of necessity to feed himself and his sister—but still...

"I'm not much of a cook," she continued. "Not at all a cook, actually. I'm more of a leftover takeout and soup-from-a-can kind of person."

He didn't like that. Bronwen's job was physical, day in and day out. She needed more than canned soup.

"Then you definitely need to come have dinner at the house," he said firmly. "It's the least I can do after your help with Hades."

Bronwen glanced over to where the horse in question was grazing quietly. "I told you I don't mind helping."

"You still need to eat. And...and I have more leftover cake than I can possibly eat."

This was all true, but he knew he was pushing. The fact was, he wasn't ready to let her go for the night. Back to her apartment with just a hot plate and microwave, far out of his reach. He wanted her close by, just a little while longer.

And she needed to eat a real meal.

"Cake!" she exclaimed. "How on earth do you have left-over cake? You never even leave the house." She slapped a hand over her mouth. "I'm sorry. That was rude."

He shook his head. "You're not wrong. I thought if I spent some time alone I could get my head back on straight."

She tilted her head, considering him. "And?"

His mouth twisted in a wry smile. "Still working on it."

"And what about the cake?"

"Cooking and baking… I find them relaxing."

Her expression softened into sympathy. "That's great that you have something like that." She grinned at him. "Plus, then you have cake!"

He grabbed the bucket they'd used to carry the feed out to the shed and, when Bronwen held out her arm, handed it over.

"I don't actually like sweets," he confessed. "Just the process."

"Oh my God." Bronwen laughed her infectious laugh that sounded like sunlight breaking through clouds. "Well. In that case, I'd better come for dinner. I can't let perfectly good cake go to waste."

"Exactly." Satisfaction sat comfortably in his gut. He should feel the opposite. He should tell her not to come, that she'd do so much better to avoid him. He should feel regretful and guilty.

But he didn't.

"All right. Let me just check in with Abigail about things, and maybe jump in the shower. I'll be up in a bit."

He nodded. "And…thank you. For helping. I'd still be sitting on my ass on that bucket while Hades ignored me, if it wasn't for you."

Bronwen shook her head as if dismissing his thanks. "I think we still have a ways to go with the big guy."

"We?" He didn't like the hope that took up residence in his chest at the word. He didn't have room for hope. Not until he figured out his life, which definitely wouldn't be anywhere near Morning Song Farm.

Bronwen looked offended. "Obviously. I'm invested now.

Maybe in a few days we can see if he'll let you lead him. We need to get him into the barn at some point."

She made it sound…if not easy, then achievable. And maybe it was. With her help.

"All right." He shoved his hands into his pockets in case they got ideas, like reaching for her before he could make his escape. "I'll see you in a while, then."

She smiled at him, and he knew he was making all kinds of regrettable mistakes. But he couldn't regret them quite yet.

"Yep. See you in a bit."

Nine

Bronwen sat at the kitchen table, a plate with a huge piece of cake in front of her. Ian was stationed at the sink, rinsing dishes.

"I can't possibly eat all of this," she protested.

Ian slid a look in her direction. "Try. You can't exist on canned soup."

She laughed. "I don't. Really." She couldn't resist adding, "Sometimes I make ramen noodles."

He turned to glare at her, but she knew him just well enough now to see the hint of a twinkle in his eyes.

"Anyway, you already fed me chicken and homemade soup and bread—I'm hardly going to starve." She watched as he washed the dishes by hand, since the old house didn't have a dishwasher. "And if you give me a minute, I'll do the dishes. You don't have to cook for me and clean up, as well."

She'd arrived at the house after checking in with Abigail and satisfying herself that the horses were tucked into their stalls and comfortably munching on their hay. She'd taken a shower, run a comb through her hair and told herself for the millionth time that she'd go get a proper haircut soon. Then she'd put on her only clean pair of jeans and a decent long-sleeved T-shirt—Ian had so far only seen her filthy and covered in hay and horse hair, so she figured this was a major improvement.

And then she'd headed up to the house and found Ian, devastating in a plain white button-down shirt and jeans, hair still damp from his own shower, and an entire meal better than she'd had in months in process. They'd eaten and talked horses, Ian asking about the farm's various residents and noting everything he'd learned about Hades's rather strong personality during his time observing him. It had been...companionable. Comfortable.

But the memory of their kiss was never far from her thoughts, tugging at her to decide whether she wanted Ian as a temporary friend or a temporary...something else.

"You're a guest," he said now. "Besides, I haven't had the chance to be this domestic in years."

She was sure that was true—the professional show-jumping circuit was grueling and involved a lot of travel. But she wondered about the last time he had been domestic. What was he doing, years ago, that had given him experience with all of this cooking and cleaning?

She didn't ask, but instead took a bite of cake. It was some kind of vanilla almond, with what she guessed was lemon icing. "Oh my God," she said. "This is incredible."

Ian dried his hands and turned to lean his back against the counter. "Good."

"You made this whole cake and didn't even try it?" If she had these kinds of baking powers, she'd have eaten the whole thing in one sitting.

But he shook his head. "I used to, when I started baking. But like I said, I'm not really a sweets person. And I already know my cakes are good."

He said it without an ounce of arrogance, someone wholly confident in the simple fact of their abilities. He had probably been the same about his riding, which had been at least as successful as his baking. But he could still make an incredible cake, while the riding... What a waste, she thought. And then called herself the hypocrite she was. She might not have been on Ian's level, but she'd been a good rider with a bright future in front of her. And now she hadn't been on a horse in years, when physically she could go down to the barn right now and hop onto her horse's back.

Unlike Ian.

"When does your sister get back?" she asked, thinking the future was probably a safer topic of conversation than the past.

Ian shrugged. "I'm not sure. A few weeks, I think. It's a postdivorce getaway. So, a little open-ended."

Bronwen considered that. A few weeks—there were a lot of possibilities in a few weeks. With Hades, with Ian, with herself and Ian. If he was even interested. But she wasn't going to bring that up. Yet.

"Good for her," she said. She took a bite of cake and swallowed. "What will you do then?"

If she had been looking down at the cake instead of at Ian, she would have missed the way his body tensed, the way the warm light went out of his blue eyes. Maybe the future wasn't any safer than the past after all.

He didn't answer right away, but she didn't push. She didn't let him off the hook, either.

Eventually, he said, "I don't know."

And she thought that might be the end of what he was willing to share, so she ate the rest of her cake in silence and brought the plate up to the sink, washing it herself.

Maybe the fact that she was occupied made it easier for him to continue, because he did.

"I don't know where I'll go or what I'll do. In the meantime, I'll make sure everything here keeps going. Whatever help you need. But once Anne gets here, I'll go somewhere else." She sneaked a look at him. His hands were in his pockets, his forehead furrowed as he stared across the room. "Somewhere without horses. That much, I've decided."

Bronwen started. "Really? I know you can't ride anymore, but—"

"No horses," he repeated firmly. "No horses, and no horse people. I'm done with that whole world."

Bronwen blinked at the force behind the words, as if he was trying to convince her of something. Or himself.

"But you could train, or teach, or…or do anything you wanted in the showing world. People think so highly of you."

She'd learned that much. Every online article about Ian emphasized his strength, his integrity, his humor—the last of which she'd only seen the tiniest sliver of, it seemed. They said he was a wizard with horses, that he could ride anything. Get the best out of any horse. How could he turn his back on that kind of talent?

But he was shaking his head. "I'm done. No more riding, and no more horses. I need something as far from that as I can get. And while I'm here…" The edge that had been in his voice that first morning when she'd barged in on him was making a reappearance. She thought now that it must be a defensive mechanism. Or a way of convincing himself he was colder than a man who'd willingly take on the care of an unmanageable stallion could possibly be. "I'll help, but I'm not getting any more involved with the barn or the boarders—or their horses—than I have to."

Well. That was clear enough. Although…

She turned to face his side, leaning her hip against the sink. His profile was something to see, all hard planes and sharp angles. Like a marble sculpture.

"The barn, the boarders and their horses," she said. "Noted. What about the barn manager?"

There was a pause, but Ian was so still next to her that it was easy to see the tick of his jaw, the way his Adam's apple bobbed as he swallowed before answering.

"What about the barn manager?" he finally asked.

She bit her bottom lip, and didn't miss the way his gaze flicked in her direction.

Sure, he'd said back in the hay storage room that he wasn't looking for anything, either. That being with her was a bad idea. Maybe it was. But she'd been thinking about it, and she'd decided like the adult person she was that it was a mistake she was happy to make. She didn't want a relationship—was actively avoiding them, in fact—but Ian was the first person she'd met in some time who made her want anything. Feel anything. She missed feeling things, and she wanted to feel some more.

The plain fact of it was, she'd really, really enjoyed kissing him. And she was fairly certain he'd enjoyed it, too.

So, what was the harm?

"Well, inviting her into your house and stuffing her full of dinner and cake is hardly not getting involved."

"It's not my house."

She suppressed an eye roll. "Ian."

He gave a little huff of impatience.

She waited it out, and finally he turned to face her. She looked up at his pale blue eyes, anything but cold now. They burned into hers, roiling with emotion and what she hoped was desire. Yeah, she was willing to make this mistake, if that was what it was.

"You agreed that it could get complicated. That this would be a bad idea." His voice was as tightly wound as a nervous horse.

She couldn't help teasing him with a half smile. "This?" she asked, as if she didn't know exactly what he meant.

That jaw tick again. She wanted to reach up and soothe it with her fingers, so she did, the skin rough with nearly invisible blond whiskers. The scratch of it sparked the tamped-down embers that had been lying in wait since that day in the hay storage.

He turned to glare down at her, lips pressed in a firm line. Then he shook his head.

"You know what I mean. *This*."

And he leaned down and kissed her, as if he was proving a point, as if it wasn't exactly what she wanted.

She kissed him back, trying to convince him through her actions that, mistake or not, this would be worth it. That they both deserved a little pleasure for once.

She opened to him as he demanded, his mouth on hers almost punishing, but also everything she needed. There was no hesitation, no question of his desire, as he feasted on her lips, his tongue sweeping against her teeth in a way that made her knees weak, made her belly swoop like she was falling from a great height.

But he had her, holding her securely in his strong arms, a palm against the nape of her neck and his fingers gripping her hair. She could hardly draw air into her lungs—only him. His scent, his feel, the hard length of his tall, lean body blotting out everything else.

He pulled back slightly, his breath warm on her face in the chill of the old house. "You're not what I expected to find here," he said softly.

She blinked her eyes open. His were still closed, so she pinched his side to get his attention. He jumped a little and scowled down at her. But there wasn't any anger in his expression.

"What did you expect to find?" she asked, and then held her breath. For some reason, she wasn't sure she wanted the answer.

He shook his head slightly. "Not this. Not you."

She didn't know whether that was good or bad, but he lowered his mouth again and she decided it didn't matter for now. His tongue caressed her bottom lip before he broke their contact again.

"I want to do this every time you bite that lip." His voice was a rasp and her body thrilled to it. "It drives me up the wall."

She didn't have words to respond, not when his large hands slid downward to cup her ass, squeezing as he kissed her again, his erection jutting urgently into her stomach through his jeans. She instinctively ground up into him and he groaned, a desperate sound that went right to her already damp core.

"Fuck," he grunted against her lips as her fingernails dug into his shoulders where she'd braced her hands for stability.

And then she was flying, or it felt like it, as he lifted her easily up onto the kitchen counter next to the sink. She gasped in surprise and he swallowed it, kissing her again. And again. At this height her head was level with his, his hips between her thighs. She wrapped herself around him, arms around his neck and legs around hips.

"I don't want to wait." He tore his mouth from hers, his fingers coming to the button of her jeans. "May I?"

She blinked stupidly at him, her brain unable to make sense of anything after he'd obliterated her logic with his kisses. But whatever he wanted to do was fine with her, so she nodded.

He kissed her once more, hard. And then he unzipped her jeans and tugged them down, off her legs along with her underwear and sneakers.

She inhaled sharply as he knelt in front of her, finally catching up to what he intended.

"Ian—" He glanced up, gaze scorching her to her center.

"Do you not want me to?" His voice was rough as gravel.

She had no idea why she'd even said his name. It certainly wasn't a protest. If anything, it had been something awfully close to begging.

"I...I do. *Very* much," she gasped out.

He was on her like a starving man, strong, calloused hands holding her knees apart. Her heart thundered in her chest, fingers grasping the edge of the counter to hold herself upright as he licked up her swollen folds and back down, tongue darting inside her just long enough for her to stifle a cry.

"I want to hear you," Ian commanded from below.

And it was his lucky day, because when he slid one long finger inside her, tongue still teasing, she couldn't hold back. Moaning and whimpering, arms shaking. Head thrown back as if she didn't have the strength to hold it up.

Her skin was so feverishly hot, she was amazed she didn't burst into flame right there. She should have been shocked at how quickly the pressure building low in her belly came close to the breaking point, but there was no room in her mind for anything but waves of sensation and need as Ian's brilliant tongue coaxed her higher and closer to the summit.

He was voracious, but every time she neared the precipice, every time she came *this* close to tumbling over, he held back. He brought her to the edge over and over again, the whiskers on his cheek rubbing her inner thigh with just enough roughness to heighten her pleasure. Two fingers now, pumping slowly in and out of her while his tongue circled her clit, orgasm deliciously just out of reach.

"Ian," she whined, and the vibration from his answering chuckle was what pushed her right over, coming harder than she could remember ever doing before. The sensation lasted so long she wondered wildly if it would ever stop, but eventually she floated back down to reality, her entire body tingling with aftershocks.

She was sure if she looked down she'd find her legs had actually turned to Jell-O. Which seemed fitting, she thought feverishly, given that she was on a kitchen counter. She swallowed and took a steadying breath. When she opened her eyes, Ian was standing upright again, looming over her in the best possible way, arms braced on the counter on either side of her legs. His lips were swollen, hair mussed and cheeks slashed with red.

He looked perfect.

"Hi," she said nonsensically.

The corner of his mouth turned up, but it did nothing to soften his almost feral expression. His hands clenched the countertop, and he kissed her, hard and deep, before declaring in a thick, low voice, "Bed."

Bronwen was light but substantial in his arms as he made his way determinedly up the stairs. For the first time, he felt real gratitude that his injuries hadn't been worse. His hip twinged only slightly as he carried her to the bedroom, his back mostly keeping any complaints to itself.

He wouldn't have missed this for the world—his arms were full of satisfied woman, and the way she looked at him as he laid her on the bed and crawled over her made him feel like he was whole again. Like maybe his worth wasn't measured by his ability to ride horses for other people, no matter what everyone in his previous life apparently believed.

Bronwen reached up and ran her fingers through his hair, a smile illuminating her gorgeous face. "You look a little wild."

That wasn't him, not usually. He was a lot of things: competent, driven, focused. And now, broken. But not wild.

Here, though, he liked the sound of that. She *made* him wild. She made him feel things when he wasn't sure he had the ability anymore. She made him want; she made him imagine something he hadn't been able to before: the future.

The imagined future didn't go very far, or past this room. But at this moment he was doing a lot of imagining. What he wanted to do to her, with her. What she'd look like when he stripped off the shirt she still wore. All of that imagining pumped blood through his veins, air through his lungs. All of that imagining made him feel *alive*.

And wild.

Wild enough to kiss her again, the way he wanted to: ravenously, endlessly, laying his body on hers until he could feel every curve and swell of her under him.

She wrapped her legs around his hips and arched up into him, the pressure against his aching dick almost too much. He groaned into her mouth, knowing he needed to slow down but not wanting to stop kissing her. Ever.

Her hands on his back, his spine, the warmth through his shirt and the soft scratch of fingernails on the fabric had him growling with desire. He wrenched his mouth away from hers and sat up, wiping his mouth with the back of his hand. She stared up at him with bright green eyes, all lust and humor and need, and he was undone.

"Off," he commanded, tugging at the bottom of her shirt. Trying to ignore the way his body all but howled in protest at the pause in the proceedings.

She smirked at him, but wriggled her way out of the top, tossing it to the side and propping herself on one elbow to unsnap her bra as he watched.

He was so far gone he could hardly see straight, but he kept watching, trying to memorize the slide of the thin straps off her shoulders, the way she removed the bra slowly, teasing him. He growled again.

And then she was bare to him, full breasts and strong arms and wide hips all in front of him like a buffet. He trailed his fingers down her sternum to her belly, taut with muscle from heavy work but softened by padding he wanted to sink his teeth into.

"*Fuck.* I don't know where to start."

She huffed out a laugh. "Seems like you already made a pretty good start downstairs."

"Mmm." He had. A very good start, but not enough. Not anywhere close to enough.

He braced his hands on either side of her head and leaned down to kiss her collarbone. She gasped, and he kept going, his mouth over her heart, between her breasts, along one side of her stomach. Down to where she was wet and ready for him. He inhaled deeply, her musky scent almost enough to push him right over the edge.

But he wanted to be inside her when he came. He *needed* that. Still…

He pressed a kiss right to her core and was rewarded with a groan.

"Ian."

He teased her with his tongue, storing up her taste and feel for whenever the day came when she was done with him.

"Ian." She tugged on his shoulder, and he stopped long enough to look up at her.

"What? I'm busy."

"Take off your damn clothes already," she demanded.

His forehead fell to her thigh. "If I take off my pants I'm going to be inside you in two seconds."

He felt her silent laugh as her body shook. "You say that like it's a bad thing."

He made himself stand, immediately mourning the loss of her touch. Warning bells went off in his mind, telling him that this was too much—too much to feel, too much to lose as he inevitably would. Too addictive for someone who was going to move on as soon as possible.

But there was no way he was stopping now. Not when Bronwen lay on the bed, naked and waiting. Wanting *him.*

He tore off his shirt like it didn't have perfectly good buttons to make taking it off easier. His shoes, socks and jeans were next, underwear last. Everything in a heap on the cold wood floor. But he was burning, on fire with want. So, when Bronwen crooked a finger at him, knowing smile on her lips, he was over her in a second, pulling her with him as he rolled to the side.

Her hands were everywhere. Down the long muscles of his arms, across his chest, skimming the sensitive skin of his nipples as he gasped at her touch, down the planes of his stomach to where his dick jutted between them, hard and hot and aching almost painfully. She moaned and leaned in to kiss his throat while her hands stroked *almost* where he needed it most.

He nearly came right then, the muscles in his stomach contracting and a wave of dizziness and need stealing his breath.

"Jesus, Bronwen," he whispered on what oxygen was left inside him. "I fucking want you."

"I love your body" was her reverent answer, hands still exploring every inch of him.

He'd never thought of his body as anything more than functional. It worked; it rode horses; it did the things he needed it to do. At least, until his accident. Sure, it also brought pleasure, to himself and his partners, but this, too, had always been primarily functional.

The way Bronwen was looking at him, like he was... beautiful. Worthy of desire exactly as he was. It was almost too much.

"I think—" he began, but then her hand brushed his cock and words were impossible. He groaned again, almost a whine. Fuck, he wanted to be inside her. "I have condoms... somewhere," he managed.

"Somewhere, huh?" Her words were a whisper into his ear, as if she was as breathless as he was. "Is this like some kind of kinky scavenger hunt?"

That surprised a laugh out of him. How could he be laughing when his body was ready to erupt?

She rolled away from him and sat up, and he fisted his hands to avoid hauling her back.

Slowly, he rose from the bed and headed for the closet. His skin was hot and feverish, prickling as if being away from Bronwen for even this long was causing some sort of allergic reaction.

"Just give me a minute."

He ripped open one forlorn box sitting in the closet, tossing the contents onto the floor. Nothing. He unzipped the duffel bag next to the box with such force he almost broke the zipper. But—*there.*

Triumphant and trying to ignore the fact that he was still so hard walking was uncomfortable, he strode back to the bed, condoms in hand. Bronwen sat in the middle of the bed, wide-eyed and laughing.

"I thought you were fighting someone in there." She grinned at him.

And then she shrieked as he grabbed her and kissed her, hard. She lay back, and he was between her thighs on his knees, her arms up over her head. He took a moment despite the clamoring of his body to get on with it already.

He simply...looked at her, kneeling between her legs, condom in hand. Long brown hair spread out like a cloud around her head. Eyes shining and liquid with desire. Cheeks and lips flushed, spectacular breasts rising and falling with every quick breath.

God, she was beautiful. Warm and real and strong, gorgeous and lying beneath him, open and wanting. Waiting.

He couldn't wait anymore. He leaned down and took one perfect nipple into his mouth, suckling until she groaned and her hands clutched at his hair. The sweet pain of her grasp drove him close to the edge, and he slipped a hand between them to play with her clit, stroking until she squirmed under him.

"Ian—now. I need you *now.*"

He could no more have refused her demand than he could have leaped out the window and flown away.

With an agonized groan, he sat up just long enough to rip open the package and roll the condom on his swollen length.

He settled over her, sliding inside slowly, almost unbearably slowly. He didn't want to hurt her, or do anything other than bring her as much pleasure as she could stand. His body shook with the effort of holding back.

"Ian—please. *More.*"

He snapped. His control broke and he drew back and then slammed into her with a groan that matched hers.

She was hot and wet and absolutely perfect. He opened his eyes to meet hers, as dazed and hazy as he felt.

"More," she said again, and how could he do anything but obey?

With an impatient sound, Bronwen wrapped her legs around his and clutched her fingers into the meat of his ass. They found a rhythm, desperate and a little shaky and so fucking good he couldn't think of anything beyond the feel of her, the little cries and sounds she made with every thrust, the way he could feel how close she was.

He slipped his hand between them again, needing her to get there before he shattered. With a cry she came again, her body tensing and her channel squeezing him almost to the point of pain.

His orgasm ripped through him, an earthquake so powerful his vision went white for a moment as waves of pleasure tore him apart and left him in pieces right there on the bed.

When he eventually returned to his senses, he rolled to the side to dispose of the condom, then gathered Bronwen's limp body to him, her back pressed to his front.

"You okay?" he asked quietly.

"Better than okay," she answered sleepily. "Perfect."

Ian knew he wasn't perfect. But maybe, just for tonight, he'd been able to be a little sliver of who he'd been. Or maybe, with Bronwen, he was something new entirely— still not perfect, but perfect with her.

Too bad there was no way he could stay, no way he could take the time to see if that theory was correct. Bronwen would never leave horses behind—that much was clear. And he'd never ask her to. But he needed to get as far away from that world as possible, if he was ever going to find a new place, a new life.

He told himself it was fine, that tonight was only an interlude. An evening out of time, where both he and Bronwen grasped at fleeting pleasure while it was at hand. They'd both be able to move on—it was only one night.

And if part of his brain knew he was lying, sleep took him away soon enough that he didn't have to think about that anymore. The moonlight shone through the window, bright in the deep, dark night, and Ian slept better than he had in months.

Ten

A week later, Bronwen led Hades from the field into the barn.

She'd been working with Ian on getting the horse to allow her to lead him, and after a few false starts and a couple of close calls with teeth and hooves, Hades had been convinced—bribed, really, with sugar cubes and treats and lots of praise—to walk through the barn aisle and out the other side several times. Before calmly walking into the stall prepared for him as if he was a king and had planned to take up residence there all along.

She'd been wary of releasing him out into the field the next day, but Ian had said firmly that the horse needed to be turned out. And needed to learn to be caught and brought inside more than once. He had a point.

Ian had walked along on the other side of Hades's head each time she'd led him, and eventually the big horse grudgingly allowed him to take the lead rope, as well.

Bronwen felt as if she'd won the lottery, and Ian had offered a rare grin.

They'd talked while working with the horse, about everything but mostly nothing. Nothing too personal or painful.

"You grew up around here?" Ian asked one day while they were practicing leading Hades back to his pasture.

"In Boston," she replied absently, patting Hades on the neck. As always, he was alert while being handled, as if waiting for the other shoe to drop. If she had anything to say about it, it never would. "A little duplex in Brighton, surrounded by apartment buildings and triple-deckers. Hardly bucolic farm territory."

His gaze was focused, like everything about him was focused. She liked that—the way when he asked a question he listened attentively, as if the answer mattered. As if he really wanted to know about her childhood, instead of just making small talk while they worked with Hades.

"How'd you end up in the horse business?"

She couldn't help but smile. "I was born horse crazy. I used to stampede up and down the stairs, and jump over all the furniture like I was in the show-jumping ring. Drove my parents absolutely bananas. I begged for years to have riding lessons, and finally my mom caved, I think more to shut me up than anything else."

Ian grunted, but his continued focus encouraged her to keep going.

"My mom drove me out an hour away to a lesson barn for *years*." She shook her head, still amazed that her mother had put up with that. "She had to stand there and watch in the heat and cold, even though I know she found the whole thing terrifying."

"Did you fall off a lot?" Ian asked with a grin.

"Doesn't everybody?" Bronwen laughed. "But yeah, I was so fearless back then…" She trailed off, real grief for the loss of that fearlessness eclipsing her nostalgia for one moment before she pushed it away. "I always rode the problem horses, the ones no one else wanted to ride."

"Makes you a better rider," Ian commented.

She nodded. "Once I got my driver's license, I borrowed my mom's car until I mucked enough stalls to buy the worst car in the world so I could go for lessons a few times a week."

Those days were a million years ago and also just yesterday. She could remember the shiny bay pony who could jump anything but once bit another girl's finger nearly off. Or the big brown ex-racehorse who'd developed the habit of sticking her tongue over the bit so Bronwen had zero control. The skinny paint who'd been a stopper, teaching Bronwen to never lean forward before a jump or she'd surely end up on the ground.

She remembered her mom forcing herself to watch the shows Bronwen entered on borrowed horses, even though she'd been scared to death that Bronwen would fall. Her dad slipping her money they didn't have to spare so she could buy a decent helmet and boots.

She owed them all so much: her parents and the horses alike, for what they'd given her. She'd tried to repay them by studying equine science in college and making horses her career. And she'd managed to make a little money on the side, training and schooling and braiding other people's horses at the shows she'd attended with Charlie, which she'd slipped back to her parents when they weren't looking.

Now she was barely breaking even, with no real potential for things to improve, as far as she could see. But what she could control was the way she managed the horses in her care, the small things she could do to help their owners, the time she spent with her parents now that she wasn't scrambling for the next show, the next ride. She was doing her best, even if it wasn't the best she'd hoped for.

"What about you?" She took Hades's halter off as Ian opened the pasture gate, and spared a moment to scratch the horse's ears. He'd already come so far, such a long way from just a few weeks ago, when he would have taken off across the field at just the sight of them.

When Ian didn't respond, she turned her attention to him. He rubbed a hand over his face and sighed.

"Not such a heartwarming story, I'm afraid," he finally said, what sounded like years of fatigue and sadness coloring his voice to gray.

Bronwen almost told him to stop, never mind the past. She knew well enough that reliving hard times was rarely worth it. But she was curious, and she'd shared something of herself. Not everything, not the truly dark parts, but something. If Ian was willing to talk, she'd listen. So, she waited.

He leaned back against the pasture fence, long legs crossed in front of him, eyes on Hades as the horse ambled away and lowered his head to munch on the fresh spring grass.

"The last however many years were pretty great," he said, starting at the end of the story. "You never think you've made it when you're in the middle of everything, but…I did, you know? I was good. I'd gone further in the sport than I ever thought I could."

She knew this, from her internet sleuthing. The years of striving, competing, traveling around the world with top horses. It sounded exciting, exhausting, stressful, glorious. Her own dreams as a kid had been so similar to his.

"But at the start... Well, you had the worst car in the world." He shot her a grin. "I only had an old, rusty bicycle at first, but luckily we lived in an apartment in the middle of nowhere, close to a bunch of horse farms."

"Virginia," she remembered.

He nodded shortly. "Born and raised. Those farms had everything I wanted—beauty, freedom, structure, routine. And horses."

"Freedom from what?" Curiosity made her push, just a little.

Ian sighed, but he didn't refuse to answer. "My dad was... not great. It was a relief when he left, honestly, even though he took his salary with him. He was hardest on my sister, mostly because I wouldn't engage with him. I avoided his rages, but Anne never met a fight she'd back down from." He shook his head, but Bronwen thought she saw pride on his face. "My mom wasn't thrilled to be saddled with two kids by herself, though she was probably also glad to see the end of our dad."

"I'm sorry, Ian. That sounds awful."

He shrugged. "Anne and I spent as much time as we could at the farms in the area. Kind of amazing to think now that they put up with an angry teen and his little sister, now that I know how much work those places are. But thank God they did."

"And they let you ride?"

"Some did. Others were happy enough to throw me a few bucks if I mucked stalls and mostly stayed out of their way. There was one trainer who saw something in me— God knows how. He taught me to ride, taught me about horses. I was hooked."

"And your sister? Was she a rider, too?" Bronwen hadn't seen any mention of her in the articles she'd read, but after all, his sister was the one who'd bought an entire horse farm.

Ian pushed off from the fence, and together they started the walk back up the hill. Bronwen breathed in the mossy spring air, noticing the lightest of green on the tips of the tree branches, the way the other horses in the fields lounged beneath the sun rather than huddled in or next to the sheds.

"Her favorite was the breeding farm down the road from where we lived. She pestered the people there until she knew every bloodline, every tip and trick they had about breeding sport horses, and handling pregnant mares and foals. But she didn't work for them—she went to college while I caught rides where I could, scrambling from barn to barn until we ended up in Florida, where the big shows were, and I made a decent enough living to support both of us. We got out of Virginia and never looked back."

Pride suffused his voice, and Bronwen thought about the support she'd had, and all that Ian had accomplished without anything like that. Again she thought what a waste it was that he was determined to turn his back on his talent, his determination. But really, who was she to talk? And what did Ian really owe to anyone after going through such hardship and finding such success?

Bronwen thought now about what Ian had said, quietly impressed and moved by his story. She knew he didn't want her sympathy, or even her admiration—but he had both.

There had been no repeat performance of the evening up at the farmhouse. Mostly because Bronwen had been busy: a regular vet visit took up all of one day, another horse had colicked and Bronwen had spent the evening and a good part of the night walking him to get rid of the dangerous bellyache. Her dad's birthday had taken up one of her days off, and Olivia's the other. And then two horses had thrown shoes. Luckily, the farrier had been on the schedule already, thanks to Ian.

She was exhausted, quite frankly.

And also…also, something had settled between the two of them, herself and Ian. Something fragile and tender that neither of them seemed willing to poke and risk disturbing. When they worked with Hades—Bronwen leading him or brushing him or otherwise thoroughly handling him, followed by Ian carefully doing the same—Ian would casually touch her. A hand on her waist or her shoulder. Leaning close to her as they watched the horse absorb his lessons and new life. She wasn't complaining. But neither of them seemed willing to take things further again, even though she, at least, definitely wanted to.

Maybe Ian thought that his insistence that he'd be leaving the horse world behind once his sister returned had scared her off. Sure, she thought he was making a mistake, wasting his incredible talent. And since horses were her world, she could never consider a long-term relationship with anyone who was so set on having nothing to do with that world.

But she didn't want a relationship at all—she'd been burned too badly last time, when personal betrayal had also meant the complete uprooting of her professional life. That betrayal had turned her world on its head, and four years later she was still on shaky ground. It would take time for her to be able to trust again. And time was something she and Ian didn't have.

But that didn't mean they couldn't continue what they'd started up at the house. For a while.

She was so absorbed in her thoughts that she nearly walked Hades right past the farrier. Luckily, or possibly unluckily, the stallion took issue with the enormous strange man standing in the barn aisle and kicked out at a passing stall door.

She started at the loud thunk of hoof on wood and came back to the present. She smiled apologetically at Xavier, the farrier.

"Sorry. This one's going to be a little iffy."

Xavier nodded stoically.

It took more than an aggressive stallion to get a reaction out of Xavier. Nearly as tall as Ian, he was burly enough that rare was the horse who could push him around. And his silent, methodical way of working soothed most nervous animals.

She just hoped Hades could hold it together. His hooves badly needed trimming.

"Ian, this is Xavier. He's been the farrier for Morning Song longer than I've been working here, anyway."

Xavier nodded in silent greeting at Ian, who returned the movement, and then raised his eyebrows at Bronwen, who shrugged and smiled. She'd tried many times to entice Xavier into conversation, but he wasn't a talker.

Now he approached the stallion cautiously but confidently while Bronwen and Ian stood at his head.

"I'm beginning to think it's just me he doesn't like," Ian muttered.

"He likes you now," Bronwen said.

"Only because I've given him a gallon of treats since he got here."

"Whatever works," Xavier offered, surprising Bronwen with actual words. "He's a nice one. Worth the effort."

He held a hand to Hades's neck, slowly stroking him down to the shoulder and down his leg to his front hoof. One ear was pinned sharply back and the horse's body shook almost imperceptibly, but he held still.

"His name is Hades," Bronwen said. His name was as good a warning as she could give, honestly. But Xavier just grunted and leaned into the horse, shifting his weight to encourage him to lift his hoof. Hades complied immediately.

"Someone's trained him well," Bronwen commented.

"Maybe the breeder," Ian said. "Probably not whoever made him aggressive. I tried to ask Clover Farm for more details on his history, but apparently they bought him at auction. Couldn't believe a horse this nice was there—and then they found out why."

Xavier got to work, hunched over Hades's feet in a way that made Bronwen's back ache just watching him. Hades was stiff as a board, skin twitching wherever Xavier dared to touch him, but as long as Bronwen and Ian stood by his head and told him all of the ways he was a wonderful horse, he held on.

At long last, the farrier finished up with Hades's feet, which looked much more comfortable to stand on. He was trimmed and shod, all set for the next few weeks. He'd been barefoot when he'd arrived at the farm, but Ian insisted he be shod for work. Bronwen had kept silent about it, hoping he wasn't still expecting her to be the one to ride him.

"Good boy," Ian said, scratching the velvety black nose. Hades snorted at him and nipped at the sleeve of his shirt.

"I think that's a 'give me treats for being good' nip, not a 'leave me alone' nip," Bronwen laughed.

She unclipped the cross ties from Hades's halter and led him into his stall. He'd started spending nights in there recently, but it would be good for him to spend time in the barn while there was activity going on. He stuck his head over the door when she closed it, looking at Charlie as Abigail led him out of his stall for his turn.

Bronwen walked back to where Ian was standing with Xavier, examining Charlie's feet.

"This one's yours, isn't he?" Ian asked. "Great conformation. Jumper?"

"Hunter," Bronwen said. "We were all style and just a little substance back in the day," she joked.

She'd enjoyed the jumper classes, where jumping ability and speed were all that mattered. But Charlie had always been too laid-back for that, uninterested in speed-jumping around a tough course. And he was pretty enough to win in hunters, where looks were everything. She'd bought him for basically nothing after college from a family who hadn't known what to do with the young, gangly horse. Bronwen had trained him, and he'd turned out to be better than she'd ever hoped.

"And now?" Ian asked with one eyebrow raised.

She was hardly going to tell a former professional show jumper why she wasn't still competing. If his body could magically go back to the way it was, he'd be over those enormous fences again in a heartbeat. Horses were in his blood, just as they were in hers—Ian said he wanted nothing to do with them, but she couldn't swallow that line no matter how many times he offered it. Horse people didn't walk away so easily. Just like how she was still here in the barn, even though she might never ride again.

She just shrugged. "Too busy—and Olivia likes riding him." Both of which were partly true, so maybe together they made a whole truth.

Luckily, she was interrupted by Brian and Scott entering through the big barn doors, Brian carrying a stack of pizza boxes and Scott with what looked like cans of soda. Rachel was right behind them.

"Mom dropped me off," she said by way of greeting. "And look—*pizza!*"

"I should be getting back to the house," Ian murmured.

I'm not getting any more involved with the barn or the boarders— or their horses—than I have to, Bronwen remembered him saying that night after dinner.

But Brian was having none of it. "Come grab some pizza," he said to Ian, more or less shoving him toward the tack room. "I'm Brian, by the way. I heard all about you from Martha. We got way too much food, and someone's got to save it from the bottomless stomach over here." He nodded at Bronwen.

"Hey, I shovel shit for a living," she said. "I have a right to be hungry."

Ian raised his eyebrows at her. "That's why you need more than soup."

"And it wouldn't kill you to have pizza," she shot back, pushing him as Brian had done, if a little less forcefully. Reluctantly, he followed the group of them into the tack room.

Rachel grabbed a piece of pizza as soon as Brian set the boxes on the counter, and she flopped down dramatically on a couch.

"Mom wants to take me horse shopping," she said, in the same tone that someone might say, *Mom wants to take me out back and shoot me.*

Olivia walked into the tack room in time to hear her, and she and Bronwen exchanged a look.

Scott took a piece of pizza and sat down gently beside Rachel.

"And are you…are you going to go?"

Bronwen winced. This particular topic was a minefield. She was grateful to Scott for responding, because she no longer knew what to say.

"No!" Rachel took a fierce bite of pizza and spoke with her mouth full. "I don't want a new horse—I have Applejack."

Ian stopped in the middle of pouring himself some coffee and turned to throw a questioning glance Bronwen's way. But she couldn't explain with Rachel right there. She knew the kid sounded like a spoiled brat. But there was no love like a person's love for their first pony. Rachel and Apple-jack were *friends*, and the fact that Rachel had grown far too big for the little guy didn't mean anything in the face of that friendship.

Still, at some point she wouldn't be able to ride him at all, and that wasn't fair to either her or the pony, who was still young and had so much to teach a small rider. And Bronwen knew there was no way Rachel's family could afford to board two horses—even one was a big hit to their budget—so Applejack would have to be sold.

It was heartbreaking to watch the inevitable disaster unfold, and Bronwen felt helpless to make it any better for Rachel. Or her parents.

To her surprise, Ian took his coffee and sat on the chair facing the couch, directly across from Rachel.

"Which one is yours?" he asked casually.

Rachel stared at him.

"That's Ian," Bronwen said. "His sister is the farm's new owner."

Rachel nodded, luckily not asking why the new owner's brother was having pizza with them while no one had yet seen any sign of the actual owner.

"Nice to meet you," Rachel said politely, and Bronwen stifled a smile. She was a good kid, and she wished there was a way to make all of this a little easier. "Applejack. The paint pony."

"Ah," Ian said. "I've seen him out in the field—he's a really nice animal."

Rachel smiled despite herself. "He's the *best* pony. I just... I'm..." She broke off.

Ian waited patiently for her to continue while everyone in the room held their breath. The thing was, Rachel had never actually admitted out loud that she'd outgrown her pony, as if by not saying it aloud it might make it untrue. And everyone else had tiptoed around the issue for over a year.

She wondered now if they'd really been doing Rachel a favor.

"I don't want him to think I don't love him," Rachel finally whispered. Tears brimmed in her eyes, but she swallowed visibly and fought them back. A good kid, and also tough as nails in her own way. Bronwen could imagine herself, if she'd had the good fortune to have her own pony at that age, reacting similarly. Emotions on overdrive but unwilling to show any weakness.

Bronwen's heart squeezed. Ian simply nodded as if this was a completely casual conversation, even though she knew he must feel the tension in the room. He sipped his coffee.

"I know I'm too big for him, and I want him to feel useful and happy, but if we sell him, he's going to think I don't love him." The words came out in a rush, and Bronwen busied herself getting some pizza so she didn't just stand there staring.

She'd always assumed—they all had—that Rachel simply didn't want to let her pony go. But this sounded like something else. More than that. And also…something solvable. Why hadn't they just *asked* her about it? She mentally shook her head at herself.

She found a seat and covertly watched Ian, who was giving Rachel all of his attention.

"If he found a good home, and you could visit, would you feel differently about looking for a new horse?"

Rachel nodded. "Of course. I just want him to be happy forever."

Scott appeared to unfreeze from where he'd been sitting absolutely still next to Rachel. "Or you could lease him," he offered. "If your parents agreed. Another kid could enjoy him—and pay the bills—but he'd still be yours."

Rachel brightened considerably. "Do you think so?"

Brian chimed in from where he stood by the coffeepot. "You could at least ask them about it."

"Or you could sell him locally, so you could visit," Olivia added. "That way he'd know you still love him."

"I'm going to talk to my parents," Rachel said a little cautiously, as if it had never occurred to her that selling Applejack might not mean losing him entirely, or result in the pony feeling somehow rejected.

Bronwen's gaze met Ian's, and he smiled slightly. She bit her lip, and he raised his eyebrows.

I want to do this every time you bite that lip...

She nearly choked on her pizza, remembering his lust-roughened voice saying those words.

He grinned at her and turned back to Rachel.

"When I was a little older than you, I didn't own any of the horses I rode," he said. "I'd ride them for their owners at shows, and then sometimes they'd move away, or decide to have someone else ride them. Sometimes I never saw them again."

Rachel looked horrified. "Didn't you miss them?"

Ian shrugged. "Of course. But they weren't mine—and

I'm sure I wasn't as close to them as you are with Applejack. But still." He looked up and met Bronwen's eyes, before turning back to Rachel. "It was very hard."

He took a breath, and Bronwen glanced around the room to find everyone listening attentively to his story.

"But one day I was at a show," Ian continued. "And I ran into an owner I'd ridden for before, and the two horses. I don't think I'd seen them in a couple years." A smile crept around the edges of his mouth, like the memory still made him happy. "They remembered me—the horses. Nudged at me for treats like they used to do, ears pricked like they were about to ask me how I'd been all this time."

Rachel giggled. "Horses have good memories."

"They do," Ian agreed. "So, I don't think you have to worry too much about your pony feeling unloved. Those two horses remembered me, and remembered how much I'd...loved them. I'm sure of it."

He turned his head to gaze out the window, and Bronwen suspected that the happy memory was still tinged with pain. He'd loved the horses, but so much had been taken from him over and over again. There had been no stability, no certainty. And then, when he'd finally reached a place of security and success, it had all been yanked away in an instant.

Her heart ached for him, and she wished she could tell him he had a place here. That he should stay. But it was the last thing he wanted, and what could she offer him, really? Could she trust someone with her heart again? Ian needed—deserved—trust, and love, and stability. And she deserved someone who would stay, who would support her in the world she belonged to.

It could never work between them.

"They remember we love them," Rachel was saying.

Bronwen swallowed a lump in her throat. How would she feel if she'd had to let go of Charlie, the only horse who'd ever been hers? She was lucky to have a job that provided a place to live for them both, and a friend who was willing to ride him when she wasn't.

"And no one loves their pony more than you do," Olivia said with a smile. "So there's no way he's going to have anything but a great future."

The tension dissipated, and Bronwen sighed with relief. They all cared about Rachel—and Applejack—and none of them had known how to address the elephant in the room. But somehow Ian had.

She glanced at him, wanting to telegraph her gratitude, but he was already talking to Brian. Olivia had gone to sit with Rachel and discuss nontraumatic things, and Martha had just blustered into the room and grabbed Scott to talk his ear off. Bronwen watched them all, her barn family plus one, and wondered if, when Ian left, there would be a hole in their group.

And how she'd ever be able to fill it.

Eleven

"Angle his head slightly to the left," Bronwen called across the outdoor ring. "No, the other left. No, not that far—just... Oof."

Charlie refused the jump again, scooting over to the right side at the last minute, and Bronwen sighed.

The sun shone brightly across the sky over the ring and the fields behind the barn, tipping the surrounding trees with gold. A warm breeze came in from somewhere spring had already settled, gently lifting Charlie's mane from his neck as he trotted through the new arena footing. His feet lifted happily over the soft surface after pulling another one on his inexperienced rider, and Bronwen stifled another sigh. It was perfect weather for riding, the outdoor ring had never looked better and Charlie—despite his jump refusal—was fit and ready to go.

But things once again weren't going to plan.

"Ugh! Sorry. I can't get him straight toward the fence."

Olivia pulled the brown horse to a halt, then walked him over to where Bronwen stood by the arena gate.

"He's wiggly, I know." Bronwen looked up at her friend. "He needs a little half halt a few strides away, and then a very slight bend to the left, because he loves to dart out to the right."

Olivia gave her a wry smile. "I noticed that."

Bronwen gave her horse a quick pat on the neck. He snorted and pawed the ground, looking all too pleased with himself.

"I'm sorry," her friend said. "I'm trying to do what you say, but I'm just not that good of a rider."

Bronwen shook her head. "You're a great rider."

"For a beginner, maybe," Olivia said.

"And Charlie's not really a beginner's horse."

They'd had this conversation a million times. Olivia and Charlie weren't a great fit—for one thing, before Bronwen stopped riding, she'd been the only one to ride Charlie since she'd bought him and trained him. She knew all his buttons, but somehow couldn't articulate them to Olivia. She was no teacher, and Olivia wasn't an advanced rider. And Charlie was set in his ways.

Olivia was kind to stick it out with Charlie, knowing that if no one was riding him he'd just become an out-of-shape lawn ornament. Or Bronwen would need to sell him to give him the work he wanted.

And then I'd be as distraught as Rachel, she thought.

Olivia preferred to ride on trails, which Charlie enjoyed, as well. But he was a hunter, and despite being in semi-retirement, Bronwen wanted to keep him in good shape and trained, in case…

In case what? she asked herself for the umpteenth time. Olivia was frustrated with Charlie, Charlie was frustrated with Olivia, and Bronwen was frustrated with herself.

She should just get on her damn horse and show her friend what she meant, since words clearly weren't cutting it. Should ride her own horse and let Olivia find one that fit her better. Should stop being such a wimp and do what needed to be done.

Should, should, should…

"I think there's actual smoke coming out of your ears," Olivia said, amusement threading her voice.

"I just—"

"I know," her friend said, cutting her off. "It's okay."

It wasn't. Bronwen's irritation with herself had only grown since Olivia started riding Charlie. She knew she could demonstrate what she meant, and it would make sense to her friend when she saw Charlie approach the jump.

And if she did it once, maybe she could do it again. Maybe she could ride her horse, let Olivia off the hook, keep Charlie fit, and everything would be right with the world.

But she couldn't make herself say the words, and she couldn't make herself move to take the reins from her friend.

It was never going to happen. And once again she felt like a failure, letting down both horse and friend.

Olivia moved Charlie off toward the right at a walk.

"Is this a lesson?" The deep voice behind her caused her to jump.

She turned to find Ian approaching the gate.

Her stomach did a little flip while her heart fluttered, and she wanted to roll her eyes at her own body for its reaction to this man. No matter how many times she saw him—and that was daily, since they'd continued working together with Hades for the past couple of days after the impromptu pizza party—it was always a bit of a shock to the system.

"I guess," she said and turned back to watch Olivia press Charlie into a canter. "The teacher's not much good, though."

She felt more than a little self-conscious, having a professional show jumper watch her horse, her friend and her questionable teaching skills.

"He's a great horse," Ian said. "How old is he?"

"Just turned fifteen," Bronwen replied, and she couldn't keep a bit of pride out of her voice. "He looks pretty good, doesn't he?"

She sneaked a look at Ian's profile, all hard, chiseled lines and focused concentration as he watched Olivia urge Charlie to a canter.

"I wouldn't have guessed he was that old. He'd still win at a show, that's for sure."

Bronwen understood the unspoken question: If she owned such a wonderful horse, why wasn't she riding him? Showing him?

She said nothing.

Olivia turned Charlie in a big circle and headed for the jump again.

"How long has Olivia been riding him?" Ian asked.

Bronwen chewed her lip. "About two years. He had a bit of a...retirement before then. But she helps keep him in shape."

"He's thinking about refusing the jump," he said quietly.

Bronwen could see it, too. His side angled over to the left like he was thinking of taking a hard right turn as they approached the low cross rail.

"Head a little to the left," she called across the ring. "Use your right leg, harder—right leg…"

Charlie darted to the right just before the jump, looking extremely pleased with himself. He gave a little buck, which jolted Olivia out of the saddle, but she hung on and pulled him to a walk.

"I'm guessing she hasn't been riding very long?" Ian asked as Olivia and Charlie headed toward them.

"Just about three years—though she rode a little when we were in college. She was taking lessons nearby, and then I suggested she ride Charlie."

"He's not a beginner's horse," Ian said, like Bronwen didn't know that already.

"Sorry," Olivia said as she pulled to a halt in front of them.

Bronwen could tell she was discouraged and tired, and honestly, she felt the same. Charlie wasn't the right horse for Olivia. But her friend was a good rider, if inexperienced, and she just wanted to be able to show her what she had to do to keep him straight to the fence.

She glanced at Ian, wishing selfishly that he could ride again. What a demonstration that would be!

Ian stepped forward and gave Charlie a pat.

"It's just an issue of timing—getting his body straight and head turned away from the direction he wants to run out. He knows he can get away with refusing, so the more he refuses, the more he's going to try."

"That's what Bronwen said," Olivia said miserably. "But I don't get when or how to do that. There's too many arms and legs involved—mine and his."

"I'm not very good at explaining it," Bronwen admitted. She'd never tried to teach anyone before, and it was very clearly not her talent in life. She could *feel* what Olivia needed to do, but she couldn't express it in a way that made sense.

Ian took hold of one of the reins and turned to Bronwen. "Why don't you hop on and show her?"

Olivia's eyes widened and she shook her head at Bronwen, who was suddenly frozen to the spot.

Olivia understood, but Ian? She didn't want to tell him how afraid she was, how weak. Stupid pride, yes, but pride was important, dammit. Some days she felt like it was all she had: her competence in her job, with the horses, with the people around her. She'd built her whole life around that competence, all while knowing that in one single area, she was anything but.

And the way Ian was looking at her, like he had every confidence that she could do as she suggested. He saw her as that competent person, and he believed that with one demonstration she could show Olivia what to do. It was humiliating that her stupid nerves said otherwise.

And the thing that killed her was that Ian was right. Charlie could jump that fence in his sleep and look like a million dollars doing it. And she *knew* that if she could just show Olivia what she meant, her friend could learn how to keep him from refusing.

She was so tired of being afraid, of letting herself and others down. Olivia. Charlie. And now she'd have to tell Ian that she was less than what he believed her to be—not a fearless, fierce manager of barn and boarders after all.

Instead, she was someone afraid to ride her own horse, despite being perfectly capable of doing so. While Ian would give anything to be in her shoes. He'd already be cantering down the line to the fence.

"Yeah," she croaked. "Okay."

"Bronwen—" Olivia began, but Bronwen shook her head at her friend. She didn't want to be this person anymore.

Slowly, Olivia swung her leg over and slid to the ground. She whispered to Bronwen, "You really don't have to—"

"I know," Bronwen said, cutting her off. "I *do*, though." She took a deep breath in. "At some point, I have to try."

Olivia silently took off her helmet and handed it to Bronwen. God, she'd nearly forgotten. She shoved it on her head, grateful that it fit well enough. If she'd had to go back to the barn for another, she'd never come back.

Olivia backed away with a frown on her face, clearly unhappy but trusting that Bronwen knew her limits. Bronwen wasn't so sure. As she gathered the reins at Charlie's neck, she walked herself through the steps she'd taken a million times before.

Left hand at the withers. Right hand on the saddle. Left foot in the stirrup. Now just get up and on the horse!

Her hands were shaking so hard she was surprised Ian

didn't comment on it. But he just backed away until he stood next to Olivia by the gate, unaware of the storm inside her.

Charlie knew, though. He turned an ear back toward her, as if to ask if she really wanted to do this.

"It's okay, Mr. Charles," she said through rattling teeth. Her stomach wasn't just in knots—it was an entire rope factory twisted into an unsortable mess. Her hands were frozen on the reins, but she let her muscle memory take control and she pushed Charlie forward with her legs.

After so long out of the saddle, she felt as if she was in a race car with no seat belt. Her brain kept trying to push scenes of the last time she'd ridden to the forefront of her consciousness, and she forcefully pushed those scenes back down.

Muscle memory. Don't think, just ride.

Charlie cantered like a rocking horse, as carefully as if he balanced a dozen eggs on his back. He knew something was wrong, and she forced her body to relax, even as her mind spun and her stomach roiled.

She turned him to the jump. She could just hear the sound of Ian's voice as he described what she was doing to Olivia.

"She's bent him to the inside," he was saying, "so he has no way out. Just at the last minute, she sets him completely straight, and then *up*—and over."

And she was. *They* were—over the jump and cantering away. Charlie dropped to a trot and then a walk almost immediately, turning his neck all the way around to bump the tip of Bronwen's boot with his nose.

"Good boy," she managed.

And then the whole world spun like she was on an amusement park ride, and she gripped Charlie's mane, sure she was going to be sick. She retched once, but luckily nothing came up. Pressed one hand to her stomach, willing it to hold on.

"Bronwen!" Olivia's voice barely penetrated the sudden roar between her ears.

She could feel herself shaking, felt strong hands on her left thigh, her other leg instinctively swinging over Charlie's back, and then she was on her feet on the ground, still shaking. Her knees gave out and Ian's arms held her to his solid chest.

"Bronwen—are you all right? What happened?"

Another hand lay on her shoulder. Olivia.

Her breath came in short gasps and she couldn't look at either of them. This was what she'd been afraid of—that her nerves would get the best of her and she'd lose control. She'd humiliate herself in front of everyone around her.

And it was happening.

"Bronwen?"

Ian's voice was soft and reassuring in her ear, and she wanted to snuggle into him, to let him take her weight and her fear and all of it from her. But the idea horrified her— her weakness was so tiny and laughable compared to what he'd been through. He'd had his whole life taken away from him. He couldn't ride. And she could—as she'd just demonstrated—but her nonsensical fear betrayed her and made her into a fool.

"Bronwen—you did it!" Olivia's voice was sparked with hope, excitement that Bronwen had finally sat on a horse again.

But Bronwen didn't feel excitement. Or triumph at losing

control of herself after one tiny jump. Her stomach was sour with embarrassment as her knees still wobbled beneath her.

She pulled away from Ian, unable to make herself meet his eyes. He must think she was silly, weak, ridiculous. She certainly felt all of those things.

She'd wanted to avoid this moment at all costs, even before she'd met him. And having him here witnessing her failure made it so, so much worse. Her face burned and tears pricked at the corners of her eyes. She tugged the helmet off her head and thrust it at Olivia.

"I…I have to go…"

"Bronwen." Ian reached out and clasped her wrist with his hand, but she pulled free and shook her head.

"Please." Her voice was as shaky as her legs, and she just needed to escape.

She stumbled away, gaining strength as she ran from the scene of her most embarrassing moment, out the gate and down the path toward the barn.

Ian and Olivia called her name, but she didn't stop. She didn't even turn around. She ran, hoping she could put enough distance between herself and her failure that maybe it wouldn't feel so all-consuming as it did at that moment.

She slowed to a walk when she reached the barn, forcing herself to walk calmly past the horses to the stairs to her apartment. Upstairs, her knees gave out and she collapsed on her bed, and let herself give in to tears.

Ian stood at the bottom of the stairs at the far end of the barn, looking up toward the landing above and wondering what the hell just happened.

He hadn't thought anything of his suggestion that Bronwen jump on Charlie and demonstrate what Olivia needed to do—clearly the verbal instructions hadn't been working. But now, in the aftermath of everything that had just occurred, he cursed himself.

He'd wondered why he never saw Bronwen on a horse. He'd wondered why she wouldn't still compete Charlie—who was obviously still fit and happy to work. And he'd wondered why Olivia, clearly not experienced enough for a horse like Charlie, rode him regularly while Bronwen stayed on the ground.

He should have known—or at least suspected the possibility—that something kept Bronwen from riding. If he hadn't been so wrapped up in his own problems, he would have been more perceptive. He should have at least asked her before putting her on the spot.

When she'd pulled Charlie to a halt and clutched at her stomach, something cold and panicked had shivered inside him. He hadn't known if she was ill, or injured, or if something else was wrong. He'd only known that he *needed* her in his arms. Safe. Where he could help.

But she'd pulled away and run for the barn. Olivia took one look at him and demanded that he go after her.

He hadn't needed to be told twice.

But he hesitated now, as he listened to the silence from above. He'd never been upstairs in Bronwen's apartment, and he had no idea if she even wanted his help or his comfort. She hadn't wanted either out in the ring. But his need to know that she was all right overrode his hesitation, and he climbed the steps.

The apartment was dim, with small windows along one side the only source of light. He had the impression of one large room, a basic kitchen in the corner, a few scattered pieces of furniture. Homey, but a little ramshackle and thrown together. The sweet, earthy scent of hay and horse permeated the space. In another corner was a large bed, and as his eyes adjusted he could see Bronwen sitting on the edge, her back to him.

He shoved his hands in his pockets.

"You should have told me," he said, his voice rough. And that wasn't even what he wanted to say. Bronwen didn't owe him anything. There was no *should* here. "You could have said no," he amended in a gentler tone.

Her head turned so he could see her profile. He thought her cheeks might be streaked with tears, although it could have been the light. But his chest twisted just the same.

He took a few steps forward. "You shouldn't ever feel that you have to get on a horse just because some asshole tells you to." He tried a little humor, and he could have sworn the corner of her mouth turned up, just a little.

She shrugged. "You were right to tell me to show Olivia. Telling her wasn't doing any good."

At least she'd responded to him—and importantly, didn't tell him to get the hell out. "Teaching is hard. Especially when we're trying to explain things our bodies know but our brains haven't formed into words."

She nodded slowly. "I never tried to teach anyone before I came here. I thought since I know both Charlie and Olivia so well, it would be easy. And I'm not much better with the other boarders—it's all in my body, not my head."

A few more steps, and he stood just on the far side of the bed from her.

"Well. Teaching might not be your calling, but you can definitely ride."

Charlie had been a different horse with her on his back. Willing, forward, ears pricked toward the jump and only the slightest hint of resistance as they approached. Resistance that Bronwen nipped right in the bud—in the show ring, a judge might not have even seen it.

She huffed a little laugh. "Can, but won't, you mean."

His eyebrows rose at that. "You were just on a horse, weren't you?"

At that, she twisted around and looked at him with disbelief. "And then I fell apart! One jump and I thought I was going to be sick!" She shook her head and turned back around.

Ian walked around the bed and sat beside her, holding out his palm for her hand. If she didn't want his comfort, she could refuse. But she placed her hand in his, fingers lacing together. Her grip was tight, as if she was seeking stability, something to hold on to. He was happy to give it to her.

He watched as she took a few deep breaths. He wasn't going to push her for information, and he'd certainly never push her to ride again. But he wanted her to understand that whatever she believed her limitations were, and for whatever reason, she *had* just jumped beautifully on her own horse.

"We all fall apart sometimes," he said. "But it doesn't change what we've done. What we've been able to do."

She blinked a few times and squeezed his hand. "I did get him over that jump, didn't I?"

His long-frozen heart thawed a little more, the way it always seemed to do when he was around her. "Beautifully." He swallowed. "I'm sorry. I didn't even think before I asked you to do it. I knew I'd never seen you on a horse, but—"

"It was a fall," she said quickly, as if she wanted to get the words out before she changed her mind. "I was riding Charlie at our old barn, a show barn south of the city, getting ready for a show. It was my fault—I heard a truck coming up the drive, and I knew he's spooky with big vehicles like that, but I was…I was overconfident. He's my horse—I trained him, right? I didn't think he'd try anything."

Ian winced. All riders had made mistakes like that with horses they knew well. Assuming that surely the horse wouldn't dare act out with *them*. But the animals were nothing if not creatures of habit, and if a horse was spooky around trucks, then…the horse was going to spook at a truck.

"So, yeah. We were headed toward a big triple, part of a really tricky combination of jumps. I should have waited, just circled around once, but I didn't. He spooked, obviously. Which would have been fine, but the truck backfired right next to the ring. Any horse would have lost his mind. Charlie shot sideways right into a fence. And I went flying."

"Were you hurt?"

He couldn't help but think about his own fall. You just never knew—you could get right up from what looked like a horrible tumble and be completely fine. Or you could land wrong that one time, and everything changed.

"Broke my arm," Bronwen said. "And Charlie…he had a bad bruise on his left hind leg. He was lame for weeks. I felt *horrible*. Why hadn't I just stopped him for a minute? It wasn't even at a show."

Ian released her hand and wrapped his arm around her. There wasn't much he could say. People made mistakes, and sometimes horses got hurt. Or people. Or both.

"I was...I was glad, in a way, that my arm was broken. And even a little glad that Charlie was injured, so I couldn't ride. Every time I even looked at my saddle I felt sick."

"You're not at that barn anymore."

Bronwen shook her head. "I was cobbling together a living as the assistant barn manager, riding and showing other people's horses while also training and showing Charlie."

"Sounds a little familiar," Ian said with a smile.

Bronwen smiled weakly back. "Hardly on your level. These were local shows, mostly. The big ones in the area, but still nothing like the Florida or international circuit. I thought maybe someday I'd get there, but..."

Ian turned to her, curious. "Is that what you wanted? Would you still want that?"

She laughed a little, bitter and resigned. "I mean... It doesn't really matter, does it? I don't think so, not really. I never quite had that ambition, and I don't actually like all the travel. But...it would have been nice to have the choice, you know?"

He watched her for a moment, wondering if this was the right moment to push, or if she just needed someone to agree with her. But he didn't agree. Getting over a bad fall took time, and it was the mind that often put up the most resistance. But she had done it—she'd ridden again, and here she was, in one piece.

"You did it, though," he said. "It took you some time, but you *did* ride today. And if you wanted to, you could keep trying until it feels easier."

She nodded slowly. "I just used to be totally fearless, you know?" Her voice caught as she spoke, and he pulled her closer. "It hurts to lose that."

"Sometimes a little fear is a good thing. Especially around horses." He'd always had a healthy respect for the big animals—not fear, exactly, but in many ways it was safer to have that little warning voice in your head than to believe you were invincible.

Not that it had done him much good.

"Maybe," Bronwen said quietly. "I don't like it, though. I miss being the old me."

Something kicked around in Ian's chest. Wasn't that why he'd been a reclusive bastard these last weeks himself? In some ways Bronwen had done the same thing, closing herself into the little insular world of Morning Song Farm, leaving her dreams behind and giving in to her fear and disappointment that things couldn't be exactly how she wanted them.

Sure, she could ride, physically. And he couldn't. The loss was still something he didn't know if he'd entirely get over. But change was change, and they'd both experienced it and then turned inward instead of dealing with it head-on.

Maybe they both needed to face their lives as they were, and stop focusing only on what they'd lost.

"You were brave today," he said. "If I'd known how brave you'd have to be, I never would have asked you to do it. But you did. You might not be fearless, but it didn't stop you."

She turned her head and smiled almost shyly up at him.

"It didn't, did it? I always let that fear tell me it wasn't possible, but it is. I *could* ride again, even if it's hard."

"I told you I wanted you to ride Hades," he half joked. He could see it, though, her muscle memory and intuition and skill on that powerful stallion—they'd make quite a pair.

She laughed and turned to fully face him on the bed. "Let's not get ahead of ourselves."

She bit her lip, and for once he didn't stop himself from reaching out and tracing her mouth with his thumb. Her eyes lit with heat, and the banked fire always present when he was near her flared to life.

"Maybe, though. Maybe I could." She spoke quietly, almost to herself.

"I think you could do anything you wanted," he said and meant it. She was all resilience and determination under a caring and empathetic exterior, and he believed she could do whatever she set her mind to.

She placed her hand on his thigh, the warmth of her skin like a brand through his jeans.

"It's been a while since we were together anywhere near a bed." He heard the question in her voice, and he answered honestly.

"I'm still leaving, Bronwen. When my sister gets here—I didn't know if you'd still want...you know. When I'm leaving soon."

He'd said the words so many times, to himself and out loud, but this time they sounded off to him, like an out-of-tune note on a piano. He *was* leaving, though. Even if he had no idea where he'd go or what he'd do. Even if right now, he felt more at home than he had since the accident. Being around the horses at Morning Song hadn't been as sharply painful as he'd expected, but it was still hard. An ache in his gut every time he saw one of the boarders carrying a saddle down the barn aisle, or warming up in the outdoor ring he'd fixed but would never use. Eventually, it would wear on him, pretending everything was fine when inside the pieces of who he was were cutting him apart. Eventually, everyone here—even Bronwen—would see that he wasn't the Ian Kingston he'd been, the one they expected and no doubt wanted. He knew he couldn't take seeing that disappointment in their eyes. None of this was permanent. Change was coming for him again, and he'd do a better job of facing it this time.

He wouldn't make promises to Bronwen that he couldn't keep.

"So you thought you were doing the noble thing, leaving me alone because you're going away?"

It sounded a little silly when she put it that way. Bronwen had made clear that she was fine with a short-term arrangement. He just thought... He thought she deserved better. She deserved everything, and he wasn't the person to give it to her.

Still, she'd been more than clear that night at the house, and he'd run right over her wishes.

"I guess I did." He laughed at himself. "I'm sorry."

She rolled her eyes. "What a waste of time. God save me from men being noble when I want exactly the opposite."

That sounded promising. "What exactly do you mean when you say 'the opposite'?"

She slid her hand up his thigh to his belt buckle. "I think

you know. You certainly did that night after dinner. Or have you forgotten already?"

As if he'd ever forget that night. She'd blown his mind.

"Maybe you can remind me."

She smiled, a slow, sensual smile, and once again he was lost to her.

Twelve

Bronwen paused with her hands at Ian's belt, her breath stolen by the desire in his eyes.

Noble. She almost rolled her eyes again. If she'd known that was why he hadn't requested another round of what they'd done at the house, she would have disabused him of that notion right away.

"No more being noble," she said. "If you're leaving, I want you as many times as I can have you before then."

He swallowed visibly, then nodded, his pupils blown wide. "Deal."

"May I?" She nodded her head at her hands. The bulge in his jeans made it pretty clear that he was interested, but she still wanted to make sure he was entirely on board.

He leaned back on his elbows, which only made his arousal more obvious. "Whatever you want."

"Mmmm…" she all but purred. "Those are the magic words."

She started on his belt buckle, taking her time. Her fingers might have brushed his erection a few times. By accident, of course. Ian's chest rose and fell with a deep breath.

"And torture is what you want?" he said on a rough laugh as she finished with his belt and started on the zipper of his jeans.

She shrugged. "Either that or let's tear our clothes off as quickly as possible so I can feel you inside me again."

He grunted like he'd been punched in the stomach. "I vote for the second option."

He grabbed her wrists and flipped her over onto her back before she could catch her breath, both of them laughing and breathless.

Ian rose and turned to her. "Well? Wait—let me. Stand up."

She complied, and they stood facing each other in the dim light of her apartment. She could hear his breathing, imagined she could hear his heart beating. She could certainly hear her own heart pounding in her chest. He licked his lips, gaze intent on her. A zing of awareness sparked down her spine. That focus, that concentration, all on her.

She stepped closer, until she could feel his breath on her forehead. His hands came to frame her face, so gentle. But she could feel the tension in him. The want. It made her want in return.

His palm slid around to rest at the nape of her neck, as if to hold her there. Like she was going anywhere. They gazed into each other's eyes for a long moment, the fingers of his other hand grazing her jaw. He leaned in, lips brushing hers, then trailing along her jaw to the sensitive skin of her neck.

She shivered under his light kisses, her entire body wound tight like it was just waiting for release.

Ian pulled back and slid his hands down her sides to the hem of her long-sleeved shirt.

"May I?" He repeated her words back at her, his voice that gravelly pitch that sent a bolt of heat down to her core.

She nodded. He pulled the shirt up and over her head, letting it drop to the floor. He had her sports bra unfastened and off before she could draw another breath, and then his hands were on her, long fingers tracing the slopes of her breasts, the heat of his palms searing her where they touched her skin.

With a groan, she stepped away and slid off her pants and underwear. Then she grabbed his hand and tugged him back to the bed, Ian half laughing and half growling with desire.

He kissed her, his lips capturing hers, plundering, his body heavy and welcome on top of her.

"Ian," she gasped. "Wait."

He raised his head and gazed down at her, his eyes gratifyingly hazy with lust. "What is it?"

"Your clothes." She glanced meaningfully down at his body. "Off. Now."

With a pained groan, he peeled himself off her and stood, shucking his already unfastened jeans and tossing his shirt over his head. She took a moment to look, really look at him.

So tall in her little apartment. Lean and lanky, but solid muscle. A dusting of hair over his chest that matched the gold on his jaw. Dusky nipples she wanted to lick. Legs that looked as if they were forged from iron, that spoke of hours in the saddle. Little dips above his hips that begged for her to trace them with her fingers. His cock, fully erect and hard—for her.

Heat punched through her, need stealing her breath.

"Come here," she whispered into the quiet.

And he was on her, over her, blocking out the light until all she could see, all she could feel, was him. Around her, over her, and hopefully soon, God willing, inside her. Her body clenched with want.

"Ian."

He kissed her again, not the desperate, forceful kiss she'd expected, but lingering, soft strokes of his lips. His tongue. The bristle of his unshaven jaw scratched across her cheek, only highlighting the slow, tender brush of his mouth on hers. She arched up against him, wanting more, and he chuckled, his breath filling her lungs where she'd gone breathless.

He nipped at her bottom lip, and the sting reverberated down to her hot, wet core. She whimpered, and he groaned.

"Are you sure?" he asked, and she both wanted to smack him for questioning this and deeply appreciated his thoughtfulness. When was the last time someone had been so careful with her?

"I want you," she replied with absolute certainty. "I want this. As much as I can have of you before..."

She didn't finish the thought. There was no room for the future here, no place for what might come to ruin what was in this moment. She refused to speak it aloud. They both needed to find their way, alone, but right now, they were together.

He kissed her again, deeper, harder. *There* was the urgency she needed, the desperate press of his groin into her belly, his hand slipping behind her back to pull her closer. She thought she could feel the pulse of his cock in time with his heartbeat, in time with her own heart. He was hard, more than ready for her, and she knew she was ready for him.

"Ian, please."

He lifted his head, looking down at her with dazed eyes as if he wasn't sure where he ended and she began.

"Turn over." His command was the last thing she expected, but she suspected she'd do anything he requested in that deep, whiskey-rough voice.

"You'll have to move first," she gasped as he pressed her into the bed again.

With a grunt, he rolled to the side and off the bed, his hand on her thigh as if he couldn't bear to let go of her completely.

She rolled to her stomach, and his hand came to the small of her back.

"Jesus," he rasped. "Your ass is amazing."

She wasn't particularly self-conscious of her body. She used it in her work all day, and it did the job. Functional. Strong. But she could *feel* his hot gaze on her, feel how much he wanted her. Her ass, which was maybe a little larger than she might have liked it to be in an ideal world, the object of his focus and desire.

She felt beautiful. Powerful in a way that had nothing to do with physical strength. A man like Ian Kingston wanted her, as much as she wanted him.

And she was going to have him.

Suddenly, strong hands came to her ankles, tugging her down the bed until her legs hung off the sides, toes touching the floor.

"Ian! What are you—"

She heard a soft thunk, and then felt the heel of his hand press between her legs, right where she throbbed for him. Her words broke off in a gasp. She turned her head and saw him behind her, on his knees. She squeezed her eyes shut and groaned, that image burned into her memory forever.

"What are you doing?"

She heard him shuffle around, and then her legs were being spread open by what she imagined were his elbows as his fingers gently stroked against her core. She moaned, a helpless, needy sound.

"I'm doing this," he said, and then his tongue was on her.

She was fully exposed to him, butt in the air, the skin on her back tingling with sensation. The cold floor against her feet contrasted with the heat of his tongue right where she needed it most.

He was good at this—really top-notch skills, she had to admit—but what had her close to the edge faster than she'd ever gotten there was the way he licked and sucked her as if he could never get enough. As if he'd missed more than a few meals and she was the one thing he'd been craving. She could hear—*feel*—him groan against her as he teased her, her orgasm rushing toward her like a tidal wave she didn't have a chance to escape.

Not that she wanted to escape, not when his hand on her ass pinned her to the bed, his other hand braced on her hip. If he wasn't holding her down she thought she might float away, or simply explode into pieces right there in her apartment.

Another groan and his fingers bit into her butt as if he

was himself only just holding on to his control. The pinch of pain from his hand and another stroke of his clever tongue caused her to fall apart, spinning into pleasure so strong it took everything and rearranged it, her whole world just exploding and then reknitting itself together, the same but entirely different.

"So good," he grunted against her thigh, his breath hot on her already feverish skin. "Now roll over."

The command in his voice made her squirm, somehow reigniting the fire he'd only just quenched. But she lifted herself onto her elbows and turned to meet his eyes.

"No. Like this."

His eyes widened and then darkened, that possessive hand resting on her back again as if to claim her.

"Like this," he said softly. It wasn't a question. His fingers trailed down the sensitive skin of her spine, sending a shiver right down to her aching core. "Hmm."

He stepped between her legs and leaned down to press a kiss against the nape of her neck, lifting her hair up and to the side. His fingers lightly scratched her scalp, and she whimpered.

He groaned behind her and she heard the crinkle of the condom wrapper, the sound of his sharp intake of breath as he pressed himself to her entrance. His weight leaned against her and she had to push her hands into the bed to steady herself.

"You ready?" he asked, bending down again close to her ear, his voice like sandpaper.

"Yes. *Now*." Her own voice was barely more than a gasp.

With a grunt of satisfaction, he slid inside, the thick length of him filling her so full she couldn't take a breath for a moment, then two. Finally air rushed into her lungs and he began to move, his big hands gliding up her back, both soothing and enhancing sensation.

"You feel so fucking good." She could hear the strain in his voice, the effort it was taking him to hold back.

She didn't want him to hold back.

"More, Ian. Don't stop."

He pulled out, nearly to the tip of him, then slid back in, slowly, inch by inch until she was moaning with the need for more. And he gave it to her—harder this time. Hard enough that she gripped the bed quilt, fisting the fabric as he began a rhythm—not gentle this time, but demanding. Exactly what she needed.

Liquid heat like molten metal poured through her veins, every part of her body entirely attuned to the man behind her. She could feel herself coiling again, tension building as he continued to push into her, the heat of his body just above her back, his breath hot on her ear. He was whispering nonsense to her, his voice as needy as she felt.

"Ian, I need—"

She didn't have to say more, as he pulled her against his chest with one strong arm, his knee braced on the bed, his other hand coming to her sensitive folds, stroking her in time with his thrusts.

"Come for me," he said in that rough voice that she knew even now meant he was close. "Give it to me."

Every cell in her body lit up at his words as if they'd been waiting for his demand, and she came. Endless waves of bliss crashed over her as she cried out, his fingers finding the exact right spot to send her even higher, spiraling out of control and then slowly floating back down to earth.

His rhythm broke and he slammed into her, his control finally gone, his body shaking over her as he came with a shout, shuddering for a long moment until he collapsed onto her with a groan.

Silence engulfed them, the occasional rustle of activity in the barn below the only sound.

Eventually, he eased away as if he was afraid he'd hurt her, and she heard his feet pad on the floor as he disposed of the condom in the bathroom.

She scooted up onto the bed and rolled to the side to make room for him.

Ian lay down beside her, chest still rising and falling as if he'd been running. His hair stuck up in untidy locks, his mouth red and swollen from kissing her—everywhere.

He was a far cry from the cold man she'd first encountered at the farmhouse, and she loved it. This man was warm and real and messy. Not to mention naked in her bed.

She moved closer to him, his arm coming around her, and reached up to touch his cheek with her hand. He gazed down at her with an unfathomable expression, and she wondered if he was having thoughts of being noble again.

She'd need to nip that in the bud.

"I don't want you to avoid this—or me—because you need to move on," she said. "I want you to know I understand."

He was quiet for a while, and she wondered if he'd answer. Eventually, he said, "I just don't want to hurt you." A soft laugh rumbled through his chest. "Or myself."

Bronwen chewed her lip. She already knew it would hurt when Ian left. She'd accepted that. She'd miss him no matter what, so she'd decided that they might as well make the most of their time together.

And then, of course, there were her own issues.

She sighed and rolled over onto her back, staring up at the ceiling. "Let's just say I don't have a great romantic track record."

Ian chuckled. "I wouldn't say I do, either. Does anyone who isn't happily partnered?"

She smiled. "Good point. But…I've had a couple of real clunkers in the past few years and I know I'm just not— I'm not in a place where I can do it again. My last boyfriend really messed with my head, and on top of my fall…"

Ian took her hand, his fingers stroking hers. "You've been licking your wounds."

"Yeah," she said quietly. "He was just… He promised a lot. Big things, small things. He'd promise to meet me at a show to cheer me on. Then he wouldn't show up. There was always some excuse I couldn't argue with. He stood me up more times than I can count. Told me I shouldn't be so clingy when I pushed him on it. And I know he was busy— he's one of the best riders in New England. A big fish in a smallish pond, I guess." She laughed without humor. "But that was the pond I was swimming in. It felt good that he was even interested in me. He told me he'd take me to meet his family, but he never did. He'd promised to be faithful…"

She saw Ian's head turn toward her out of the corner of her eye. "Let me guess. He wasn't."

She shook her head. "Nope. Word got around the barn.

Just rumors, little ones at first. Then more obvious comments. You know how horse-show people can be sometimes."

Cutting. Competitive. Happy to knock someone down to size, if it made them feel better about themselves.

Ian grunted. "I certainly do."

"That's one reason I love it here. It's...safe. The people are honest. Supportive."

Ian said nothing. But his hand tightened almost imperceptibly on hers, and she wondered how close to home her experience with the darker side of the horse world was for him.

"I went to a show with a friend, just to watch. I wasn't riding that day. I just decided at the last minute to go along. I caught him behind the stables with someone else who kept her horse at my barn. He wasn't even sorry—just said he'd never committed, which wasn't true. But what could I do?"

"Dump his sorry ass, I'm hoping."

"Yeah. I told him what I thought of him. And then went back to the barn and..."

Ian shifted toward her. "That's when you fell, isn't it? When you were hurt."

She nodded. "The same day. After that... When Charlie's leg was healed enough for him to move, I brought him here. I knew Ruth, the former owner, a little bit, and she offered me this job. She'd been doing almost everything herself up until then, but it was too much at her age. So we came here."

"And you've been here ever since."

Something in his tone had Bronwen rolling to her side. Their eyes locked, the now-familiar zing of awareness shimmering across her skin.

"Yeah. And?" She raised an eyebrow at him.

He shrugged, then took a long inhalation and exhalation, like he didn't really want to answer her. But she was patient.

Finally he said, "You were hurt. Physically, emotionally, mentally. By your boyfriend and by the fall. But…"

A chill chased away the residual warmth inside her. "But what?"

He sighed. "I just think… Look, I know I'm the worst kind of hypocrite. I *know* that. But it's easier to see someone else's situation than your own, isn't it?"

She sat up on the bed, staring down at him. "And?"

He sat up, as well, resting his hand on her thigh as if to keep her there. "You were licking your wounds in a place where you felt safe. That's important—believe me, I know. But now…you *can* ride. You could work toward competing Charlie again. Slowly. You don't have to push yourself beyond what feels safe, like what happened today. But you don't have to…hide."

She blinked down at him, anger and surprise squeezing her chest. "Hide? Is that what you think I'm doing?"

"No more than I am," he said with a wry smile. Which took some of the sting out of his words.

But not all.

"And what about you?" she pushed him. "You've been hiding, and now you're getting ready to run. From what? To what? You have all this talent, and you're throwing it away because…"

He stiffened visibly. "Because of what? Because I lost everything, Bronwen. *You* could ride again. Go back to your old life. Find someone to love who isn't a complete ass.

Your boyfriend was a jerk—but not everyone's like that. I know you know that. You don't have to hide yourself away on this farm."

It all sounded terrible to her. Scary, certainly, but...also just wrong. She didn't want to go back to that competitive show barn. She hadn't even missed it once she got to Morning Song. She didn't particularly want to compete again. The stress and backstabbing wasn't for her. As for love...the only person she could imagine being with was here with her.

And that was a problem.

"I'm not hiding," she said. And they both knew it was a lie. She let out a breath. "Okay, maybe I'm hiding a little bit."

"Well. You're not alone in that." He pulled her closer, and she tucked her chin into the crook of his neck. "You don't have to do everything all at once. Maybe just try sitting on your horse for a bit. See how that feels."

"Will you help me?" she said before she could think better of it.

"Of course. I promise."

She let herself believe him, because she had no reason to do otherwise. Her trust might have been shattered in the past, but Ian had always followed through, on small things and large.

It was a fool's errand, but she carefully placed her fragile, healing trust in his hands, at least for this. Only for this, for now.

Early that morning, before the horses clamored for breakfast, before the sun edged over the tops of the tree branches surrounding the farm, Bronwen quietly descended the stairs from her apartment and made her way to Charlie's stall.

As always, the barn was a soft landing first thing in the morning, serene and quiet and magical in expectation of everything another day full of horses might hold. The early light tried its best to barge in under the sliding door and through the stall windows, but in the aisle and in Charlie's stall everything was still dim and gentle, from the sleepy rattle of horses nosing their feed buckets in hopes of breakfast to the scent of wood chips and grain and earth.

Ian lay in her bed upstairs, snug and warm under the blankets, and she'd been tempted to lie there with him, listening to the quiet hush of his breathing. She was an early riser by necessity, but this particular morning she'd woken with a start well before her alarm went off.

She'd drifted off into a dreamless sleep in Ian's arms that night, and later they'd woken each other up with sleepy kisses and strokes that led to more. Now she was tired and smugly satisfied and desperately in need of coffee, but there was something she needed to do before she started her day.

"Hey, bud," she said quietly as she unlatched the stall door and slipped inside.

Charlie's roomy box stall smelled like sweet feed, hay and wood shavings, underlaid with the earthy smell of horse. He turned quickly when he heard her voice, whickering a greeting.

"Shh," she said. "Don't tell your roommates I'm here, or everyone's going to want their food right now."

The other horses no doubt had already heard her with

their animal-sharp hearing, but so far no one was kicking the wall or whinnying to be fed.

She took the time before the equine demands began to do what she'd come for. As Charlie stuck his velvet nose against her chest, sighing heavily, she reached up and stroked his ears the way she used to do before shows, when they were both a little wound up anticipating the challenge to come. She couldn't remember the last time she'd just...stood with her horse, listening to the sounds of his breathing, letting him inhale her scent and nudge her with his soft nose.

Tears came unexpectedly, apologetic and regretful.

"I'm sorry, Charlie," she whispered into his forelock. "I'm sorry I've been ignoring you."

That wasn't really it, though. She'd made sure he was cared for, found him a rider, groomed him and paid as much attention to him as she had to the other boarders.

But it wasn't enough. Because he was *her* horse—the one she'd found, trained, ridden in her best moments as a competitor. He was her friend, her confidant, the one constant aside from Olivia between the before and after of her life. He deserved more than maintenance care.

Maybe she'd compete him again; maybe she wouldn't. But even if she never rode him again, he deserved so much more than she'd given him. She'd put a wall between her feelings about the past and anything that reminded her of what she'd lost, and that included Charlie.

Something cracked inside her as it thawed, years' worth of emotions spilling out in tears. She buried her face in Charlie's mane and let it out: unresolved sadness over what had happened, the injuries—external and internal—they'd both suffered. The abruptness with which her life had changed, everything old falling away and her life at Morning Song becoming the entire circumference of her existence. The pain of now leaving behind the safety of repressing her emotions and telling herself that shoveling stalls and managing boarders was all she needed to be happy. Fear of what the future might bring.

But with the unknown was also the known: the family she'd found here. Charlie. Olivia. Those were constants, real sources of comfort she could depend on.

"Thank you for waiting," she told Charlie, stroking a hand down his neck, soft hair and familiar contours.

Charlie snorted and stamped one hoof, probably realizing that she'd been in his stall for some time and no breakfast had appeared.

Then he turned his head and nosed her arm, and she lifted her head to look at his brown, liquid eyes regarding her patiently. He nosed her again, and she stroked one silky ear with her hand. His eyes slowly closed, head nodding.

It wasn't breakfast he wanted. Just her—his person. She leaned against his solid shoulder, one hand on his back and one on his ear, watching him doze.

Whatever came next, she had this. She understood why Rachel was so desperately set against selling Applejack. She'd never let go of Charlie for anything—whether she rode him or not. She'd been taking him for granted, setting him aside so she wouldn't have to think about the past, the future or anything other than her routine at the farm. Each day circled with an unshakable boundary, letting her off the hook for processing what had happened, or thinking about what the future might hold.

She needed to do better than that, as Ian had said. She *deserved* better than that. She'd needed safety after her fall, but safety wasn't going to bring her happiness. She needed to stretch herself again, figure out what she really wanted. She needed to enjoy the privilege of owning this marvelous horse, even if past memories occasionally reared their unwelcome head.

She needed to live in these moments—with Charlie, with Ian—because no future was guaranteed. She'd been existing, not living. And it had to change.

Thirteen

Ian had broken her. He'd addled her brain with sex and now she had no will of her own.

That was the only explanation for why she was currently in the indoor ring, enormous stallion in a borrowed saddle in front of her, Ian holding the reins of a bridle she'd scrounged up and adjusted to fit the large horse.

"He'll be fine," Ian was saying. "I tacked him up the past four days, and he barely even blinked at me."

"And I put my weight on his back a couple times while you were busy with the vet," Olivia offered.

"And he let us walk him over some ground poles yesterday," Scott added from his spot by the edge of the ring.

"He only bit me twice!" Brian offered. His husband swatted him with his hand. "Sorry. He didn't really bite me—he was very good."

Despite herself, Bronwen smiled. Hades had become a bit of a pet project of the whole barn, and had progressed so far from his first days at the farm. Her heart warmed with pride at the thought. The "unmanageable" stallion was still nervous at times and took a while to accept new people. Especially men. But with a little patience and a lot of bribery, many of the boarders had now taken a turn handling him, and there really were no more major milestones to accomplish.

Except this one.

Ian and Olivia had taken the "get Bronwen back on a horse" project seriously, the three of them meeting up every day for the past week while she got used to riding Charlie again. No jumps—she wasn't ready for that, and diving in the deep end that way had clearly been too much for her poor nerves. But she'd ridden him first at a walk, and she found that the distraction of talking through everything she was doing for Olivia's benefit had gone pretty far in quelling the ever-present fear and nausea. She'd worked up to a careful canter yesterday, Charlie on his best behavior and Olivia and Ian cheering her on—quietly, so as not to spook Charlie.

Every time she slid to the ground, Ian was there to catch her, whether she needed it or not. And each night, he told her how brave she was and how much progress she was making, and then proceeded to show her how much he'd wanted her all day while they were being professional and businesslike around the horses.

The fear was always there, every time she set foot in the stirrup. But it wasn't overwhelming *all* the time. More like an unwanted companion as she rode carefully around the ring, building her riding muscles back up and remembering that she actually enjoyed the activity.

Strange how fear and joy could live together in the same moment.

She still hated that she'd lost her fearlessness, and that maybe she'd always feel this way—happy and determined, but afraid under it all.

She was trying to be okay with it.

Now she poked around at her feelings as she stood beside the huge horse. Hades appeared the picture of calm, almost dozing while she took an assessment of her fear to see if it would telegraph through the reins to the animal under her. Or if it would overcome her once again and cause her to embarrass herself in front of the boarders who'd gathered in the ring to watch the momentous event.

She felt...not great. But not terrible, either. She'd spent so much time with Hades—more than she had with her own horse, until recently. She knew all of Hades's quirks, the things he liked: food, exercise, having his ears rubbed while he dozed in the wash stall. She knew that new people scared him, but loud noises or sudden motions didn't.

He was perfectly comfortable with everyone present, with the indoor ring, with everything around him. She was the one whose stomach was making slow, careful flips inside the confines of her body.

"You okay?" Ian came around to Hades's side, reins in hand. "We can wait."

They could. But they had an audience. And Ian had let slip that he wanted to see what Hades could do under saddle so he could plan to send him to shows to find a buyer. That little piece of information was like a splinter just beneath the skin. She already knew Ian, let alone Hades, wasn't here to stay. But the fact that he had *plans* for unloading the horse so he could make his getaway from Morning Song...

Well. It was his life. He had every right.

"I'm not going to be less nervous later," she finally said. "And honestly, each time I do this, it gets a little better. Like you said," she added with a little smile.

"He's a different horse from Charlie, though," Ian said. "It's okay if it's too much."

She shook her head. "It doesn't feel any different than with Charlie." She laughed, and Hades flicked a curious ear in their direction. "If anything, Hades is much better behaved."

Ian nodded. "On the ground, sure. And I'll lead him the whole time today until we know what he's like under saddle."

She nodded, and before she could overthink it any more than she already had, she swung up into the saddle.

After riding Charlie for the past week, sitting on Hades was like straddling a wide, overstuffed sofa. An incredibly powerful sofa that flicked its ears back as if to inquire whether she really knew what she was doing.

Ian, bless him, didn't waste time. He led Hades off at a walk before she could change her mind, and after one trip around the ring, her fear settled into a little ball of nerves at the bottom of her stomach.

She could live with that.

"Let go of the reins," she said.

Ian glanced back at her. "Are you sure?"

"Yep. I'll make it quick, but I just want to see what he can do."

Another glance. "No jumping, though, right?"

Bronwen smiled. "No. Not today. I'm not ready for that—and who knows if Hades has even been trained over fences?"

Someone *had* certainly trained the young stallion, though. As Ian released the reins, Bronwen let him stretch out into an extended walk, loose and eating up the ground in a way Charlie could never aspire to.

"Warmbloods," Bronwen muttered. "Such show-offs."

She tightened the reins and Hades immediately collected himself, hind legs coming underneath his back end and jaw flexing softly on the bit. She pushed him into a big, swingy trot, and as she passed by the group by the fence, she heard Olivia's *"Wow."*

She urged him into an extended trot down the long side of the ring, then collected him back on the corner. He wasn't a subtle horse to ride—an animal this big needed firm commands—but he was responsive, and his trot was so big and flashy it made her giggle with joy, even as the ball of fear continued to make its presence known.

Fear and joy, together.

After a short and sedate canter on a circle—she wasn't going to push her luck—she pulled him to a walk and dismounted near the group of observers. The ball of fear dissipated quickly once she was back on the ground, and instead there was only triumph and excitement.

"Holy shit," Brian said.

"Hey, language!" Rachel admonished him. "But…yeah. Holy shit."

"He can really move—none of the other horses here look anything like that!" Olivia said, eyes wide.

Bronwen shrugged. "That's the difference between our Thoroughbreds and quarter horses and whatever, and a super-fancy warmblood."

"I mean, Charlie's a gorgeous mover, but this is something else," Scott said.

"He could definitely go in the dressage ring," Ian said. "Not just the movement, but how he's right there on the bit, and listening all the time to his rider. I bet he's done some dressage tests before."

Bronwen laughed. "Oh, God, I haven't ridden a dressage test in years."

She'd always been more interested in flying over jumps, much less in following a prescribed test of walk-trot-canter around the ring to show obedience and proper movement. But now...jumping was still scary. Dressage? She thought she could handle that.

She might not have much time with either Ian or Hades, but she planned to make the most of it.

Ian sighed with relief as Bronwen gave Hades's neck a pat. He'd encouraged her to ride the big horse, but once they were in the ring, he'd done nothing but worry.

He was about 90 percent confident that Hades would behave, but you never knew with any horse, let alone one who'd suffered trauma in the past. And while he knew by now that Bronwen was an extremely capable rider, he worried for her well-being. He wanted her to push her limits, to find a way through her fear.

But he never wanted her to be afraid or uncomfortable.

Now that it was over, relief flooded his insides and pride

swelled in his chest. She'd done it. She'd ridden almost every day this week, culminating in this effort on Hades. It was huge for her.

She was so much closer to getting her life back. Her choices. Whether she decided to go back to competitive riding or not, a person like Bronwen should never be forced to hide away due to fear. When he left, he wanted her to know one thing: she could do anything she set her mind to.

When he left…

"Ian." Rachel's voice traveled over the sound of the others, all telling Bronwen and Hades how well they'd done. "Do *you* know anything about dressage? Can you teach me to do what Bronwen did?"

"Ooh, me too. I bet Percy would be great at dressage," Martha added.

All eyes turned to him, and for once he didn't squirm with discomfort. He *should* be squirming—this community of boarders had taken him in, as well as the horse his sister had foisted on him. And he was going to walk away without looking back.

He had to. Didn't he?

But it was so easy to answer with "I always trained the jumpers I rode to around first-level dressage. It's a great foundation for any discipline."

And he knew before she even opened her mouth that Rachel would follow up with a request.

"So, you could teach me?"

The girl had been following him around whenever she was at the barn and off her pony, ever since that day at the impromptu pizza party. She was sharp, and knew horses even at her young age. He just hoped she didn't lose interest, or that outgrowing her pony dampened her enthusiasm.

"Sure. While I'm here, anyway."

And again, the clear statement of his time limit at Morning Song sounded an off note, like he was missing something. But what else could he do? There was no place for him here, or anywhere in the horse world. Not if he wanted to regain his peace of mind and let go of all the bitterness that surrounded his accident and the aftermath.

He caught Bronwen's eye, a wistful smile on her face. Then she said, "Rachel, Charlie's had a little basic dressage training. Very basic. But you could try him, if you wanted."

He raised an eyebrow, and Bronwen shrugged. It was a brilliant idea, though. Charlie would be far better suited to dressage lessons than the little pony, who from what he'd seen tended to pull his rider around the ring like he was trying to get it over with as soon as possible. And this would give Rachel a chance to see what she could do on a bigger horse.

Her eyes went wide at the offer. "Really?"

Bronwen grinned at Rachel. "Sure. He's fairly easy on the flat. Just has a mind of his own over fences."

"No kidding," Olivia muttered.

"Cool!" Rachel looked like she'd won the lottery, and she gave Bronwen a quick hug.

Scott asked him a question then about training horses for jumpers using dressage, and about Ian's opinion on Sugar's sensitive feet and reluctance to soften around corners. Bronwen took Hades's reins and led him back to the barn, Rachel in tow, asking a million questions about Charlie. Martha,

Olivia and Brian stood by the fence chattering about all the little things horse people talked about when they were with people who shared their passion.

As he answered Scott's questions, Ian thought about how easy this was. How, much to his surprise, everyone at Morning Song seemed to accept that he couldn't ride, but was still useful and knowledgeable when it came to horse care and riding. What would it be like to belong to a community like this? No one here gave any indication that they saw him as a star to hitch themselves to. No one valued him for the prizes he won or for his fame. No one expected him to do anything he wasn't able to.

Except, perhaps, to stay.

Fourteen

Bronwen inhaled deeply as Hades picked his way carefully along the trail, air rich with the smell of defrosting earth, damp leaves and undergrowth filling her lungs. Finally, it was warm enough for a decent trail ride, and Olivia hadn't given her a moment's peace until she'd put aside her work and agreed to join her.

Sunlight dappled the woods through the branches, the light still muted as if spring hadn't quite decided whether or not it would stick around. Patches of frost lingered under fallen logs as they passed by, and Bronwen noted places where the trail could use a little maintenance in the coming summer.

Whose permission would she need in a few months to hire someone to take down that old tree? To dump gravel in that spot that always flooded with every rainfall? To finally do something about the sad, empty little caretaker's cottage moldering in the middle of the woods, the one Ruth insisted on leaving because it was "picturesque"? Would it really be Ian's sister, Anne, taking up residence in the farmhouse that now held memories so different than those she'd made with Ruth? Where would Ian be then?

She wished she could make him see himself the way she'd seen him the other day, after she'd ridden Hades for the first time. Surrounded by people who respected and cared for him, using his expertise for their benefit. And for hers. But shortly after she'd let Hades back out to his field, she'd watched as he'd made his way back up to the house. Yes, he'd reappeared that evening after the boarders had all left as she was finishing up her chores, and they'd...well, they'd made good use of the rest of the evening. But she hoped he could recognize what he had here, the people who accepted him, who wanted him around.

She'd begun hoping he'd stay, even though she knew that made her a fool.

"Earth to Bronwen," Olivia said, giving her a knowing look as they rode side by side on a wide section of the trail.

Bronwen had to look down at her friend, since she was riding Rachel's pony, Applejack, while Ian gave Rachel a lesson on Charlie.

"Hey, shorty," she teased. "How's the weather down there?"

Olivia snorted. "He's like a sports car—low to the ground and fast."

It was true. The black-and-white pony's little legs walked at double speed, easily keeping up with Hades's long stride.

"He suits you," Bronwen said, and it was true.

Olivia was petite, shorter than Rachel, who looked like

she'd end up very tall when her growing was done. While Applejack was still a bit small for Olivia, his round belly took up her legs nicely, and he was one of the best trail horses in the barn.

"He does." Olivia sounded a little surprised. "Maybe I'll ask Rachel if I can take him out on the trails more often. No offense to Charlie," she added quickly.

Bronwen grinned at her friend. "You and I both know you don't like riding Charlie."

Olivia groaned. "But it was so nice of you to basically give me a horse for free."

"More like I wanted someone to take care of him so I didn't have to feel guilty for not riding him." Bronwen winced.

Olivia gave her a look full of compassion. "And I didn't want you to feel guilty. And I am grateful. But this—" she gestured at Applejack's enthusiastically bobbing head as he marched along "—this is *fun*."

Bronwen shrugged. "So, ride Applejack, if Rachel's okay with it. I can keep Charlie busy."

"And Hades," Olivia added. "You've gone from no riding to multiple horses. Go you!" She put the reins in one hand and pumped a fist in victory.

Bronwen laughed and shook her head. "It's wild, isn't it? I'm still nervous every time, but I think I'm getting used to it? Sort of."

"You just needed a little push from a hot man," Olivia said. "Was that him I saw in the outdoor ring on our way out?"

"Yeah. He's giving Rachel a lesson on Charlie."

"Better her than me," Olivia said with a wry smile.

"Charlie's devious when he's got a rider's number," Bronwen said. "It's not your fault—you just need a horse that suits you."

"Or a tiny little pony, apparently," Olivia laughed, then glanced up at the blue sky. "God, I am so glad that spring is finally here."

They both took a moment to look around, the horses' hooves crunching on last year's leaves the only sound aside from an occasional tentative bird calling out. Little buds were barely visible on the trees, announcing that yes, winter was finally over. Somewhere in the distance a woodpecker began tapping determinedly for its dinner, and Bronwen tipped her head to the sky to see a hawk winging its way along the breeze.

They crossed the small stream that ran through the property, Hades snorting at the water before stepping carefully into it, while Applejack splashed happily through.

"You know, I've walked this trail so many times, but I've never ridden it."

Everything was different on horseback, as if a door had opened onto a parallel, more magical world. The air was crisper, the sounds of the forest more defined, the colors more vibrant. The tree branches themselves seemed to reach out toward them as if greeting them along the way. She'd almost forgotten this, how sitting on the back of a horse made her feel like a part of nature rather than a mere observer.

"Shit, I didn't even think of that!" Olivia exclaimed. "We should order cake or something when we get back. It's a milestone!"

Bronwen happened to know where they could get a cake. Ian had made a devil's food cake the other day while she was at the house, and there had been shenanigans involving frosting and...well.

"I don't even want to know why you are blushing," Olivia said.

"No." Bronwen gave an embarrassed laugh. "You don't."

"He's been good for you," Olivia said casually, but Bronwen heard all the questions under the statement.

"He has. He's...a tough nut to crack, but..."

"But full of tender meat inside?"

"Gross!" Bronwen stuck her tongue out at her friend. "He cares about things really deeply, I think. And he was hurt badly—I mean, not just physically. But the people who he thought were his friends dumped him when he couldn't ride anymore."

Olivia looked horrified. "That's terrible! They weren't his friends, then," she said firmly.

"Nope. But he didn't know that. He lost his friends, his career... That's a lot to deal with."

"But you brought him out of his shell, and now he's teaching a girl dressage and training a giant stallion with you."

Bronwen shrugged. "Maybe. But he's leaving. He said he can't move on with his life unless he leaves horses behind. Finds something totally different to do."

"Ah..." Olivia wrinkled her nose. "And you're never going to give up horses. Especially now that you're riding again."

Bronwen gave Hades's neck an idle scratch as he ambled

around the turn in the trail that led back to the barn. "Even when I thought I might never ride again—and even though it was totally humiliating to lose my nerve like that—I never thought about leaving the horse world. The first thing I thought about was how I could keep Charlie and keep living around horses, even if I couldn't ride."

"But your whole identity wasn't being a rider, like Ian's. From what you've said, riding was how he built a life for himself and his sister. Plus, losing your friends like that... It's got to really hurt."

Bronwen agreed. And she couldn't even fault Ian for his decision, not really. She disagreed with it—he had such a talent for all aspects of horsemanship, not just riding. But if he could find happiness by leaving it all behind, then that was what he needed to do.

"I just...I just wish he wasn't leaving *me* behind." She hadn't said it out loud until now, but as the words left her lips, she felt the truth of them deep inside her.

Olivia made a little sound of agreement as if this wasn't news to her.

It was to Bronwen, though. Somehow, Ian had grumped his way into her life, and all of her vaguely held notions about avoiding relationships had evaporated into the air like melted snow in the sunshine.

Could she trust him, though? She'd been badly burned in the past, and she'd do anything to avoid feeling that hurt and betrayal again. Ian had never gone back on his word with her, or said one thing but done another. But if his word was to be trusted, and he said he was leaving, then...

She laughed a little bitterly. She'd found someone to trust, maybe even to love. But if Ian was true to his word, he'd be leaving her as surely as he'd followed through on all of the things he'd promised to her.

"How was he?" Bronwen asked Rachel as the girl led Charlie from the outdoor ring while Bronwen led Hades toward the gate. She held Hades's reins in one hand, adjusting her helmet with the other. The stallion was nicely warmed up after the trail ride, and ready for a quick lesson.

Hades tugged on the reins, eager to get to work.

"Great!" Rachel gushed. "He's so much fun!"

"He didn't get stubborn on you?"

"A little," Rachel admitted. "But Ian told me how to handle it, and it was fine."

Bronwen sighed inwardly. She'd spent years trying to teach poor Olivia how to get the horse to behave, and here Ian already had it figured out. On the other hand, she'd always known that Olivia and Charlie weren't suited to begin with, and Rachel was a much stronger rider.

An idea began to form in her head.

"You know…" she said slowly. "We could maybe think about a lease arrangement, if you were interested."

Rachel blinked at her. "You mean…I could keep riding Charlie? *Really?*"

Bronwen was careful to watch for any sign of reluctance or upset, but Rachel was all enthusiasm.

So she shrugged. "Sure. He needs a strong rider. And that way you can ride a bigger horse while you figure out…you know." She remembered what Olivia had said on the trail. "Oh! And Olivia said she'd like to ride Applejack sometimes, if that's okay with you. Apparently they really hit it off on the trail."

Rachel's eyes widened even further. "Really? So, Applejack could stay here and go on the trails with Olivia, and I can ride Charlie?"

Bronwen smiled. "Sure, if your parents are okay with that."

Rachel nearly dropped Charlie's reins in excitement. "Oh my God! This is so great. Charlie was such a good boy, and Applejack loves trails a lot more than ring work. I'll ask my parents! Thanks, Bronwen!"

Bronwen laughed and waved as Charlie tugged Rachel back to the barn and Hades pulled her toward the ring.

"I think these guys have had enough of our talking," she called back over her shoulder.

She entered the ring and tried to tamp down her nerves. She was so tired of the little ball of fear in her stomach, the way her limbs tingled with anxiety each time she was about to get on a horse. She tried to be kind to herself, but it was tough. She didn't even know what she was afraid of—falling, she supposed, but she'd fallen a million times. She'd been injured before, too, and survived. Yet somehow her brain had decided that this time was different. Now riding was full of undefined danger.

She sighed and marched toward the mounting block. Hades was so big she needed the assistance, yet somehow once she was on him, she felt more secure on his wide back than she did on Charlie.

Maybe the horse swap she'd suggested to Olivia and Rachel would be good for her, too.

Until Ian sent Hades wherever he chose to send him, that was.

"How are you feeling today?"

Speak of the devil. Ian pushed himself off the far side of the fence where he'd been waiting and strode toward her. She busied herself with checking Hades's girth and her stirrup length to keep herself from staring at him as he approached.

"Fine," she answered, then mentally shook herself. Ian asked her the same question every time she got on a horse these days, and she knew he really wanted to know. It was important to him that she was never pushed too far beyond her comfort level. She knew he still felt guilty for that first day on Charlie, even though it hadn't been even remotely his fault. "Good," she added. "Nervous as usual, but he's been so good. I feel...comfortable on him."

Ian nodded shortly, his eyes raking over her in that too-perceptive way that made her feel like he could read every thought, every sensation in her body. Right now, her body suggested that getting off the horse and onto Ian would be a great idea. She told her libido to hold that thought for later.

He smiled at her knowingly as his eyes met hers. "Good."

"Hey," she continued, not even quite sure what she was going to say. "You...you help me feel comfortable. You've helped me feel okay with riding again, even when it's been hard. Thank you, Ian."

He placed a hand on her leg just above her tall boot, the heat of it warming her through her breeches. The eyes she'd once thought were ice-cold were anything but now, warmer than the early spring sun and just as bright.

"You're welcome."

She thought he might say something more, but an odd look crossed his face and he pulled away instead, backing up toward the fence.

"Okay. Let's get him warmed up."

Bronwen swallowed, then shorted her reins and moved Hades off her leg. Fear notwithstanding, riding the stallion was a joy. He was young and had a lot to learn, but his natural ability and happiness in his work made riding him one of the high points of each day. She hoped she'd regain enough nerve soon to see what he could do over jumps. Whoever ended up with him was getting a treasure of a horse, and she just hoped they deserved him.

"Do you want to try the full test today?" Ian asked.

"Yeah, okay."

Ian planned to enter Hades in a local dressage show, just to see how he took to the experience. They both agreed that as long as no one he didn't know tried to handle him, he should be fine—so far, no noise or sudden movement had startled him. He rode easily in the indoor ring and outside, as well as on trails. She could have strangled whoever had taught him to be afraid of strangers. He was such a happy, willing horse when he wasn't overcome with fear.

She could relate.

"You're still okay with the show?" Ian asked as she walked Hades past him.

Was she? She had her reservations, but not for the reasons Ian was asking.

"Yeah, I think it will be good—for us both." With a pat on Hades's neck, she pushed the horse into a trot.

She didn't want Ian to ask her about the show again. Though she did think it would be a good experience for both her and Hades. She'd gone to a couple of shows with Brian and sometimes Martha, who were the only boarders who showed regularly. But she'd stayed in the background, helping with holding the horses and calming nerves.

She used to live in that world—loading up the horses into the trailer each weekend, often sleeping in said trailer or in a cheap hotel if the show was a little farther away. They hadn't been the big, upper-level shows Ian was used to, but it had been her whole world when she was at her old barn.

She wondered how it would feel now that she'd been so removed from it all for several years. Was it a world she even wanted to belong to anymore? She was looking forward to finding out.

But... She knew, although he had only mentioned it in passing, that Ian's plan was still to sell Hades to a good home. He wasn't sure what his sister had intended by sending him the horse, aside from trying to lure him back into the horse world. But he didn't plan to keep him.

He didn't plan to keep any of them: Hades, Morning Song Farm, Bronwen.

She'd known that all along, but she was still trying to avoid thinking about it. It was going to hurt no matter what, so there was no sense in crying about it now when she could put it off and enjoy both horse and man.

She wished he would stay. She knew that he wouldn't.

She urged Hades into a long, stretchy canter, continuing to warm up both their muscles. At least she had this moment, right now. A perfect horse to ride and an incredible, talented, smoking-hot man waiting for her on the other side of the ring.

If she didn't want to compete anymore, she could take up training horses like Hades. She might not be a great riding instructor, but she was proud of the progress Hades had made. Plus, she'd trained Charlie herself, and he hadn't been easy.

Training problem horses to be happy and successful—yeah, she could get behind that. She smiled to herself.

And then it happened.

Something caught Hades's attention in the distance—a deer, a squirrel, who knew—and he tripped, front legs tangling. He tried to right himself, but his center of balance was thrown off by the rider on his back, and his feet slipped out from under him.

For a long, heart-clenching moment, Bronwen thought she'd stay on. And the last thought she had as she finally realized that she was coming off, tumbling through the air and crashing onto the hard ground below was—

Oh, this *is what I was afraid of.*

Fifteen

The air in Ian's lungs froze in his chest as he watched Bronwen fall from the great height of Hades's back.

The horse, to his credit, didn't spook or startle as he lost his rider. Instead, he scrambled awkwardly to his feet and shook himself like a dog. Ian spared a glance to make sure he wasn't obviously injured, but he ran directly toward where Bronwen lay on the ground in a heap.

Thankfully, Olivia came running up the hill to the ring and called out.

"Hey! Need help?"

Ian gestured at Hades. "Please—just make sure Hades is okay."

He sent up a prayer of gratitude that Hades's recent training and interactions with the boarders meant that he'd let Olivia grab his reins and make sure there was no clear injury.

He only wanted to focus on Bronwen.

"Bronwen—"

If anything happened to her because she was riding his horse, he'd never forgive himself. He shouldn't have pushed her. He should have... He didn't even know what he should have done, but he should have done something, *anything*, to prevent this.

Everything crystallized in the few seconds it took him to run across the ring. He needed Bronwen to be okay. He needed her to be safe. He needed *her*.

The idea of leaving her, his close-held plan all along, was laughable in this moment. But he wasn't laughing. No, his gut was gripped with fear and his legs couldn't carry him fast enough. It was as if he was running through molasses when all he wanted was to be with her, near her, to make sure she was unharmed.

He loved her. He wasn't leaving her.

Not now, not ever. Not even if she insisted on spending every minute of the rest of their lives with horses. Not even if she decided she did want to compete again, even if she reached the highest levels and dragged him back into the world he'd sworn to leave behind. Not if she'd have him. Not if she would just be all right.

After what felt like hours but was only a few seconds, he reached her side, sliding onto his knees in the arena footing.

She was already sitting up by the time he reached her.

"I'm fine, I'm fine." She was...laughing. Weakly, but still. Laughing, not crying. Or worse, not responding at all.

"Hold still. Don't move. Jesus, Bronwen. I'm so sorry— Wait, can you stand? No, don't. Don't move. Should we call an ambulance?"

He knew he wasn't making any sense. He'd seen his share

of bad falls—and had his own, obviously. He knew how to cope, in theory. But right now, he was a fucking mess and didn't even know where to start.

"Ian." Bronwen was staring at him as if he'd lost his mind. He felt like he had. "Are you okay? You're white as a sheet."

He forced himself to take a deep breath. Distantly, he heard Hades's hooves as Olivia led him over to where they sat.

"Are you hurt? Anywhere?"

"Is Hades all right?"

They spoke at the same time, Bronwen looking over his shoulder at the horse. He *should* care if Hades was all right— he did care. He did. But right now his brain was having trouble processing.

"Bronwen," he said, his voice sounding like someone else's, tight and reedy. Someone panicked. He never panicked. "Just tell me if anything hurts."

She shook her head, then winced. Fear rushed like a wave through his body again.

"I think I bumped my elbow." She moved her arm experimentally. "But it's all working. Just got the wind knocked out of me for a second."

And then she was laughing again. Ian ran a hand over his face, the relief that she wasn't badly hurt almost more than he could bear.

"You serious horse people are so weird," Olivia commented from behind him. "You sure you're okay?"

"I'm sure. It's just… God, I was so scared all this time. About exactly this, I guess. Falling off. But here I am, dirty and sort of lacking any dignity, but I'm…fine? Mostly."

She moved her arm again and grimaced.

"You want to get back on?" Olivia asked. "Or should I take Hades back to the barn? I think he'll let me untack him and everything."

"Yeah, I think I need to see if my arm is okay before I get back on—let me just look at him before you take him back."

And then she was up and standing by the big horse, while Ian tried to gather his wits around him down on the ground.

He shook his head and stood, clearing his throat. "He look okay?"

"Mmm." Bronwen ran a hand down each leg. "Seems fine. Just a little klutzy moment, I guess. Poor guy—haven't quite grown into your feet yet, have you?"

"It's a lot of legs to keep track of, to be fair," Olivia said. She gave Hades's neck a pat. "Let me get him taken care of while you make sure you didn't do any real damage to your arm, and then you can take another look later? I'll put him in his stall with some hay, just in case."

Bronwen nodded. "Thanks. You're the best."

As soon as Olivia started for the gate with Hades, Ian grabbed Bronwen's hand and pulled her toward him. He took her face in his hands and pressed his forehead to hers. She smelled of horse and dirt, her face wonderfully warm beneath his palms. He wanted to drink her in, alive and mostly unhurt, until his heartbeat returned to normal instead of the rapid, erratic thunking it had been doing in his chest since she'd first fallen.

"Tell me you're okay." The words came out a little more urgently, more commanding than he'd intended.

She pulled back to look at him, a quizzical expression on

her face. "Yeah. I mean, I'll need to see how my arm feels tomorrow, but I'm in one piece."

He sighed heavily. "I'm so sorry—I shouldn't have pushed you to ride again."

She reached up and pressed a firm kiss to his lips. "You never pushed me. Okay," she amended with a little smile. "Maybe a little push. But one I *needed*. Ian, without you I don't know if I would ever have gotten back on a horse."

He closed his eyes. "But then you wouldn't have fallen. Your fear—"

"I would have fallen eventually, fear or no fear. That's just part of riding. You know that."

She reached up to touch his face, and he pressed her palm to his cheek with his hand.

"You don't have to keep riding him. Hades. If it's too much…"

He took another deep breath. He knew he was hovering, that he was being irrational. Bronwen was all right. Hades was all right. He was the one falling apart.

She tugged him close and wrapped her arms around his waist.

"I'm fine, Ian," she said into his chest. "It was just a fluke." She tilted her head back and smiled up at him. "My fear—what I was afraid of, falling, getting hurt again, all of that. I don't know how to explain it, because it's not like I'm not still afraid. But it *happened*. The thing I was afraid of happened, and I'm okay. My nerves are still a big mess when I think about getting back on and riding again, but it's like…like that big, heavy cloud of what might happen is a little lighter now. I'm not going to let one fall stop me from riding." She tilted her chin stubbornly. "I'm not going to let anything stop me. Not ever again."

Ian was torn between wanting to wrap her in cotton and never let her anywhere near another horse, and cheering her on. He chose the latter, because he'd never keep Bronwen from doing what she wanted.

"Okay," he said. "Okay. Good." He kissed the top of her head. "But you have to let me do one thing."

"What?"

"This."

He swept her up into his arms and carried her right out of the ring.

"Ian! I can walk by myself."

"Don't care."

He wasn't letting her out of his arms. Not now, probably not for the rest of the day. Or night. Maybe not ever, although that would eventually get awkward. He squeezed her tight.

"Just let me hold you. Just for now."

"Aww. It's a lot harder to watch someone else fall than do it yourself, isn't it?"

That was true. But this was different from when he'd worried over his friends, or his sister, or anyone else he cared about who found themselves tumbling off a horse's back.

Because this was Bronwen, and he'd only just found her. Only just realized what she was to him. What he wanted. He wasn't ready to lose any of it. He never would be.

So, he carried Bronwen down the hill, through the barn, past the astonished boarders and up the stairs to her apartment. Her laughter at his ridiculousness singing in his ears the entire way.

And he sent up a prayer of thanks to anyone listening that she was unhurt and in his arms. That he'd gotten his head out of his ass in time and realized what he had here. Bronwen, Morning Song, a life he was willing to fight for. And he sent up a second prayer, one that asked for strength and patience. That he could learn to be the man Bronwen needed. One she wanted—one she'd be willing to take a chance on.

One that, despite her past experiences, she'd be able to trust and welcome into her life. He'd take things slowly. He didn't want to scare her off or overwhelm her. But somehow, he needed to convince Bronwen that she could trust him, and maybe she'd want him to stay.

That evening, Bronwen leaned on Hades's stall door and watched the stallion absolutely demolish his dinner.

"He's certainly a good eater," she said, leaning into Ian's side.

He hadn't left her by herself all afternoon or evening. Not that she was complaining. He'd checked her elbow at least five times, as if he thought it could somehow go from bruised to broken if he didn't keep an eye on it. Then he'd insisted on taking her out for a late lunch, which had been lovely but unnecessary. And he'd helped her with the evening barn chores, chatting with the lingering boarders as he'd swept the barn aisle and helped her prep the evening feed. She'd loved watching him fit into the barn routine like he'd always been there, even as she knew she'd feel the emptiness of his absence all too soon.

Now they were alone, and after a million reassurances that her fall hadn't been his fault, Ian appeared to have finally relaxed.

"He does love food," Ian replied. "I don't know how Anne found him, but other than his issue with strangers, he's an incredible horse."

Bronwen hummed to herself. Hades wasn't hers, but she'd miss him terribly if—*when*—Ian sold him. Then a thought occurred to her, and she could have kicked herself for not wondering about it sooner.

"When your sister sent him—she was definitely giving him to you? She'll be okay with you selling him?"

Ian turned his head toward her, rubbing his hand over his jaw.

"Her note said she was sending him my way, and that I'd know what to do." He laughed, then groaned. "I guess she never really said he was *mine*. Or that I could sell him. But as far as I'm concerned, if she didn't want me to do what was best, she shouldn't have sent me a horse."

Bronwen gazed steadily at the horse in front of them. "And is it? Best? To sell him to another home."

Ian was silent, and she couldn't tell what he was thinking.

Finally, he said, "Maybe not. Maybe he belongs here."

At that, she turned her head and met his eyes. There was a wariness there, a caution, that she couldn't read. She didn't want to ask what he meant, because it could be anything from leaving Hades with her, or in the care of his sister when she returned, or...

She didn't trust herself to articulate the other option. It was too much to hope for. Wasn't it?

"I'm still trying to figure out who I am now," he said quietly. "I don't even know. But maybe...maybe there's a place for us both. Hades and me. If there are people here willing to have us."

The words were tentative, and Bronwen didn't want to push in case they blew away like the wind currently howling over the barn roof. It had turned cold again after the warm spell, winter unwilling to release its hold just yet. She shivered in her coat.

Ian's hand found hers and squeezed. His eyes searched hers, looking for something she couldn't understand. Maybe he wanted reassurance, or maybe he wanted to know that she wouldn't *push* him.

And she wouldn't, even if her heart demanded that he tell her he was definitely staying, that he couldn't imagine leaving. Her, Hades, the barn. That was what she wanted to hear, and she knew he wasn't ready to say it. Or commit to it. How could he be, when he'd been so clear all this time that he was leaving?

She swallowed. "There's always a place here. For both of you."

His smile was like the sun that had warmed the whole farm these past few days. "Good," he said simply. He squeezed her hand again. "I promise we'll figure the rest out."

I promise... She'd heard so many promises in the past, ones that had so rarely been fulfilled. She didn't even know what Ian was promising, exactly. Would he stay for now? Forever?

Did he plan to leave and come back to visit her? What was he offering, if anything?

But she didn't ask, because she didn't want to be disappointed. Which was ridiculous—she'd be more than disappointed if he left after raising her hopes. She'd be heartbroken. But at least here, now, in his words…there *was* hope. He wanted to try. He wanted to figure things out. For now, that would need to be enough. If he wanted a place here, it was his, as far as she was concerned. But she wouldn't push him for promises on the scale of what she truly wanted—not yet.

Instead, she asked for what she needed now. What she knew she could count on him to deliver.

"You're coming with me to the show, right?"

The dressage show with Hades was the day after tomorrow, and she was, quite frankly, nervous as hell. Her emotions were a mess, all of the uncertainty ratcheting up her anxiety around riding to a new level. How would Hades behave? Would he enjoy it, or would it set him back? Would she lose her nerve in front of everyone?

She needed Ian to be there, anchoring her. She needed him to keep this promise.

He pulled her into his arms, the movement causing Hades to look up and snort in their direction before returning to his feed.

"Of course I'm coming," he said firmly. "I wouldn't make you do this alone."

She sighed in relief. She *could* do it alone—the show was only a few miles away. She only needed to groom Hades that morning and load his tack into the trailer. They were signed up for one dressage test, and then they'd be home before they knew it.

But she wanted Ian's support. Needed it.

"Good," she said, echoing the simplicity of his words a moment earlier.

Hades finished his food in his feed bucket and turned his attention to his hay.

"Are you worried?" Ian asked.

Bronwen almost laughed. She was worried about so many things: the show, the future of the barn under Ian's sister's ownership, whether or not Ian actually meant to stay when he'd said all along that he was leaving, Hades's own future...

So she just said, "Yes." And let that cover it.

Ian smiled, something hopeful and a little tentative in his expression, and she both wanted and didn't want to ask what it meant.

Instead, she turned and grasped his head in her hands and kissed him, longingly, slowly, savoring the taste of him while she still had him. As always, the warmth that always took up residence in her belly when he was near burst into flame at the contact, its heat urging her to *feel*, to get ever closer.

A groan rumbled in the back of his throat, and his hands slipped under her coat, her shirt.

With a gasp, she broke off the kiss, breath already coming hard and fast. Ian kissed along her jaw and down to the tender spot under her ear. She shivered, this time not from the cold.

"Scared me to death today," he whispered against her throat, his arms tightening around her. He raised his head and looked at her. "You're sure your arm is okay?"

She stopped herself from rolling her eyes with a smile. "Definitely. Just a bruise where I landed. You've seen it. It barely hurts anymore."

"Barely isn't not at all," he grumbled, pressing a kiss to the top of her head.

She tried to ignore the squeeze of her heart. She could get used to this—*was* used to this. Ian worrying about her, caring for her. Encouraging her when she needed it. She shouldn't have let herself come to depend on it. Should put a stop to all of this now, until Ian told her what he planned for his future. She'd assumed that since she wasn't ready for a relationship, she'd be safe—that somehow, her heart would understand the logic of that and protect itself.

How foolish. She'd never stood a chance with this man, and she should have known it that first night in the cold, dark farmhouse. But she'd charged ahead anyway, and if he didn't stay, she'd pay for it.

And she was still a fool, because instead of stepping away, she held him closer, as if she could keep him with her through force of will.

"I'm fine," she said, as much to herself as to Ian. And she kissed him again, choosing sensation over heartache for now.

He turned them both and pressed her into the wall next to Hades's stall door. His tall frame blocked out most of the light from the bulbs hung along the aisle. The barn door was closed against the wind, a distant shushing noise that only highlighted the cozy quiet of the barn.

"You're fine," he repeated, as if trying to finally get that fact through his head.

He held himself very still, palms warm against the skin

under her shirt, forehead pressed to hers. She breathed in his air, breathed out to his lips. Somewhere in the barn a horse pawed the ground, another rattled their feed bucket, hoping for a second dinner.

She smiled and heard Ian's quiet laugh.

And then his fingers curled into her, and his body shuddered against hers.

"Bronwen," he whispered urgently.

And he took her lips with his, desperate and demanding, as if he needed to prove to himself that she was here with him. Her hands clutched at his shoulders, the world tilting with the intensity of the kiss.

"I need you," he said, his mouth brushing her cheek. "I'm aching for you. Bronwen—"

She turned her head to kiss him again, cutting him off. He didn't need to ask, not for this. She was fine after her fall, but still rattled, if she was completely honest with herself. His mouth on hers—hot, desperate—his hips pressing into her stomach, all of it grounded her to this moment, this place. To the fact that she was here, *he* was here.

She needed more.

With a groan, he slid his hands around to the small of her back, then down to cup her ass through her sweatpants, pulling her closer. The wall behind her was solid, and as she wound her hands around his neck she felt *held*. Secure.

His tongue slid across her lower lip, the scruff on his face scraping against her skin, echoed in the lick of heat between her legs. The sudden shakiness of her knees. The tug of desire and need in her belly. The whimper that pulled itself out of her.

He swallowed the small sound, and without moving his mouth from hers, he shoved a knee between her thighs, the friction and pressure drawing out another whimper. She struggled for breath, turning her head and pressing her lips to the tender spot where his collarbones met just above the buttons of his shirt.

His breath hitched, his chest rising and falling far too fast from a few kisses. She felt as if they were dry branches just waiting for a spark, and when his fingers smoothed around the waistband of her pants and tugged, lightning struck.

Her hands fumbled with his belt, the buttons of his jeans, tugging and shoving the fabric down just enough to allow his erection to spring free. She reached for it but he was already pushing her own pants down, somehow also co-ordinated enough to pull a condom from his pocket and tearing it open.

She took the small packet from him, holding his gaze as she slowly rolled the condom onto his hard length, intentionally slowing down the inferno. Stopping time for this one moment. Savoring the agonized pleasure on his face as she gave him a squeeze. Letting her thumb stroke him back down to the tip.

He licked his lips, chest heaving, all tightly wound energy and tension.

She reached up and stroked his cheek, her own body screaming for her to move, act, anything to douse the flames threatening to consume her.

But the moment held, one second, and another, both of them right on the edge of something unnameable. Like an arrow drawn in a bow, held for an endless point in time and paradoxically only for an instant, just before the inevitable explosion of release through the sky.

And then Ian was kissing her again, messy and reckless, hauling her up the wall with his hands under her hips, sliding into her in one deep thrust with a grunt of satisfaction. Her fingernails scraped his scalp and he groaned, a rough, hungry sound.

The cold fabric of the inside of her coat brushed against the side of her hip, a delicious contrast to the heat where they were joined, the heat of his searing kisses as he began to move.

She felt him harden even more inside her as he built a rhythm, something about the sensation so erotic the beginning of her orgasm tightened and tingled between her legs.

"Ian—" she gasped, and he slid a hand between them, rubbing her swollen clit with his calloused thumb, rough and demanding. His other arm held her up, pressed against the wall and his hard body, keeping them together just as she herself began to fall apart.

His lips broke from hers and he mouthed her jaw, her throat, inhaling as if he wanted to consume all of her.

He stroked her steadily in time to his thrusts, sensation lighting her up like summer sunshine, hot and inescapable. And then it all burst, sparks behind her eyelids and liquid desire flooding her limbs to her fingers and toes. Her orgasm shot through her like a rocket, fireworks exploding into a million little stars blasting into the sky.

She cried out in the silence of the barn, and then she could feel him joining her over the edge, one more hard, powerful thrust that jolted her back against the wall. The force of it somehow completing and enhancing the tail end of her pleasure as he groaned and shuddered against her. After a long moment he stilled, breath still coming heavily and in time with her.

She palmed the back of his neck, warm and damp with sweat, clasping him to her as he lowered her to the ground, her legs wobbly like rubber. She hooked an arm around his waist for stability. He slid out of her with a groan, and unexpected little bursts of pleasure drew a moan from her at the movement.

On a long exhalation, he laughed, a low rumble.

"Just give me a…moment," he said. "Before we move."

The cold night air chilled her skin where it was exposed, and she wriggled with one hand to pull up her sweatpants.

At her motion, Ian pulled back slightly and frowned. "You're cold." He blinked a few times as if just now coming back to himself. "I'm sorry—I wasn't thinking." A little huff of breath and he pulled her to him again, burying his face in her hair. "I just needed you."

"I needed you, too," she reassured him, and it was true. For a thousand reasons, some of which she understood and some…not so much. She'd needed the sudden unleashing of the tension between them, the physicality of it. Now she felt complete, grounded, centered on the man holding her with firm and sure hands.

She stroked his back through the fabric of his shirt. "You must be freezing. Where did the spring go? It was just here."

He made a sound of assent, then pressed a kiss to the top of her head before straightening. "Let me just duck into the bathroom to…" He gestured to where his pants still hung open with a wry smile. "You head upstairs and get warm." He lifted an eyebrow in a question, and she took one of his hands to give it a squeeze.

"Meet me up there," she said firmly, and he smiled wider. "Good," he said.

And he released her hand reluctantly, as if he didn't want to lose contact for even a moment. She felt the same, as if everything was right and safe and as it should be when they were touching. But as soon as he released her, all of the worries and doubts and the ever-present shadow of the unknown future came swooping down, crowding her in the dark staircase as she made her way up the stairs to her apartment.

Sixteen

Ian kissed Bronwen again, and then again, and she laughed.

"With this many good-luck kisses, Hades and I are definitely going to win tomorrow."

She stood on the porch of the farmhouse, wonderfully disheveled and blushing. Not half an hour before, they'd been tangled up in bed, and Ian would have given a lot to be back there instead of kissing her goodbye for the night.

"That seems like a good excuse to keep kissing you," he replied.

Bronwen swatted him on the shoulder. "You're the one sending me home. This was all your idea."

Ian groaned. "You need a good night's rest before the show. We have to be up in a few hours."

Bronwen sighed dramatically. "So practical. But you're right. I'll take Martha's example—she said she slept nine hours last night before heading out with Percy for the hunter show this weekend."

"You don't have nine hours left, but you'd better go before I change my mind and haul you back inside."

He didn't know why he was so reluctant to let her go, aside from the obvious. They'd spent most nights together over the past couple of weeks, but he did want to make sure she was well rested for tomorrow. He'd see her again in just a few hours to get Hades ready and set off for the nearby show. There was no reason to cling.

He settled for one more kiss. He wanted to tell her everything—that he'd decided to stay, that he wanted to know if she would be willing to keep him. He didn't even know what that would look like, but he wanted to find out. His sister would likely return soon, and so much depended on her plans. But whatever it took, he would make sure that Morning Song was in good hands. And if Bronwen was willing, he'd stay with her as long as she wanted him.

But he knew she was wary of relationships, and that his sudden decision would be a surprise at best and unwelcome at worst. He could hardly spring it all on her right before the show. She was nervous and didn't need anything else to worry about.

So he tucked her into her coat and turned her around by the shoulders.

"Scoot," he said. Her arms shook as she laughed at him, and he smiled despite everything. "See you in the morning," he murmured into her ear before releasing her.

With a wave, she took off down the path to the barn, and he watched her the whole way.

Then he went inside and to the little study off the living room. He'd kept the door shut since he arrived, most of the boxes of his things from Florida still stacked against the wall. The rest of his belongings were still in storage down there. It was a silly gesture, he saw now, refusing to unpack these boxes. It wasn't as if he had much—clothes, kitchen items, papers and photographs, books, a few pieces of furniture from his old apartment.

When he'd first arrived at Morning Song, he'd only removed what he absolutely needed and left the rest in the small room, colder than the rest of the house. He wasn't sure whether he'd simply refused to commit to even his short stay at the farm, or if he'd been punishing himself, unwilling to make any place feel more like home.

Now he grabbed scissors from the kitchen and began opening boxes—knowing he might need to pack them right back up if Anne planned to live in the farmhouse, or if Bronwen kicked him to the curb. He shoved that thought away and started pulling things out. For now, he needed distraction. And finally, he felt like he could let the remains of his past back into his life.

None of it was particularly special, or valuable, but he could almost breathe the Florida air as he opened one box after another. His books on training horses. His riding clothes, including the show jacket he'd planned to wear at a big show he'd never made it to. That one stung. But even as the hurt was still there, he didn't feel the same resentment as he had in the past. He'd lost a lot. Nothing could change that.

But he'd gained something, too. A group of people who seemed to like him for who he was and not what prizes he could win. More time, less stress—some of his happiest memories now were of cooking in the old kitchen while Bronwen watched, or leaning on the fence simply watching Hades graze in the field. Knowing he didn't need to hop into a trailer or on a plane the next day. That he could do the same tomorrow, and the next day. It was a stability he'd never experienced, and he realized now that given the choice, he'd gladly choose stability over the excitement of the show circuit.

He'd been mourning something he'd achieved by necessity, without ever wondering if it was what he really wanted.

And Bronwen, of course. He'd gained her, too. For now, and hopefully forever.

A few photographs spilled out of a book as he lifted it out of the box. He rifled through them. There was one of him on a horse he'd ridden years ago, midway over an enormous fence. He missed it. He'd never deny that he'd always miss riding. But it didn't hurt as much as he would have expected to see the evidence of his past life. Pride and satisfaction outweighed the pain. He'd *done* something with his life. He'd taken care of himself and his sister and he'd achieved more than he'd ever thought possible. And he'd gained skills that people still wanted—expertise, knowledge, training.

It hadn't been a waste after all.

A knock on the door interrupted his thoughts. He rose and dusted off his jeans, wondering what had brought Bronwen back to the house. He should scold her and send her back to her apartment, but he knew he probably wouldn't.

But when he opened the door, it was the last person he could have expected.

"Anne!"

His sister raised her eyebrows at him. "Why are you so surprised? I told you I was coming. Also, this is my house."

Ian let out his breath with a huff. "A house you've never been to. And you didn't tell me you were coming."

Anne pushed past him and into the mostly empty living room. "I've been here. When I bought it—I was hardly going to buy a farm sight unseen."

For some reason, he'd thought that was exactly what she'd done. Anne always followed her intuition, which sometimes made her seem impulsive. But usually, her instincts were onto something.

"And I texted you two hours ago from the airport on my new phone," she added, holding up the device in question. "I had to get the world's most expensive Uber when you didn't answer."

Ian tried and failed to stop the flush that he could feel creeping up his neck. Two hours ago he'd been in bed with Bronwen. His phone was probably still upstairs.

"I'm not even going to ask what that reaction is all about," his sister said and turned in a circle in the middle of the room. "It's hardly homey in here, Ian. You've been here for weeks!"

He shrugged as if it was no big deal, but in the face of Anne's scrutiny he felt foolish. He'd just been telling himself that refusing to settle into the house had been silly, and it was true. But maybe he'd needed to brood, to live in the worst parts of himself, to figure out what he needed.

He'd thought it was to run away. But now he knew it was to stay.

He cleared his throat. "So. Are you moving in?"

Another eyebrow raise. "'How are you, dear sister? How was your postdivorce getaway? Are you well?'"

No one could make him feel like an ass like Anne.

"Sorry," he said sheepishly. He hadn't seen her in well over a month, and he *did* want to know how she was doing.

"I'd think you'd fallen madly in love with the farm and were worried I was going to kick you out," she said with a smirk. "But clearly you don't feel *that* much at home." She gestured to the cold and empty room.

He ran a hand through his hair. "I was…just dealing with some stuff."

Her smirk softened into a sympathetic smile. "I know. I know you were."

Impulsively Ian crossed the space between them and pulled his sister into a hug. Neither of them were huggers, really, but having Anne here after so long, after so much had happened—he wanted to *feel* that she was okay. That she was really here.

He breathed her in, the grown-up version of the girl he'd raised as best he could. It hadn't been perfect, or even a particularly good childhood for both of them. But they were *here*, dammit. They were here and together. And they'd both be okay, accident and divorce be damned.

"What was that for?" Anne asked shakily when he finally released her.

Ian shrugged, awkward in his own emotions. "I just… missed you." He let out a long breath. "How are you, anyway? Did the vacation do…whatever you needed it to?"

Anne nodded slowly, as if she was trying to figure out the answer. "Yeah. I think so. I just needed to remove myself from my past, from the divorce—from everything, you know? Just for a little while."

Ian did know. Wasn't that exactly what Anne had given him by sending him to the farm?

"Oh—Ian! Why is all your stuff crammed into this room?"

He'd left the door to the study open when he answered the door. Now Anne bustled into the room and looked at his half-opened boxes.

Then she looked at him as if she could see right through him to exactly why he'd never unpacked. Uncertainty crossed her face like a cloud.

"I'm sorry, Ian. Was it a mistake? I just thought, since I'd found this farm but wasn't moving in right away, it might give you…" She laughed a little. "Something. I don't know. I didn't have a clue what you needed, honestly."

The last time he saw Anne, he'd been just out of the hospital, bitter and in pain and discovering how much he'd really lost. Her divorce was recently finalized and she'd already made plans to go away for a while. He'd all but forced her to take her trip despite the mess he was in. And then she'd suggested that he farm-sit while she was away. He hadn't really been in a mood to ask for specifics.

"It was exactly what I needed," he said, giving her arm a squeeze. "I didn't know it then, but…it was perfect."

She sighed with relief and nudged the side of one box with the toe of her boot. "Thank God. I thought I'd get here and you'd rip me a new one—for the farm, for the horse, for everything."

"I mean…" It was Ian's turn to raise his eyebrows at her.

"It was all a bit of a surprise. The fact that this is a working boarding barn, for one. The horse, for another. I wasn't thrilled at the time."

She met his gaze, a smile playing around her mouth. "But you are now? Thrilled? Or at least not furious?"

"I'm not furious...anymore," he teased. Then he grew serious. "At the time, I was pretty pissed off—I thought at you for sticking me with all of this, but really, it wasn't you. It was everyone and everything. You were right that I needed to rejoin the human race. And the equine one." He laughed a little, amazed at how true that was.

"I just wanted to take care of you for once," she said quietly. "The way you'd always taken care of me." She shook herself much the way Hades did after a roll in the field. "Anyway. This room is freezing. Let's pull this stuff into the living room and then you can make me a snack."

In a few short minutes they'd pulled the boxes and furniture into the living room, some spilling into the kitchen. Just the presence of his things chased away the emptiness that had haunted the house since he'd arrived.

He grabbed the makings for a sandwich out of the fridge and started putting together something for his sister to eat. She sat at the table and watched.

"How is Hades, anyway?" she asked while he worked. "Clover Farm said he was a little difficult, but his breeding is incredible."

Ian snorted. "A *little* difficult? Anne, the horse was untouchable when he got here. Someone really did a number on him before Clover got him."

Anne's eyebrows furrowed as she frowned. "Really?

That's horrible! Have you made any progress with him, or did you toss him in a field and leave him?"

Ian rolled his eyes. "You know I wouldn't do that. And yes, he's made a lot of progress. Actually, the barn manager is riding him in a little dressage show tomorrow. You should come."

"Oh right, the former owner said the manager is great. What's her name? Brooke or something?"

"Bronwen," he tried to say as casually as possible, but Anne grinned at his tone. She saw right through him.

"Aha, I see."

He brought the sandwich-laden plate to the table and sat across from his sister.

"You see nothing."

"Uh-huh. If I'd known there was a *Bronwen* here on the farm, well—I'd still have sent you here. But with even more enthusiasm."

"We were talking about the horse, Anne," he said repressively.

"Uh-huh. Sure. Anyway, if you and *Bronwen* are taking him to a show tomorrow, I think I'll hold off and meet both horse and woman when you get back." She yawned, then took a bite of the sandwich. "I'm exhausted, honestly. I needed to get away, but now I just want to stay in one place for as long as possible."

Ian grabbed a sandwich just for something to do. He'd made pasta for Bronwen earlier, determined that she'd eat a good dinner before the show.

"So," he began.

Anne gave him a half smile. "*So.* You want to know what the hell I'm doing."

He really did. "I think…" He stopped, then tried again. "I'd planned to hide away here until I figured out what to do next. Something far away, something as different from riding horses as I could find. I wanted to leave it all behind."

Anne reached across the table to squeeze his hand. "Ian…"

"But," he forged ahead, "because of your totally inappropriate interference—" Anne rolled her eyes at him "—I realized that I had my head solidly up my ass."

She gave him the look that said he was being too hard on himself. He'd seen it a million times before, when he'd fallen from a horse, or ruined dinner because he was still learning how to cook.

"I had reason for it," he admitted. "But still. I was wrong, and I needed this place—the people in this place—to figure that out. So…thank you."

"You're welcome," Anne said simply.

"And…yes, I fell for the barn manager." They both laughed. "I have no idea if she wants me to stick around, but I'd like to. The people here—the boarders, hell, the horses, too. They're just trying to do their best. And to take care of each other. And they seem to like me okay." He shrugged. "I've been teaching a few lessons, just to help out a little."

"That's great, Ian. You're such a good teacher."

He smiled a little. "Maybe. It does turn out that my horse skills extend beyond catching rides."

"Of course they do!" Anne's expression turned thoughtful.

"I want to stay here," Ian said, because he might as well

lay all his cards on the table. "Assuming Bronwen doesn't kick me out," he added. "I want to stay at Morning Song."

"I see." Anne didn't appear unhappy about the idea, but she didn't seem happy, exactly, either. "You know what my plan for the farm was, of course."

He had absolutely no idea. "Anne," he said a little irritably. "I can't read your mind. Especially when you're God knows where and I can't reach you."

She shook her head at him. "Remember when we were teenagers, and I always hung around all the babies at that one farm you rode for?"

He remembered. She'd come with him most days after she'd gotten out of school, and spent hours learning about handling foals, studying bloodlines, helping the breeding arm of the farm he'd been riding for any way she could. He'd never thought that much of it—who didn't like baby animals? And Anne had always been more interested in that area of horsemanship than in riding, which was all he'd focused on.

Suddenly, he got it. Buying Morning Song hadn't been a whim. It hadn't been a random act of a woman grieving a bad marriage and divorce. Or an un-thought-out purchase because she'd needed somewhere to live when she returned from her trip. It hadn't even been a pity purchase, just for his benefit, because she knew he needed to be here.

"You want to start a breeding operation."

Anne's face lit with excitement. "Yes! Obviously. I know Clover's not too far from here, but I was thinking of a smaller business. Just a stallion or two, and a few mares. Something just active enough to be profitable, but small enough that we can really pay attention to the horses and any clients."

"Hades," he said.

She nodded. "All part of the plan. Honestly, buying this farm took up most of my money. I could hardly go off to Europe and import some already successful stallion. Hades was such a bargain for what he is."

Ian could see it. The fields of Morning Song jubilant with playing foals, mares calmly grazing while their little ones ran in the spring sunshine. Hades the foundation, passing on his talent to generations. Anne could work with the babies, and he could help train the young horses. It was a beautiful vision, and he wanted to be part of it.

But...

"The boarders. Bronwen."

Anne wrinkled her nose. "I have to admit I thought we'd just convert the farm over."

Ian suppressed a groan. He loved his sister, and he loved the idea of raising horses together. But Morning Song was a community. They weren't professional riders, their horses nothing like the expensive high-performance animals he was used to. But they were loved, treasured—as much as the people who cared for them loved and treasured each other.

"But," his sister continued with a little smile, "I'm open to suggestion."

"Really?" He had no idea how that would work.

"Yes, really. I'm hardly going to kick your friends—not to mention your lady friend—out on their ass, if that would hurt you."

"Oh."

"*Oh*, he says." Anne shook her head. She wiped her hands on a napkin. "Ian. I want to do this, but more than anything, I want to do this with *you*. If you're willing." She took a deep breath and stared off into the distance. "We used to be together all the time, you know? You and me against the world. But then we grew up, and these past few years you were traveling the world while I…" She sighed. "While I made a huge mistake and got married."

"You didn't know he was an ass."

"Mmm. I probably did. I just didn't want to admit it. But I missed you, Ian. And then, with your accident, I thought maybe…maybe I'd lost you." Her eyes filled with tears, and this time he reached across the table for her hand.

"You didn't. You didn't lose me, and I'm not going anywhere."

She smiled at him. "Good. I think this could be good for us both. And for me, well…I just want a *home*. Finally. Somewhere safe and happy. With horses and my brother— and anyone else he wants to bring into our family."

"Let's not get ahead of ourselves." He didn't even know if Bronwen wanted him around on a permanent basis.

Anne huffed a laugh. "I think you'll be fine."

Ian wasn't so sure, but he had hope. And that was something he hadn't had for a while.

"Anyway," Anne continued. "It's a big farm. Plenty of room to build another barn for the breeding operation. I'd need to try to take out a loan for a new barn, but for now we can make do. And we've already got a barn manager who knows how to run the boarding side of things. Seems to me like we're already on our way."

Ian sat quietly for a moment, filled with gratitude and hardly believing how much things had changed in the past months. The grace other people had shown him… Bronwen, everyone at the farm, now his sister, willing to adjust her plans just because he cared about the people here. Grateful didn't even begin to cover it.

"I guess we are," he said and let it sit there for now.

The ring of the landline phone in the house woke Ian from a deep sleep.

The sky was black through the windows and he had no idea what time it was. He would have thought the landline would be disconnected by now—he certainly hadn't been paying that bill. He only knew it existed because of a wrong-number call some weeks ago.

He nearly tripped over his clothes from yesterday, piled on the floor in the living room where he'd left them by the couch after settling Anne in the one bed in the house. His back complained as he moved, and he resolved to buy a second bed as soon as possible.

He grabbed the phone once he'd made it to the kitchen.

"Hello?" His voice was rough with sleep.

"Ian? That you?"

The voice on the other end of the line sounded worried—panicked, even. And familiar. He tried to jog his brain into some form of wakefulness.

"Um. Martha?"

"Yes, it's me. Are you at the house?"

She must be panicked if she was asking if he was at the house where the landline she'd just called was.

"What's wrong?"

His brain began catastrophizing. The barn, Percy, one of the other horses. A person injured. But all of the horses should be tucked into their stalls this time of night, owners home in their own beds. And Bronwen would have called or come up to the house if something was wrong, wouldn't she?

"I'm at the show—you know, at Old Oak Stables?"

Right. Martha had taken Percy that morning, possibly now yesterday morning, to a show a couple of counties over, planning to stay with her sister overnight. It was a big show for Martha and Percy, who usually stuck to day trips when they wanted to get out and see what they could do. Martha had only decided to head farther afield because the farm was close to her sister.

"Okay? Yes." He glanced down at his watch. Three thirty in the morning. He groaned—he'd be heading down to the barn to meet Bronwen in just a couple of hours.

"It's Percy—I think he's colicked. I'm here at the farm with him, but no one is around. They don't have an on-site barn manager. He just lay down and I can't get him up. I don't know what to do—I don't want to bother Bronwen when she's got her own big show."

As she spoke, Martha's voice sped up and she sounded out of breath, like she was bordering on a panic attack.

Martha wouldn't have been able to reach Bronwen anyway. Ian had told her in no uncertain terms to turn off her phone last night. She needed the rest, and nothing that wasn't happening right below her apartment in the barn was so important it couldn't wait until daytime.

Or so he'd thought.

And even as his mind worked on Martha's problem, part of him was touched that he'd been the second person she'd thought of to call for help. She could have picked anyone—another boarder, her own sister, another friend. But she'd turned to him, and he wasn't going to let her down.

"Okay. Martha, it will be fine." He wasn't sure that was true—colic could be a simple upset stomach in a horse, or it could quickly grow serious and life-threatening.

He thought he heard a quiet sob through the phone. "I didn't bring Percy's feed with us. The feed they have here is so similar, I didn't think it was necessary. They said it would be okay."

Ah. Most horses could take a slight change in feed, but some horses were sensitive. And that plus the stress of being away from home could certainly start a horse colicking. Poor Percy.

"Okay. I'm going to come to you, okay? You're only forty-five minutes away, and I can get there in thirty this time of night. Keep trying to get Percy up, and walk him if you can. Just don't let him roll. If it's serious we can get the vet over."

With a few more reassurances, he hung up and sprang into action. He left a note in the kitchen for his sister, thought about texting Bronwen, then decided against it in case he could resolve everything before she woke up—no sense in adding to the stress of her day. He'd call her by the time they were supposed to meet at the barn.

The roads were deserted this time of the morning, and he made it to Old Oak in decent time. He found Martha in a stall in the dark, Percy curled up on the bedding. He was breathing heavily but turned his head and whickered a greeting at Ian as he quietly entered the stall.

"Hey, big boy, feeling a little under the weather?" He crouched down next to the horse and was almost knocked over by Martha, who threw her arms around him.

"Oh my God, thank you for coming!" She released him and sat back on her heels, tears in her eyes. "I didn't know what to do."

He gave her a reassuring smile. "It's no problem. Let's see if we can get him up and walking, okay? And I'll leave a message for Dr. Forster."

Morning Song's vet knew Percy, and he should be willing to come to Old Oak that morning. And the barn staff would be arriving shortly, if they needed additional help. Percy didn't look like he had much more than a bad tummy ache, but Ian wanted to be careful. He knew how much the horse meant to Martha, and how worried she was.

Percy was, however, as stubborn as ever, and it took some time to convince him to get up off the comfy bedding and to his feet. And even longer to get him out of the stall and walking. By the time Martha had him in the barn aisle, it was past the time he was supposed to meet Bronwen at the barn.

He left her a detailed voicemail and hoped she checked her phone soon. With a sinking feeling, he realized that at best he'd be able to meet her at the show before her class. At worst, he'd miss it entirely and she'd have to go alone. He groaned and his stomach clenched as if he was colicking himself. He'd promised Bronwen he'd be there for her today—and he knew how she felt about broken promises.

He squeezed his eyes shut, then opened them again. Surely she'd understand? She cared about the Morning Song horses more deeply than anything. If one of them was away from home and sick, surely helping them was the priority?

Bronwen could handle a small schooling show on her own, no problem. But he'd promised...

There was nothing to do about it, though. Percy's health had to come first, and all he could do was hope that Bronwen could forgive him.

Seventeen

The first rays of sunlight hit Bronwen like a slap to the face.

She sat bolt upright in bed, then scrambled out of the blankets to the floor. What time was it? She glanced down at her watch. *Shit.* She'd turned off her phone as Ian had commanded last night, not realizing that she'd also turned off the alarm clock function.

Now she was late.

She threw on her nice breeches and show shirt, which she'd carefully laid out the night before, with an old long-sleeved shirt and sweatpants over them to keep everything clean, and ran down the stairs to the barn.

No sign of Ian, even though it was half an hour past when they were supposed to meet. She took a moment, breathing deeply, trying to slow her heart rate. Oversleeping and running downstairs to a missing Ian felt like some sort of anxiety dream. She tried to calm her racing mind, still adjusting from the abrupt transition from sleep to panic.

Hades whickered at her from his stall. Abigail was already in the feed room getting ready to dole out breakfast.

"Hey, have you seen Ian?" she asked, trying not to sound as freaked out as she felt. She'd have to load Hades into the farm's trailer and get on her way in less than an hour.

Abigail shook her head. "Nope, quiet as mice around here. I wondered where you were—isn't that show this morning? I thought you'd be up before I got here."

"Overslept. Ugh!"

Abigail gave her a sympathetic look as Bronwen grabbed Hades's feed. She quickly dumped it into the bucket in his stall so he could eat before they left. She'd already put hay and all of the equipment she'd need in the trailer yesterday.

She made herself walk up the path to the house instead of running flat out like a maniac. Let the cold air of the morning root her into the present moment. She was fine. She'd be ready to head to the show on time. A little extra sleep wasn't a terrible thing.

And there would be an explanation for Ian's absence. Maybe he'd overslept himself. Maybe he was just running behind. She could hardly blame him, since she was in the same boat herself.

She let herself into the house with the key Ian had given her. It was dark and quiet, and she let out a sigh of relief. He'd just overslept, as she had.

She walked to the kitchen and peeked out the window at the driveway. Her breath stopped halfway into her lungs, and then came out in a rush. His car was gone from its spot. He hadn't overslept—instead, he'd left the farm. For what?

A small, scared part of her suggested that maybe he'd

changed his mind. About what, though? That part of her mind wasn't big on offering specifics. About the show? About Hades? About the farm? Staying? Her?

He'd never made any promises. Maybe he'd heard from his sister and she was coming to take over everything. And maybe that easy out was too much like exactly what he said he wanted for him to turn it down.

She shook her head and firmly told herself that she was being silly. Ian would have told her if any of that was the case. He'd never just disappear, not without telling her. Especially not today, when he knew she needed his support. He'd *promised*.

She turned on a light in the living room. And she saw what she'd missed as she darted to the kitchen window.

Boxes.

Maybe fifteen moving boxes scattered around the room, as well as pieces of furniture she'd never seen before. A couple of modern-looking chairs. Some sort of wooden chest that might be an heirloom. A bag for a jumping saddle embroidered with the name of one of the best saddle makers. Books piled next to one box. A bunch of photographs stacked haphazardly beside another.

She reached down and picked up a photo. It was an old color print of two teenagers next to a tall brown horse. The people in the photograph were clearly related, tall and blond and with identical smiles. The boy was Ian, younger but still the man she…

Well.

She placed the photo back where she'd found it, slowly and as carefully as if it was a bomb.

She took a few calming breaths. Her nerves about the show combined with her nerves about whatever the hell was happening here at the house until she was basically just one big ball of nerves.

Okay. Ian wasn't here, but she knew he'd slept in the house last night. And his stuff—stuff she'd never seen—was being boxed up just as if he was…

Moving.

Leaving.

What other explanation could there be? The house belonged to his sister, who as he'd said should be arriving soon. He could hardly be moving *in*. And the only other direction to move was out, right?

Which was what he'd said all along that he was going to do. She should have believed him. When he'd said in vague terms that they'd figure things out together, he could have been talking about anything. The farm, his future, Hades.

But if they were working things out together, then where was he? He'd promised he'd be here with her for the show, and he was nowhere to be found. Even if she'd misunderstood what was going on here, she couldn't get past that. He'd *promised* to be here, and he wasn't.

And he'd begun packing up his stuff without talking to her first.

Much more slowly than she'd arrived, she left the house and trudged back down the hill to the barn. She still had the slightest hope that she'd just missed him, and he'd be at the barn when she got back—although where his car was continued to be a mystery.

But in the barn, the only sound was the horses eating

their breakfast, soft chewing and snuffling sounds coming from each stall. She could faintly hear Abigail rustling around in the feed room, probably getting ready to muck out the stalls and turn the horses out for the day so Bronwen was free for the show.

She rubbed her hands together in the cold and pondered her options. She could completely lose her shit right here in the barn aisle, or she could go up to her apartment and do it there.

Or she could be the grown-up person she was and get herself and her horse to the show.

Hades had worked hard, done everything they'd asked of him. He was ready, and deserved to have his chance in front of whatever audience turned up for a local dressage show. She didn't know what the future held for him, but whatever it was, he needed to start showing the world that not only was he tremendously talented, but he also wasn't aggressive or dangerous when handled properly.

And she had worked hard, too, if not overcoming her fear, then learning to live with it. Ironic that she'd been looking forward to the show she'd once dreaded the idea of. Whatever Ian was doing, she wouldn't let him take that away from her.

She nodded to herself and mentally drew a boundary around whatever was going on with Ian and all of her associated emotions. After braiding Hades's mane as best she could, she grabbed the last few things she needed from the barn, loaded up the big stallion and got on her way. It was only when she was a mile down the road in the trailer that she realized she'd forgotten her phone in her apartment.

But, she figured, she didn't really need it anyway. She was doing this by herself, and she didn't need anyone's help or support after all.

Ian waited at the back of Martha's trailer as she slowly backed Percy down the ramp.

"Good boy," he said as he gave the horse a pat.

Martha stood by Percy's head, lead rope in hand. Her expression was almost comically similar to Percy's: tired, relieved, a little stunned.

He probably looked the same.

"What's going on?" Scott emerged from the barn, Brian right behind him. "Ian, did you go with Martha to the show?"

The two men walked the short distance to the trailer.

"Ian saved our bacon, is what happened," Martha said, her normally assertive voice a little shaky. "Percy colicked last night, and I panicked."

"You didn't panic," Ian reassured her. "You did exactly the right thing—called for help and stayed with your horse."

She gave him a grateful look. "I'm never doing an overnight show again, that's for sure."

Ian didn't like the sound of that. A brief colic episode shouldn't hold Martha back from whatever shows she wanted to do with Percy. "No," he said. "You will. You'll just take this experience and learn from it—bring Percy's feed with you, and know that his belly has some issues with being away from home. Keep an eye out for anything else that might bother him while he's away. You'll be fine."

In the end, they'd had the vet come out to Old Oak just

to be safe, even though Percy seemed to be improving all on his own. Ian hadn't wanted to risk the trailer ride home if there was any chance it would set him off again. So, they'd waited, explaining the situation to the farm staff as they'd arrived for the morning, and then again to the riders arriving for the second day of the show.

And in between explanations, walking Percy and talking to the vet, Ian had sent Bronwen several increasingly worried texts and voicemails.

No answer.

"Is Bronwen back yet?" he asked now, trying not to sound like he was climbing out of his skin.

Scott and Brian exchanged glances.

"Oh, shit," Scott said. "Today's her show with Hades—weren't you going with her?"

Martha started to lead Percy toward the barn, and the rest of them followed.

"She was really nervous, I think, although it's hard to tell with Bronwen," Brian said. "I know she went—the trailer is gone and so is Hades. Did she end up going alone?"

The leaden feeling in the pit of his stomach that had been weighing him down all day increased severalfold.

"I guess so," he said. "I went out to Old Oak to help Martha early this morning. Bronwen hasn't been answering her phone."

"Well," Martha said, "Bronwen would be the first to say that a sick horse takes precedence over everything." Her eyebrows knit together in concern and she glanced at Ian. "But I'm sorry, Ian. If I messed everything up for you and Bronwen. I didn't even think—"

He cut her off. "No. You were right to call and get help. A colicking horse is no joke, and you needed to make sure Percy was taken care of."

He wondered if he should head over to the show and try to find Bronwen—but her class was likely over by now. He checked his watch and realized that there was a fairly decent chance he'd pass right by her on the way there as she was on the way home and miss her entirely. He also didn't like the idea of leaving Percy, even if the horse seemed to have recovered.

After several minutes of anxious waffling, he decided that there was nothing to do now but wait and try to focus on the people around him until the woman who held his future in her hands arrived home.

They entered the barn and Ian had never been so happy to walk through the big sliding door. Had he really avoided this place when he first arrived at the farm? Now it felt like a homecoming, bringing a sick horse safely back where he belonged.

Martha put Percy in his stall and shut the door, leaning back against it.

"I'm pooped," she announced. "And starving."

"Let's order breakfast," Brian suggested.

"And coffee," Martha added.

"And doughnuts," Scott said.

"We can take turns checking on Percy today, so you don't have to spend all day on watch, Martha," Brian offered.

His husband nodded. "You should even go home for a nap. Or take one in the tack room, if you want."

Martha smiled gratefully at them. "Breakfast, coffee and a nap? That sounds great. God, I'm so glad to be back."

"Well," Ian began, a sense of dread taking hold of his insides now that the Percy situation was more or less resolved, "I should probably..."

"Probably nothing—you're having breakfast on us for helping Martha," Brian said firmly.

Martha gave him a knowing smile. "There's no escaping it. You're stuck with us now."

A month ago he would have balked at the idea of belonging to this group of riders—of belonging to anyone or anything. He'd wanted to cut himself off from everything, everyone. He could give his past self grace, standing here now. Like Hades when he'd first arrived at Morning Song, he'd been doing whatever he could to protect himself until he felt safe again.

Now he could feel himself unfurl like the spring leaves at the thought of being stuck with these people, these horses, this farm. He could do breakfast and coffee. He could take his turn making sure Percy continued to improve.

He could belong here, if...

"Did anyone see Bronwen before she left this morning?"

He had to ask. The fact that she hadn't answered any of his messages made his emotions veer between absolute panic that she either hated him or wasn't okay, and belief that she was fine and simply busy with the show.

Bronwen was more than capable of taking one horse to a local show for the morning. She'd be busy, of course, and possibly unable—or unwilling—to take her focus off Hades to stare at her phone. He understood.

But the not knowing was the problem. She'd confided in him about her most recent relationship, full of broken promises and betrayal. Her skittishness about relationships stemmed directly from the fact that she'd thought someone was trustworthy and had the rug pulled out from under her. And now he'd done exactly the same thing, even if he'd had good reason. He'd promised her he'd be there, and he simply hadn't followed through. For all he knew, she believed the worst of him, and he mentally kicked himself for everything and anything he could have done to prevent that.

He should have told her how he felt, as soon as he'd worked it out himself. As soon as he'd gotten his head out of his ass about staying. About loving her. Damn the risk to his own heart and pride, the risk that she'd run screaming in the other direction. Bronwen deserved honesty, and nothing less. At least then she'd have had that to depend on, to trust. Now it was entirely possible she believed he was no better than the ones who had come before.

But there was nothing he could do about it except wait.

Scott, Brian and Martha all shook their heads. Abigail had taken over feeding and mucking-out chores that morning, but she was long gone. No one knew anything.

He let himself be led into the tack room, Scott already on his phone ordering breakfast. He tried to ignore the anxiety and questions rattling around in his brain—was Bronwen all right at the show? Was she furious at him, or would she understand about Percy? Had she even gotten his messages? And after everything, even if she could forgive him for breaking his promise...would it even matter? Would she want him to stay?

Eighteen

Bronwen drew Hades to a halt in the center of the ring and saluted the judge, who sat just outside the end of the enclosed area. Then she loosened the reins so the horse under her could stretch his neck out and relax as they walked out, dressage test finished.

She resisted the urge to raise her fist in triumph. Hades had been an absolute angel that morning, everything from loading into the trailer to handling the—admittedly very small—crowds at the show to the test itself.

They'd completed one of the training level tests, a low level meant for young or inexperienced horses. Just simple walk, trot and canter and a few circles. Nothing beyond Hades's current training level. But even so, you never knew how a horse would perform away from home, or on any given day. Luckily, this particular show had been remarkably laid-back even for a local schooling show, quiet and uneventful, and there had been plenty of space in the field set aside for entrants like her to park the trailer away from other horses and their people.

There had been one moment when it looked like a man was going to approach them as Bronwen tightened the girth before swinging up in the saddle. Hades had stiffened and backed away, but the man continued past them, and after a few moments and several treats, Hades relaxed again. She was always astonished at horses' ability to remember, and also to forgive and put things behind them.

People were so much more complicated.

All morning she'd refused to dwell on what she might or might not have to forgive. Hades deserved her full attention, and whenever she found herself scanning the cars in the barn parking lot for Ian's, she told herself firmly that whether he arrived or not, her main concern was the horse and the riding.

Everything else could wait.

And now, as she dismounted and led Hades back to the trailer, she tried to focus on the triumph she felt. How far they'd both come, Hades and herself. They'd both learned to manage their ever-present fear and try something new. And they'd succeeded beautifully. The test had been obedient and correct, and Hades's little snort of happiness as they exited the ring made her smile.

She wasn't at all surprised to learn, after she'd walked Hades around while the remaining tests were completed, that they'd won their class. She took the blue ribbon with a grin, making sure to keep her body between the man handing out prizes and Hades. But the stallion barely batted an eyelid.

How far they'd come.

On the short ride home she thought about that feeling of triumph, of satisfaction in showing a horse to their best advantage. Remembered that feeling—she'd had it as she worked with Charlie and moved up the levels of hunter shows. Knowing that they were improving together, that she could ensure kind and compassionate training and treatment, that her horse was content and secure in his work and the challenges set before him.

She'd *missed* that.

And she realized that Ian—whatever the hell was going on with him—was right. She loved her work at Morning Song. Loved the daily care of the horses. But she wanted more, and she was kidding herself if she claimed she didn't.

She had no real interest in competition herself. It was the horse that interested her: How could she work with individual animals to train them to be their best? To find the right discipline, the right atmosphere, the right rider and owner for their talent and personality?

She was *good* at that—and she wanted to do more of it. Whether she could pursue training while also working at Morning Song was a question. She loved the boarders and their horses, but she was no riding teacher, and there wasn't much call for training aside from the occasional request for advice. And there wasn't room for her to start bringing in younger horses to train and sell—if Ian's sister was even willing to let her run a business out of her farm.

She sighed. The idea of leaving Morning Song sat like a brick in her stomach. But she couldn't ignore what called her. She'd wasted too much time doing just that. Hiding, just as Ian said.

She needed to be brave enough to leave behind what she loved, in order to find where she belonged.

And maybe Ian was onto something there, too. If he really needed to leave in order to find his way toward a life where he could be happy, was he any different from her? She'd still yell at him for not telling her, though. For not sitting down and discussing his decision before pulling out the moving boxes. For packing up and leaving her to fend for herself when he'd promised to support her.

But she'd done it. She'd done what she thought she might never do again—successfully ride a horse she'd trained in a show. She'd proved to herself that this seed of an idea she had for her future was possible. And she'd done it on her own.

Whatever Ian's plans were, they wouldn't detract from the direction she wanted to go. If he was leaving, if he'd really let her down the way it seemed he had, she'd nurse her broken heart, then pick herself up and figure out the next steps.

She pulled the trailer into the farm drive and parked near the barn. As she backed Hades down the ramp, she glanced around. The day had warmed up considerably since that morning. The sun shone and everything smelled of grass and mud and warming earth.

But no one was riding in the outdoor arena, despite the nice weather and the fact that it was the weekend. Horses grazed out in the fields, but there wasn't a single person to be seen.

Curious, she led Hades into his stall and unclipped the lead rope from the halter. It was quiet inside—too quiet.

Usually, Sunday midday was prime barn socializing time: people and horses in the aisle, getting ready for a ride or relaxing after one. Jokes and laughter and the ever-present sound of horses being horses.

It was unnerving when all of that was absent.

Giving Hades a pat, she went to find out what was going on. As she walked down the aisle, she noticed movement in Percy's stall, even though all of the horses should have been turned out this time of day.

It was Brian, slowly stroking Percy's neck and murmuring to him. The horse stood with his eyes closed as if he was listening to every word.

"What's going on?" she asked, and both Percy and Brian turned their heads toward her.

"Bronwen! How was the show?"

"Good," she said impatiently. "Where is everyone?"

Brian's phone rang in his pocket, and he gave her an apologetic look and gestured toward the tack room.

Concerned, Bronwen headed for the door to the tack room. When she opened it, she stood there for several moments taking in the scene.

Martha lay sprawled on the couch, and Ian in the chair. Both appeared to be fast asleep. Scott and Olivia were by the coffee maker, mugs in hand, talking softly. They both turned toward her as she blinked at them.

Olivia gave her a little wave. "Bronwen!"

At the sound of her name, Ian started in the chair and opened his eyes. The blue irises were red-rimmed and he rubbed them as he stood.

"Bronwen—you're back." His voice was rough and thick with sleep. "Thank God. I've been trying to call you all day."

She winced inwardly. She'd forgotten until just now that she'd left her phone in her apartment. Anything could have happened at the farm and she wouldn't have known it. But she'd been so upset by what she'd found at the house that she hadn't been thinking clearly earlier that morning.

Ian took several steps toward her, and she turned and walked toward the feed room, gesturing for him to follow. She was still upset, and angry, and unsure of what she wanted to say. Ian had left her on her own when he'd promised to be there that day, and after sending her back to her apartment to sleep last night, he'd started packing up his life here without a word about it to her.

He followed her into the small room as she'd known he would, closing the door behind him with a soft click. She whirled to face him.

"What the hell, Ian?"

"Bronwen, I'm so sorry—I didn't mean to flake out on you. I mean, I *didn't*, not really. I—"

She held up a hand. "We can get to the show later. I want to know why you're packing your stuff to leave. You weren't even going to tell me?"

Realization and something that she thought was regret flashed over his features. He was surprised and unhappy that she'd seen what he was doing up at the house—but what did he expect? Of course she went looking for him. Of course she was upset by what she'd found.

Pain shot through her, right in her chest, and she reached out to grab the counter near the sink just for something to hold on to. She'd known it would hurt. She'd told herself that Ian was free to make his own decisions about his life, that he was only doing what he'd said he'd do all along, that she would get through it and move on with her own life.

But right now, it *hurt*.

"Ian." Her voice shook despite her best efforts. "Are you leaving? Just like that? You promise me you'll help me at the show on *your* horse, then instead just leave me to do it on my own while you...what? Pack up and go?"

She knew she was missing something. That she should shut up and let him explain. But she was hurt, and she'd been holding in all that emotion since she left the farm that morning. She couldn't stop it from coming out now like water through a burst dam.

As she watched, he leaned back against the wall, his expression weary and hands shoved into his pockets.

"No," he said, and she watched his chest rise and fall as he took a deep breath.

"I looked for you," she couldn't help saying before he could continue. "I went up to the house to look for you. You were gone, and boxes were all over the place."

He nodded, and that same pain sliced right through her.

But then he said, "I'm not going anywhere." He ran a hand over his face. "I'm sorry. I haven't really slept, so I know I'm probably not going to make a lot of sense. But, Bronwen, I am *so* sorry I missed the show. You have no idea. I tried texting and calling—"

"I left my phone here," she said in a small voice. What had she been thinking?

"Ah." The shadow of a smile played around his lips. "I

thought maybe you'd just decided I'd let you down and you never wanted to speak to me again."

There had been a little of that, too, she had to admit.

With another breath, he kept going. "Percy colicked away at the show Martha took him to. Last night."

Bronwen's heart stuttered in her chest. "Oh no! Why didn't she call me? Poor Martha."

"She didn't want to wake you up the night before the show, so she called the house instead. I'd already been up late because my sister showed up last night."

"Wait—what? Your sister's here?" She glanced around as if Ian's sister might jump out of one of the feed storage bins.

Ian nodded. "She was still sleeping when I got back with Martha and Percy. Too much traveling, I guess." He yawned and rubbed his eyes again. "Anyway, I went to help Martha, and we made sure Percy was okay for the trip home. When we got back, everyone here chipped in keeping an eye on him while Martha took a nap. And me, I guess—I didn't mean to fall asleep."

"Oh."

Her mind was spinning. The horses' well-being came first, always. She knew that. And maybe she could have guessed that a sick or injured horse would be the only thing that could keep Ian from his promise to her. But she had never thought that one of the boarders would reach out to him instead of her for help. It had been kind of Martha to not want to disturb her, and kinder still of Ian to jump out of bed in the middle of the night to help.

He met her gaze, his eyes full of remorse she was starting to realize he had no need to feel. "I'm so sorry I let you down, Bronwen. I can't tell you how sorry. But I couldn't just ignore Martha, or Percy." He swallowed visibly.

"Of course," she said without thinking.

There was no question that the horses came first, and she would have thought less of Ian if he'd chosen anything else over Percy's health. And then it hit her like an avalanche— Ian *hadn't* let her down. He'd done the only thing he could do, and he'd tried to reach her. If it hadn't been for her own forgetfulness, she would have gotten his messages.

Relief and her own remorse had tears pricking her eyes. He had never meant to break his promise. But—

"The boxes," she whispered.

Ian grimaced. "That probably looked pretty bad—but I'm not packing, Bronwen. Not unless you tell me you want me to. I'd— Well…" He blushed then, actually *blushed*, his cheeks bright pink. "I never actually *un*packed, is the thing. It's silly—I did bring some stuff with me when I came here, but just threw it all into that room off the living room. I didn't want to remember my life before. Or maybe I didn't want to let myself be comfortable here. Or both. I don't really know. But last night I thought, what am I doing?"

His gaze darted away from her, toward the window over the feed room sink.

"I don't want to punish myself, or run away from the things I love. Not anymore. I want to start my life again. So I started unpacking. Finally."

His eyes returned to hers.

"You were…*un*packing," she repeated.

He nodded. "I just thought… Time to get my head out of my ass and learn to live with my past *and* my future."

He gave a short laugh. "And then my sister showed up on the doorstep."

Bronwen squeezed her eyes shut, then opened them. She was having trouble processing all of this.

"Hold on. Can we…? Can you…?" Tears threatened again and she buried her face in her hands. Immediately, strong arms came around her as Ian crossed the short distance between them and gathered her to him.

"It's okay," he said soothingly, his voice still scratchy from lack of sleep. "I'm so sorry, Bronwen. I wouldn't have broken my promise to you for anything else. And I'm not leaving—not unless and until you want me to."

They were exactly the words she'd wished in the most private part of her mind that he'd say, and she had barely dared hope to hear them.

She'd been…maybe more than a little foolish.

His fingers tangled in the hair at the back of her neck as he held her close, gently rubbing and soothing. All of the anxiety and anger and confusion of the past few hours found their way out of her body in tears, and they stood there together while she took several deep breaths to calm herself. Everything she'd feared hadn't come to pass. Ian was here with her, holding her. He cared enough for the boarders and their horses to drive out to another barn when he should have been sleeping. And instead of leaving, he was…staying.

Eventually, she raised her head. "I'm sorry. I was so angry because I thought you'd stood me up for the show, and that you'd decided to leave without telling me, but…I should have asked. I shouldn't have assumed—"

"You should have brought your phone with you," Ian said wryly. "What if you'd had an emergency?"

She winced. "I know, I know. I never go anywhere without it, but I was flustered and running late, and I didn't want to turn back."

"And you were upset," he added quietly.

"I was. I wasn't really thinking straight."

"It's okay to be upset. Even if I'd been able to reach you, you were counting on me to be with you at the show. There was a good reason I wasn't there, but it would still have been upsetting."

Bronwen sniffed and pushed her hair back from her face. "You did the right thing, though."

He smiled at her, and she couldn't help taking his face in her hands and kissing him. He groaned into her mouth, as if he felt the same relief and happiness and needs that she did.

"I'm glad you think so," he said when they finally broke apart. "I was worried."

She frowned at him. "I'd never blame you for putting a horse first," she said firmly. "I was just…kind of a mess."

"You were nervous about the show," he said gently.

They'd never really talked about how she'd felt leading up to her first show in years. She knew Ian was concerned that it was too much, too soon, but Bronwen had been determined. She'd shut down any thoughts of nerves or discussion of whether or not she could do it, as if ignoring her feelings would keep them from being a problem.

"Yeah." She bit her lip. "I was, and I let it mess with my head. I think I was more scared than I thought."

He lifted his hand to her face and traced her bottom lip with his thumb. She shivered, meeting his darkening gaze.

"You know what that makes me want to do," he said, his voice deeper even than it had been when he'd first woken in the tack room.

A knock at the feed room door startled them both, although Ian didn't step away. And she held him close, as if she was afraid he'd disappear somehow. Still worried that what he was saying was too good to be true.

"Ian, are you in here?" an unfamiliar woman's voice asked. "There's a person sleeping in the tack room—is that normal? And three other people are together in one horse's stall—" The woman broke off as she opened the door and saw Ian and Bronwen. "Oh! I'm so sorry."

Bronwen took a step back and tried to subtly wipe her eyes.

"Anne, you're up. Finally." Ian's voice sounded amused and mildly irritated at the interruption. This must be his sister, then.

Bronwen's cheeks heated with embarrassment. This was hardly how she wanted to meet the woman who meant so much to Ian. Not to mention her new boss.

"Oh, are you Bronwen?" The woman was much shorter than Ian, but had the same blond hair and light blue eyes. Her smile radiated humor, but there were shadows in her eyes much like Ian's. "I'm so glad to meet you—I've heard such good things."

Bronwen glanced at Ian.

"From me, yes," he laughed. "But I think she means from the former owner."

"That's right," Anne said, holding out her hand for Bronwen to shake, which she did. "Ian hasn't told me nearly enough about anything—but Ruth said you're the best barn manager around."

"Um…thanks." Bronwen tried to accept the compliment gracefully, but her mind was drawn back to her decision of earlier that morning. She probably wouldn't be at Morning Song for much longer.

"And no," Ian continued, "we don't usually sleep in the tack room or congregate in the stalls, but we had a colic situation last night."

Bronwen couldn't help but notice how he used the word *we*—had he finally accepted that he was part of this community as much as she was?

"Right! I did get your note," Anne said. "Then I went back to bed since you were gone. I was exhausted. But can I help now?"

Ian shrugged. "You could see if it looks like Percy can be turned out in the field. He seems to be doing okay now. But ask Martha first, if she's awake. We need to keep an eye on him for the rest of the day."

Anne gave a little salute, then grinned at Bronwen. "Nice to meet you. And, Ian, make sure you tell her about our plans if you haven't already. Bronwen, we have big ideas! I can't wait to talk to you about them."

Ian made a face as his sister left the room, closing the door behind her.

"Big plans?" Bronwen was sure her eyebrows were up by her hairline.

Ian ran a hand through his hair. "Right. I hadn't really gotten that far."

"I think I'm going to leave Morning Song," Bronwen blurted, then grimaced. "I mean, I have big plans, too."

She had no idea what Ian and his sister could be planning for the farm, but it seemed likely she wouldn't be around to see it. She just hoped Ian would still want to be with her wherever she ended up.

Now Ian's eyebrows lifted skyward. "Oh?" He took her hands and pulled her back to him. "You know I support whatever big plans you might have. But you may want to hear ours first."

Bronwen swallowed. "Okay."

He placed a kiss on her forehead, then met her eyes. "Anne's always been interested in horse breeding, since we were young. She loved all that stuff—bloodlines, matching the right horses together, training the little ones. And I guess she's decided that's what she wants to do—here, at Morning Song."

Bronwen stared at him, a sort of panic rising from her chest to her throat. "But—"

Ian nodded. "Yeah. The boarders. I had the same reaction." His expression was serious, sincere as he explained, "I told her I'd never support breaking up the community here. And she got it." He pushed a lock of hair out of her face, his fingers trailing down her cheek. "She suggested building a breeding facility—another barn, and more turn-out fields. And leave the boarding barn the way it is. There's plenty of room."

Bronwen blinked in surprise. "That's...that's a huge project."

One corner of Ian's mouth turned out. "My sister's good at big ideas and following her instincts. She wants me to help."

And all of a sudden, she could see it. Could envision everything that Anne had planned, understood what Ian was saying. What he was offering. And it stole her breath from her lungs so thoroughly that she couldn't speak, only stare at that man in front of her and hope it wasn't a dream.

"And luckily," Ian continued when she didn't reply, his voice a little unsteady, a little uncertain now, "I know someone who has a real talent for training, and who loves this farm even more than I've come to."

"Me?" Bronwen squeaked ridiculously, as if she didn't know exactly what he was saying. She just couldn't believe it.

Ian smiled, his hand still against her cheek, and all of her hesitation evaporated like the frost in the fields in the sun.

"You." He cleared his throat. "Bronwen, I want to stay here and build this dream with my sister. I've never really had a home, and neither has she. Not like this. And I want… I want you to do whatever your heart calls you to, obviously. But if you're interested, this dream could include you. My dreams *do* include you. Us."

She took a breath, winding her hands around his neck.

"I'm sorry I didn't make it clear how I felt—or what I wanted," he continued. "I didn't want to scare you off. I knew you were wary of trusting again, and I was afraid to just dump my feelings on you, in case…" He broke off with a wry smile. "In case you turned me down. But I thought maybe with time, you'd warm up to the idea."

"Oh," she said a little breathlessly. She understood; she really did. It was scary enough to reveal your feelings and hopes to someone. Knowing they might not be ready to hear them only made it that much worse. "I...um...I hoped you'd decide to stay. I hoped...I hoped for exactly this."

Ian let out a breath in a relieved rush, his arms coming around her again. "Then I'm sorry I didn't tell you. I'm so sorry I made you think for a moment that I wanted anything else."

Bronwen let it all sink in. He'd felt the same as her for... how long? It didn't matter. They'd both avoided being honest about their feelings because they were afraid of rejection. She wouldn't make that mistake again.

"I was going to try to set up a training business for young horses," she said. "And it broke my heart that it meant I'd have to leave this farm." She glanced away. "It also broke my heart that I thought you were leaving, and I'd have to do it all without you."

He leaned his forehead against hers, their breath mingling. Bronwen worried that if she moved, if she broke the spell of this moment, it all might disappear. As if he could read her thoughts, Ian gave her a squeeze with his arms and a quick, firm kiss.

"You don't have to do anything without me, if you don't want to," he said. "I know you *can* do whatever you want. But if you can forgive me for letting you down and for making you think I was leaving, I'll happily stay with you for as long as you'll have me."

"Ian," she breathed and lifted her chin to look up at him, meeting his clear blue gaze. "There's nothing to forgive." He shook his head, and she placed her fingers over his lips before he could contradict her. "Nothing. You did what you thought was right—Percy, the show, taking your time with us. Everything."

His relief was palpable, clear in the way his shoulders relaxed, the way his eyes softened.

"And the farm?" he asked.

She smiled, and as she thought of all the possible futures in front of them, joy bubbled in her chest like water in the stream down past the turnout fields, bright and clear.

"Well. I think I can stand to work with adorable baby horses, be with the man I love and train young horses just like I wanted to."

His smile matched hers. "It doesn't sound bad, does it?"

"Not bad at all. Especially since the first stallion on-site won his dressage class today," she added.

"What?" Ian grabbed her into a hug and spun her around. "You won? That's incredible!"

She laughed and steadied herself with her hands on Ian's shoulders. "Ian! Yes, we won, mostly thanks to Hades. I think he'll do just fine—at anything we set him to."

"And so will we," Ian replied. "We'll be just fine wherever all this takes us."

Tears pricked at her eyes again, but she blinked them back. Now wasn't a time for tears. It was a time for laughter, and planning, and dreaming.

Ian leaned down and kissed her. "I love you, Bronwen Jones. Thank you for dragging me out of my darkness and into the life I didn't even know I wanted."

She took his hand and tugged him toward the feed room door.

"I love you, too, Ian Kingston. But I think we'd better go

tell everyone what's in store for them." She laughed again. "I can't wait to see their expressions."

"Then let's go, before Anne spills it all." Ian opened the door and shepherded her into the barn aisle, where warm sunlight streamed through the wide-open doors, illuminating dust motes like drifting stars. The sound of happy chatter and laughter came from the tack room. "Let's tell them together."

Epilogue

Ian leaned on the top rail of the outdoor ring fence and watched as Bronwen pulled Hades to a stop. The big stallion snorted as if he didn't want his workout to be over, then shook his head and stretched out his neck as he walked with big, swinging strides toward Ian.

"How was that?" Bronwen asked from up on his back.

"Great," Ian replied. "He's building muscle and you can really see him engage his hind legs in that walk-to-canter transition now."

Bronwen gave Hades's shoulder a pat, then swung down from the saddle.

"How do you feel?" Ian asked, more out of habit than anything else.

Bronwen had been riding Hades almost every day for the past month, and while she was honest about her anxiety, her confidence had clearly skyrocketed with practice riding the big black horse. They'd worked on building his muscle and advancing his training, with Bronwen taking him to a couple more local dressage shows and successfully building his reputation in the area. She'd even started taking him over a few jumps.

Eventually, he'd need to compete on a bigger stage if Anne wanted to stake a breeding operation on him. Local people might be interested, but in order to turn the farm into a top-notch breeding business, Hades would need to be known nationally, if not internationally. Which would probably mean introducing a new rider, trainer, and getting him used to travel, strange barns and big crowds.

But for now, the horse was happy and productive living on the farm and having his favorite person ride him. Anne would need to figure out the next steps, and Ian would defer to her.

Bronwen gave him a knowing look. "I feel great. And… older."

"Ah, birthday blues, huh?"

Bronwen laughed. "Not really. It's just a number, right? Thirty."

Ian pushed off the fence and slid his hands into the pockets of his jeans. "It is. And I promise the thirties aren't that much different from the twenties. Just a few more aches and pains in our old joints."

She gave him a considering look. "And your aches and pains? How do you feel about what the doctor said?"

He'd seen his new doctor in Boston the other day, and had been stunned by their declaration that there was no reason why he couldn't occasionally sit on a horse, as long as he didn't push his luck with jumping, competition or risking a bad fall. Sedate trail rides, basically. Which was more than he'd been told right after his fall that he'd ever be able to do.

"Still digesting, really. I know I should be eager to get right back in the saddle, but..."

"But it feels like a big step." Bronwen looked at him sympathetically.

"Yeah."

She would know, given her own struggle. Bronwen understood in a way that few other people could. It was welcome news. Exciting. But...it had been a long time since he'd been on a horse, and that last time hadn't exactly been a good one.

She started walking Hades toward the gate, and Ian followed along on the other side of the fence.

"No rush," Bronwen said casually. "There's plenty of horses here you *could* ride, but none that you have to."

"True." And he knew that there was no expectation here at Morning Song that he do anything he wasn't ready for. If he did nothing else for the rest of his life other than ride Hades around bareback just for fun, not only would no one ask him why he wasn't trying to do more, but more than likely several boarders would join in and tell him how they also just wanted the occasional trail ride.

Thank God he'd landed here.

He opened the gate for Bronwen and held it as she let Hades out of the ring, and then he took the reins from her as she looked up at him with a question on her face.

"Go get cleaned up," he said. "And then meet me in the tack room."

She narrowed her eyes at him. "Why? What did you do?"

"So suspicious." He held a hand to his heart and pretended

to be hurt. "Nothing you won't like, I promise." He leaned over and kissed her briefly. "Go. Before I get other ideas."

"Hmm. Like what other ideas?" Bronwen stepped close to him, and reflexively he wrapped an arm around her waist.

"Well…" He lowered his mouth again, but a loud snort interrupted him, followed by a large nose pushing Bronwen several feet to the side.

Ian glared at Hades, who pawed the ground impatiently.

"He wants his post-ride treats," Bronwen laughed.

"I swear to God, this horse." Ian gave the horse a look, but really, he had plans for the afternoon, and Hades was doing him a favor. He didn't need to get distracted now. There would be plenty of time for distraction later.

"As someone who also enjoys treats, I can see where he's coming from," Bronwen commented.

"In that case, you should definitely go get cleaned up. Shoo."

"Hmm… What are you planning?"

"Go" was all Ian said in response, and he led Hades away from Bronwen and down the hill to the big field.

The spring sun lit up the trees and shone warm on his back. In another field, Applejack and Percy lay flat on their sides as if trying to absorb as much solar heat as possible. Birds sang from the trees in the distance, and Hades tromped happily next to him, large feet leaving divots in the damp grass.

"All right, big guy. This is a little different from our routine, but I've got things to do and you deserve to be outside in this beautiful weather."

He led the stallion through the gate and unbuckled his girth. He placed the saddle on the fence and made sure the horse wasn't overly sweaty or warm before removing his bridle and slinging it over his shoulder.

Hades stood in front of him, nosing the front of his shirt.

"What a change from a few months ago, huh, Hades?"

Not long ago he wouldn't have been able to lead this horse anywhere, and even if he had, the stallion would have been off and running as soon as his bridle was removed. Now he stood…if not patiently, then calmly.

Big teeth nipped at the hem of his shirt, and Ian laughed.

"Okay, okay. I know what this is all about."

He dug several horse treats out of his pocket and held them out on his palm. They were gone in less than a second. While Hades chewed, Ian stroked his neck, marveling at the change in the animal. Had he really ever considered selling him off as quickly as possible? Now Ian could hardly imagine life without him.

With a pat to Hades's neck, Ian left through the gate, latching it behind him. He grabbed the saddle and held it on his forearm.

Hades watched him with his head over the gate, big dark eyes tracking Ian as he moved.

"Sorry, bud. I'll give you more attention later, okay? Promise."

He turned and headed toward the barn, looking back to see Hades already lowering himself to the ground for a good roll. He'd be nice and muddy later.

In the barn he put Hades's tack away, promising himself he'd clean it before the end of the day. Then he walked up and down the barn aisle, catching the attention of the boarders, careful not to make too much noise, and they all followed him into the tack room.

Once inside, he closed the door.

"Do we have the cake? Pizza?" he asked the assembled group.

"I carried the cake all the way from the house myself!" Rachel said.

Ian turned to Martha, who had been tasked with getting the homemade chocolate cake safely from the farmhouse kitchen. He'd sneaked out of Bronwen's apartment well before dawn to make it, and had been back down at the barn before she'd woken up. It wasn't that he didn't trust Rachel, but...

Martha shrugged. "I held the doors."

Good enough.

"Brian wanted to get pizza from the new place," Scott said, "but I said no way are we risking an unknown pizza situation—not for Bronwen's birthday. So, it's the usual."

"The usual's good," Ian said. "Drinks? Coffee?"

"Bought and made," Olivia replied, pointing to the full coffee carafe. "Drinks in the fridge."

"Perfect."

"And Abigail and I went out and got candles," Anne added. When Ian turned toward the cake, placed in the middle of a folding table in the corner of the room, he saw the barn assistant still sticking the last few candles of what looked like the whole thirty into the top. "Sorry if we defaced your masterpiece, but it's not really a birthday without candles, is it?"

Ian glared at his sister on principle, but in reality the cake looked great, and far more festive than leaving it plain.

"Ian?" Bronwen's voice came from outside the tack room. "Where is everybody?"

Everyone fell completely silent, as if frozen in place. Ian held up a finger to his lips and moved to the closed door. He opened it wide, moving out of the doorway as he did so that Bronwen could see everyone inside.

"Surprise!" everyone shouted, and Bronwen laughed and held a hand to her heart.

"Oh my God, it's all of you," she exclaimed, moving her hand to cover her mouth. She stood there for a moment, and Ian placed a hand on her shoulder.

"All right?" he murmured.

"I know we're a lot, but she *is* happy, isn't she?" he heard Martha say in what she probably thought was a quiet voice.

Bronwen reached up to place her hand over his. "Of course I'm happy," she reassured the assembled crowd. "Just surprised. We've never done birthday parties before."

"Except for the horses," Rachel corrected.

"Well, of course for the horses," Bronwen said with a smile. "But maybe we should do more people-centered stuff sometimes." She glanced around the room at the cake, drinks, coffee and pizza. "This is lovely. Thank you."

She squeezed Ian's hand and turned in his arms. He looked down at her, this woman who had barged in on him and pulled him right back into the life he'd sworn he'd left forever. Between Bronwen and his sister, he'd never had a chance, and thank goodness. He couldn't imagine a place he wanted to be more than here, or a life he wanted to live more than this one with this woman, at this barn, surrounded by this community.

She pushed up on her tiptoes and kissed him. A few

boarders burst into applause, while he was pretty sure he heard Rachel whisper "Gross" under her breath.

"Okay, okay," Bronwen said as she pulled away from him and faced the crowd. "Enough gawking. Let's eat!"

And they did, demolishing the pizza and diving right into the cake.

As everyone mingled and chatted, Bronwen ate her last bite of cake and then leaned back against him in a quiet corner of the room, watching everyone having fun.

"I'm so full," she moaned. "I'd complain that you're always trying to stuff me full of food, but I like it."

"And I know what else you enjoy being stuff—"

"Ian. There are children present," she scolded him, covering her mouth to hide a laugh.

"She's too busy to listen to us."

"Too busy eating, you mean."

Ian glanced at the cake, which had been reduced to crumbs in short order.

Bronwen shrugged. "Horses work up an appetite."

They stood there together, quietly watching the others, content to just be in that moment.

"I'm so glad I'm not leaving Morning Song," Bronwen finally said. "I'd miss this so much."

Ian grunted in agreement. "I would have missed it, too. You know, if you'd thrown me out on my ear."

Bronwen huffed a short laugh. "I never would have done that. I wanted you to stay long before you knew you wanted to stay."

"Mmm." Ian wasn't so sure. Maybe before he'd consciously realized he wanted to stay at the farm, and with

Bronwen, but some part of him had fallen for her right away. He'd just needed some help to get his head out of his ass.

He lowered his head closer to hers.

"Do you have all your stuff packed up?" he murmured into her ear.

Anne had bought a bed for the farmhouse's spare room the day after her arrival, and Ian had spent more and more time in the barn apartment with Bronwen. After a couple of weeks his sister had declared the situation ridiculous, told Ian in no uncertain terms that he should take the house while she'd move into the apartment, and left him to the nerve-racking task of asking Bronwen to move in with him.

He'd fumbled it, of course, worried she'd turn him down. Bronwen had to ask him to clarify what, exactly, he was proposing, before she'd happily accepted and told him that he should just ask clearly the next time.

Now he felt Bronwen's silent laugh and smiled into her hair.

"Yes, it took forever."

"Really?"

Another laugh. "No, not really. I have some books, and then barn clothes and more barn clothes, and that's pretty much it."

"What else could anyone need, really?"

She turned in his arms and laced her fingers behind the back of his neck. "Nothing. Except you, and everything we have ahead of us."

There was nothing else he could do then but kiss her, gratefully sinking into the feel of her lips on his, her warm, solid body in his arms, her hay-and-flowers scent mixed with horse. He'd never get tired of this, he knew. He'd never tire of her. Somehow, against all odds and likelihood, he'd ended up with the person he'd least have expected, and who he most wanted to be with.

"You're sure your sister wants to live in the apartment?" Bronwen asked when they finally drew apart.

They'd had this conversation before, but Bronwen didn't know Anne as well as he did, and he couldn't blame her for wondering why the farm owner would want the tiny room above the barn. "Yes. If Anne says she's doing something, then she's doing it. Better for everyone to just accept it and get out of her way." He pressed another kiss to Bronwen's lips. "And it's hardly as if the house is much more luxurious than the apartment. Just bigger."

"And it's temporary."

Assuming Anne managed to secure a loan for farm improvements, she'd eventually build a second barn for the breeding operation and a house for herself on the far side of the property.

"Yep. She'll be fine—and she says it will be nice to have her own little spot to herself."

"Ah, so this is just a ploy to get away from her annoying big brother."

He grinned down at her. "And she's throwing you under the bus to do it."

Bronwen gave a long-suffering sigh. "I suppose someone has to keep you out of trouble."

He raised one eyebrow at her. "Trouble? Me?"

"Well." Bronwen gave him a knowing look. "If you play your cards right, I bet we can find some trouble for you to get in later."

"How much later?" Even knowing Bronwen was teasing him, his body tightened in response, and he wanted nothing more than to carry her up to the apartment. Or better yet, the house, where they'd have more privacy.

"Hmm…" She glanced around them. "Everyone seems pretty much occupied with either food or talking. Why don't you slip out and I'll meet you at the house in a few minutes?"

"Oh, thank God. I thought you were going to say after evening feed."

"It's not bad form to leave your own party, is it?"

Ian shrugged. "Probably. But it's your birthday. I'll let Anne know we're headed out, and she can make excuses for us."

"Okay." She smiled at him, and he groaned.

"Get going before I throw you over my shoulder and haul you back to my lair."

"Fine, fine," she laughed at him. "Go get your sister to do your dirty work. I'll see you in a bit."

Reluctantly, Ian let the woman he loved go, and watched her move easily through the crowd of their friends, the community that had accepted him wholeheartedly, and made him feel like he belonged somewhere for perhaps the first time in his life.

And then he turned to find his sister, who he knew would cover for them. The only thing he wanted more than to celebrate Bronwen's birthday with the people they cared for most was time alone with her, to explore and celebrate what was between them. And he hoped to do the same every day, starting today, and for the rest of their lives.

★ ★ ★ ★ ★

Acknowledgments

Every book I write is a book of my heart, but this one in particular has been a dream of mine since I started writing romance: a horse-girl book but for grown-ups, and with romance and sex in it! I've been obsessed with horses for as long as I can remember, which must have been quite a surprise to my absolutely non-horsie parents. Luckily for me, my mother had her own obsession: England. So, the few times we traveled across the ocean I would drag her to various London bookstores and buy all the British horse-girl books: the Pullein-Thompsons, Caroline Akrill, Patricia Leitch's Jinny books… And then of course I read *Misty of Chincoteague*, and *Summer Pony*, and the Black Stallion series. They filled my heart and my head and my imagination, and they never left.

If you, too, are or were or dream of being a horse girl (of any gender) and if you ever lost yourself in those books about girls and their ponies (or maybe you'll go read them now!), this book is for you. Thank you for reading it.

My wholehearted, deepest thanks to my editor, John Jacobson. They have unfailingly believed in my writing from the start, which is a gift I never take for granted. They have encouraged me, convinced me that my writing is Good, Actually, when I didn't believe it, and offered much-needed criticism and correction in the kindest possible way. Having an editor who understands and appreciates your writing makes that writing a joy to create, and I cannot thank John enough.

In fact, I want to thank everyone at Afterglow Books for having a vision of the kind of books that I and so many others want to read, producing them beautifully, and allowing me to participate in this new adventure. Publishing is a whole lot of work for not much thanks or personal gain, and I see and appreciate everyone who does every part, large or small, of making the books we all love.

Thanks always and forever to my agent, Sara Megibow, an absolute delight of a person, the world's greatest cheerleader for her authors and the source of basically any information about publishing a writer could ever need.

A million thanks to Cait Nary, who read the first draft of this book and pointed out errors that would make any self-respecting horse girl shake their head in disgust. I swear I know that you can't clip a wet horse!

I always have to thank Kory Stamper, who is the kind of friend you can text after going no contact for months and share a joke or ask a writing question or complain or ask to get together for coffee. She has put up with my nonsense for thirty years. Get you a friend like Kory.

Thanks to my various Discord universe friends, who are

always available to talk me down from a writing or publishing ledge and/or answer my stupid questions and/or discuss hockey or books or Taylor Swift in the greatest of detail. As a dear friend used to say, there are people in the phone!

Finally, sorry to my kid for the fact that I continue to write embarrassing books. But thanks for listening to me complain about writing (not that you had any choice) and for being my heart and my home. I am so proud of you.